Wanted: Dead or Alive (Again)

MICHAEL K. ZIMMERLI

Marshgrass Publishing
St. Marys, GA

Author contact: mike@zimmac.com

This book is a work of fiction. Any references to historical events, real people, or real places are used fictitiously. Other names, characters, places, and events are products of the author's imagination, and any resemblance to actual events or places or persons, living or dead, is entirely coincidental. Long-standing institutions, agencies, and public offices are mentioned, but the characters involved are wholly imaginary.

Excerpt from Sea Fever, by John Masefield, 1916. Public Domain.

First Printing: 2023

Cover art: Blue Bridge on H17 © 2022 by Michael K. Zimmerli

Interior Design: Michael K. Zimmerli

Interior Formatting: Michael K. Zimmerli

Hardcover ISBN: 979-8-9872713-5-3

Paperback ISBN: 979-8-9872713-3-9

Ebook ISBN: 979-8-9872713-4-6

MARSHGRASS PUBLISHING
ST. MARYS, GA

What People are saying about *Zamboni Is Not A Pasta* …

"I absolutely loved your book. I am letting a friend with a book club read it, hoping she will get the ladies to buy it. I love how you throw some 'witty' things throughout. I am definitely a glass-half-full person and like positive things, so I like a book that makes me chuckle here and there. It has a good storyline with mystery and suspense along with a lot of informative information. I'm excited to get the next one!" – Paula

"The references to our local landmarks was awesome. I was amazed at your research so you could include so much info – the size of Jax, St. Augustine, false imprisonment, AA, etc. It was fast-paced with a surprise ending for me. I can't wait for the next book to be released." – Delores K.

"My daughter got me (Zamboni) for Christmas, and it did not disappoint. The author does a good job of fleshing out the characters and making them believable. The storyline is intriguing. It contains all of the elements of a good whodunit, combined with some Perry Mason-esque mystery, and without the grossness of most modern literature … good dialogue between the characters, and some interesting geography. Any story that involves Steffens and WaHo has to be good." – Robert N.

"Zamboni Is Not A Pasta" included many familiar geographical locations in Camden County. Michael Zimmerli incorporates historical facts seamlessly into his storyline, providing a deeper appreciation for the place I call home. I believe that readers who are not in Camden County will want to visit, too!" – Trisa C.

Contents

Dedication 9

Acknowledgments 11

Introduction 13

Chapter 1 17

Chapter 2 23

Chapter 3 35

Chapter 4 47

Chapter 5 55

Chapter 6 65

Chapter 7 77

Chapter 8 91

Chapter 9 105

Chapter 10 117

Chapter 11 131

Chapter 12 143

Chapter 13 151

Chapter 14 161

Chapter 15 177

Chapter 16 193

Chapter 17 209

Chapter 18 219

Chapter 19 233

Chapter 20 245

Chapter 21 255

Chapter 22 273

Chapter 23 281

Chapter 24 293

Chapter 25 303

Epilogue 311

Loose Threads 323

About the Author 329

Books with Mike Zimmerli Fingerprints 331

Dedication

For my wife, Mary, who continues to inspire me and hold my nose to the grindstone, reminding me that I can always do better, even when I think it's good enough.

For my children – Adam and Rebecca, who endured all the stories posted on my website while you were growing up, providing fuel for my literary imagination. The stories are still funny, and they still make me smile when I think about them. Each of the old stories brings back warm memories for me. I love you more than you can know. – Dad (but I'm glad you're not teenagers anymore!)

And for my ancestors, who provided me with extra inspiration for characters, themes, and plots.

Acknowledgments

SPECIAL THANKS TO MY WIFE, Mary, the first-line proofreader/editor for all my personal projects. She is my primary sounding board for ideas, plots, twists, and characters.

My heartfelt thanks to Trisa and Keith Chancey, Karen Perez, Wendi Cordele, and Robert Nicholson for your all your help with the proofreading. You each deserve an Eagle Eye Award. Any volunteers to design one? And thanks to real-life Pepé – Robert Perez – for sharing from your past and letting me borrow your name.

Robert Nicholson – thanks for the insights about weapons. Who knew you were a master of punctuation and weaponry? Pleasant surprise from an old friend.

It seems that the more I write, the more help I need.

In for a Penny,
In for a Pound.
At least you're in.

—Jimmy Favreaux

Introduction

JIMMY FAVREAUX WOKE TO AN unfamiliar sound: someone rummaging around in his kitchen. The scratchy sounds had jolted him from his dreams, and now the adrenaline in his veins had fully awakened him.

A private investigator, Jimmy doesn't carry a gun, not because it isn't allowed—it is—but because he prefers to keep the drama in his cases to a minimum. Waving around a Glock 9-millimeter handgun while serving papers is frowned upon. In these days of concealed carry, a simple thing like asking questions about a missing person or serving a subpoena can swiftly evolve into another shootout at the OK Corral. Firearms can escalate everyday interactions to a level no one intended or wants. So, Jimmy is typically unarmed when on the job.

This is Jimmy's house, though, and Jimmy lives alone. His Glock – that one he doesn't carry as a rule – is in a small gun safe in his office. And, like most people, Jimmy doesn't sleep in his office, at least not intentionally or very often, limiting his access to his weapon in situations such as the one.

Some of his buddies tell him he needs to move his gun to his nightstand or under his pillow, but so far, Jimmy has done neither. Thus, his current situation.

He grabbed the hockey stick from the corner of his bedroom. Some people are proficient with a golf club, others with the tried-and-true Louisville slugger baseball bat. However, Jimmy was born and raised in Winnipeg, Manitoba – yes, up in Canada, eh – and he takes comfort in the feel of the hockey stick in his hands, its taped handle providing a non-slip grip, the stick's length giving him a slight reach advantage. It made up slightly for what Jimmy lacked in size and range.

At five-foot-six, a height Jimmy had sadly discovered is slightly shorter than the average woman, the hockey stick extended his reach a solid foot. That added distance could be critical for getting close without putting his body in peril. And utterly useless against a revolver or shotgun, his adrenaline-fueled brain reminded him.

However, feeling somewhat armed, he opened the door to his bedroom as soundlessly as possible, making sure not to bang the door frame with the hockey stick. The kitchen was on the backside of the house, only a few steps to the right of his bedroom. A previous owner had added the kitchen space, and Jimmy was always grateful. When Jimmy bought the house on the Georgia-Florida border a dozen years ago, he had spent half his nest egg making the place comfortable and modernized. He had remodeled the kitchen and installed stainless-steel appliances and a commercial range hood.

The stove's surface light was on, and the refrigerator door was open, providing some illumination in the pre-dawn.

The sheer curtains over the windows at the opposite end of the room revealed the birth of a new day, and Jimmy wondered what time it was. Squinting at the clock on the wall (*When did I start squinting?* he wondered), he saw that it was about six-forty-five. His intruder had graciously allowed Jimmy to sleep until it was almost time to wake up anyway.

Suddenly, the shadows began shifting, and Jimmy knew whoever was in the kitchen was backing out of the refrigerator. A shapely tan leg emerged from behind the door, accompanied by its twin. He saw that the person rummaging in the fridge was barefoot. As his eyes traveled up the legs, he arrived at a pair of shorts and a tee shirt that came down to the curve of her bottom, mostly hidden by the loose shorts and tee shirt. His mind said "her" because of 1) the shapely legs, 2) the long black hair, kept under control by two braids, and 3) because he recognized who it was.

Daani Manyeagles. From Turtle Lake, Wisconsin, where there is no Turtle Lake, she had told Jimmy. Upper and Lower Turtle Lake are several miles east of the town where Daani deals blackjack at the Turtle Lake Casino, one of the many Native American-owned casinos across the upper Midwest. This casino is owned by one of the Wisconsin bands of Ojibwe, the one Daani belongs to.

Daani had recently been a person of interest, using police parlance, in a case Jimmy was recently dragged into. Though it seemed much longer, it had only been three days ago.

The cast of that little drama had included Ruth and Doug Thompson, originally from Grand Rapids, MN, but lately from Chippewa Falls, WI. In addition to the Thompsons, there was Jimmy and Daani, and – rounding it out – Jimmy's one-time nemesis: Jack Powers.

When it was all over, everyone went their separate ways, and Jimmy and Daani went to the Waffle House. And then to Jimmy's house.

Jack went to the morgue.

Chapter 1

JIMMY SET THE HOCKEY STICK in the corner of the hallway, out of sight of anyone rummaging around in the kitchen.

"Hey," Daani said, her head now completely out of the refrigerator. "I was wondering when you were going to get up. Did I wake you? I really was trying to be quiet, honest. I'm heading out for home this morning, so I thought I'd make us breakfast," she said. "You know, to kind of say thank you for letting me crash here for a couple of days."

Jimmy had converted one of his house's three bedrooms into an office when he bought the place, leaving two bedrooms, each with its own bathroom.

Surprisingly, there was not a steady stream of people looking to couch surf at his place, and Jimmy discovered that he didn't have many close friends back in Minnesota and even fewer in his hometown of Winnipeg. No one had ever taken advantage of Jimmy's housing situation in a dozen years. Until Daani, that is.

In addition to a nearly nonexistent friends list, Jimmy had ditched his old cellphone number when he started his freelance investigation business on the Florida border. He felt it was time to make a clean break from the past, and a local number looked better. Jack Powers – in trying to complete his AA Step Nine list – had attempted to make amends with Jimmy, but he didn't know Jimmy had a new number. Consequently, Jack didn't realize Jimmy never got his apology, but it all worked out.

During Jimmy's long night with Jack's body in the hotel bathroom, he realized he owed Jack for helping him disengage from northern Minnesota and relocate to the land of sun and warmth. Amends had been made, just a tad late for Jack's Step Nine list.

Daani asked, "What kind of omelet do you want? Say cheese and ham because that's all I found in your refrigerator."

"Cheese and ham would be great, Daani."

"Perfect! Great choice, Jimmy!"

Jimmy stood in the doorway to his kitchen. He thought it was nice having someone else there, doing something for him, but it was such a rare experience – *as in never!* – that he had forgotten he wasn't alone in the house that morning. Hence the hockey stick.

His eyes took in her form, a pleasant sight. She was about the same height as Jimmy and neither chunky nor skinny. Her long, ebony-colored braids came down to nearly the middle of her back. Jimmy was pretty sure her hair would be even longer if she freed it from the braids, but on both days Daani had spent at Jimmy's, she kept it bound up. They went to the zoo one day and to one of the area's many beaches the next. They talked a lot, laughed freely, and generally enjoyed each other's companionship, but that was all – nothing physical or romantic.

While they had kept things platonic, Jimmy recalled Ruth making a comment about consenting adults as she and Doug were leaving. Her remark had prompted Daani to protest that she didn't go for "old guys." Supposedly said in jest, it was also a clear boundary.

As Daani cooked his omelet, Jimmy realized he felt lonely.

***

After breakfast, Jimmy washed the dishes while Daani finished packing her few belongings in her bag. He walked her out to her car, parked in the front next to his SUV. The situation felt as awkward to him as the night at the hotel when they were alone for the first time and no longer adversaries. Neither knew what to do or say that time.

Apparently, Daani had been thinking about it, too, because she didn't hesitate to make a move. She wrapped her arms around Jimmy's neck, gave him a squeeze and a familial peck on the cheek, and said, "Thanks for everything, Uncle Jimmy."

"Uncle Jimmy?" *You're killing me here, kid!*

"Yeah. Uncle Jimmy. In the Ojibwe world, we have many grandfathers, grandmothers, aunts, and uncles—all the older adults, blood relatives or not. It's a sign of respect and inclusion in the family. So, you're my new Uncle Jimmy."

With no amorous activity between the two during Daani's visit, there were no shenanigans to remember each other by, either, unfortunately for Jimmy. Now she had thrown a huge bucket of ice water on Jimmy's unspoken intentions. His new designation as "Uncle Jimmy" left no wiggle room.

So, Jimmy did what any good uncle would do: he wrapped her up tightly in a bear hug, ignoring her nearness.

Releasing her from his grasp, Jimmy gave her his best "relational" advice saying, "Be careful driving. Remember not to drive so long that you fall asleep at the wheel; get a hotel. You saved enough staying here that you can do that. Eat well, too. Are you sure you'll get back in time?"

"Tonya Darkmoon said she would cover for me if I wasn't back in time for my first shift. I just need to call her if I'm not going to make it."

She got in her car, closed the door, and Jimmy stepped out of the way so she could back up and leave his grassy yard. He waved, and she honked in reply. He continued to wave at her tail lights until she was nearly out of sight. Turning out onto Highway 17, she turned right toward the I95-North ramp. Jimmy had never felt this lonely out here before. A dog or cat or some chickens might help. Or work.

His cell phone dinged. He checked the message. It was from his friend, mentor, and part-time partner, Pepé. It said,

Call me. Got a case to discuss. Or better yet, meet me at the usual place for breakfast

The "usual place" was Steffens Restaurant, a historic diner on the edge of Kingsland on Highway 17.

Jimmy texted back,

Be there in ten

Chapter 2

I T TOOK JIMMY LESS THAN the estimated ten minutes to cover the five miles to Steffens. The hardcore breakfast crowd had been in much earlier and already left to make their mark in the world. Since it was now nearly nine a.m. – practically lunchtime by some people's clocks! – Jimmy and Pepé didn't have to wait for a booth.

A Highway 17 dining fixture since 1948, Steffens has been a travelers' staple for seventy-five years. The timeless eatery on the popular north-south state highway preceded the interstate that lured many businesses away. Both Steffens and Highway 17 have stoically withstood years of change, maintaining their identities by not trying to be something they are not.

Jimmy didn't tell Pepé he'd already eaten breakfast earlier. Instead, Jimmy told his partner the mirror had shown him he had picked up a couple of extra pounds, so he was eating lighter and trying to watch what he ate. Jimmy asked Emily, the waitress, for a coffee and a single order of Ms. Helen's Biscuits & Gravy, a menu staple at Steffens since 1948. They still used the same recipe, with natural sausage and peppered gravy. Jimmy turned his cup right-side up, and Emily poured the hot brown liquid in without spilling a drop.

Pepé wasn't big, but he was solid. A cop should have some substance. In a wrestling match with a methhead who weighs a buck-twenty, you want to have the weight advantage. Your adversary may have chemically-induced paranoia or rage, and applying your heftier bulk to the situation can help resolve the matter. Even several years after retiring, Pepé still liked to maintain what he called his fighting weight. If his wife, Gwynn, teased him about his extra cushioning, he jokingly replied, "It just means there's more of Pepé to love!" He ordered a Steak Bomb Burrito: three scrambled eggs, shaved steak, cheese, onions, and tater tots, all wrapped in a jumbo flour tortilla. And a Diet Coke.

Emily hadn't written anything down, but Jimmy knew she would get it right. Not because they always ordered the same thing – they didn't – but because that was just how it was at Steffens. They had good waitresses who knew what they were doing. For a small order like theirs, she could walk back and tell the cooks to start a steak bomb and a single Ms. Helen's. The waitress would pause long enough to write a couple of tickets in shorthand and clip them to the wheel before heading back to the tables and booths.

Jimmy recognized the signs of a good breakfast crew. He had worked in a restaurant for several years when he first moved to northern Minnesota after leaving his hometown of

Winnipeg. Jimmy had sojourned as a breakfast cook, so he was familiar with the particular steps required for this unique ballet. It had been many years since he had worn an apron professionally, but Jimmy still enjoyed cooking, hence the kitchen upgrades at home. He still toyed occasionally with the idea of replacing his regular stove with a commercial one, complete with a flat griddle, but the price was more than he could justify with his current income.

"So, how you doin'?" Pepé asked as they waited for their orders. The question and accent revealed traces of growing up in Brooklyn that would never fade away. Pepé might drop an occasional "y'all" into the conversation, but it usually came out "you all."

Emily swung by with a pot of coffee to warm their cups, but they'd barely had time to make a dent in what they had, so they waved her on with a smile.

"I'm okay," Jimmy replied to his partner's question. "Daani left for Wisconsin just a few minutes before you texted me. I don't envy her driving back alone. Thirteen hundred miles. But she's young."

"Wiscahnsin," Pepé mimicked, drawing out the 'ah' to an unnatural length. He did the same thing whenever Jimmy mentioned Minnesota. Pepé always repeated, "Minnesohta," making the oh-syllable about three times as long as normal.

Jimmy sipped the hot coffee from the diner mug it was served in. For all he knew, this cup had been in use since 1948 and had caressed the lips of Presidents, movie stars, and murderers. That would be something to research sometime—

the average lifespan of a restaurant cup and how many people drank from it before it ended up broken on the floor.

"How long was she here? A couple of days?" Pepé asked.

"Yeah. Just two days after the case. We went to the zoo one day and the beach the next."

"Which beach did you take her to?" Pepé inquired.

"American Beach down in Fernandina. It's never too crowded, and parts are closed off to driving. Plus, there's the historical aspect to it. You know, the old building down the street from Birney Park that was a juke joint back in the 30s and 40s. Everybody from Cab Calloway to Ella Fitzgerald to Duke Ellington played there. I would have loved to have seen it in its heyday."

Jimmy stopped, his coffee cup nearly to his lips as though the pause in conversation required another drink of the caffeine-loaded go-go juice, as he called it. But before taking another sip, Jimmy steered the cup away, almost as though teasing his mouth like Lucy pulling the football away from Charlie Brown. He gently swung the cup to one side where he could use it for a pointer as the conversation required.

"The first time I ever went to American Beach, I really enjoyed it. It was the first real beach I had ever been to, having grown up in Canada. So, when I told someone about it the next day, they bent over, leaned in close like they were going to tell me a secret, and asked, 'Did you know that American Beach used to be the Black beach?' It was an old Southern guy who had been born here, you know? The kind that never quite made it out of the 50s."

Pepé grinned and nodded. Jimmy noticed his cheeks were grizzled that day. Pepé didn't like shaving, and his wife didn't like beards, so they compromised somewhere in the middle. This was apparently a no-shaving day.

Jimmy continued his tale about American Beach. "I looked at the old guy for a second, and I leaned in just like he had, and I said, 'They never asked to see my ID.' The guy looked at me like I was an alien. I think he muttered something about 'damn Yankees' as he walked away, but I thought it was a hoot. I should have told him I was a Canadian, not a Yankee. That would have really messed with him!"

Jimmy's partner's eyes crinkled up behind his glasses, and a grin spread across his face from ear to ear. Pepé's mouth opened, and his patented laugh rolled out. There was no way of adequately describing Robert's laugh. The closest thing was probably Arnold Horshack from *Welcome Back, Kotter*, but that wasn't quite right either.

Jimmy didn't think Pepé looked much like it, but his partner – a former cop – was half Puerto Rican. Jimmy also knew that not being blessed with stereotypical Hispanic looks had probably saved Pepé from numerous fights and injuries when he began his police career in Charleston, S.C., in the mid-70s. Jimmy had asked Pepé about it, and he had explained that he had more Spanish blood in his genetic makeup, which provided his light skin instead of the usual brown skin and eyes and black or nearly black hair. Most of Pepé's hair was gone now, though, so that wasn't a giveaway.

Charleston, S.C., is definitely part of the Deep South, complete with—at the time—signs that read Whites Only or

Colored Only. Sixty years ago, it was all white or the back of the bus. There was no middle ground or allowances for being part white, which could be even worse since neither side accepted people of mixed race. Daani had told Jimmy something similar. Because her father was white and her mother Ojibwe, she was too white for those on "the rez" and too Native for the whites.

The 1964 Civil Rights Act theoretically ended Jim Crow, but the actual story was something quite different. In 1965, ninety-five percent of South Carolina's African American children still attended segregated schools. Widespread desegregation of South Carolina public schools didn't occur until the early 1970s, about the time Pepé was hired as a Charleston cop.

Their waitress brought them their breakfasts—Jimmy's second, but he wasn't telling Pepé that!—and refilled their coffees before hurrying to her next table. Ms. Helen's biscuits were smothered in sausage and pepper gravy, and Jimmy was glad for his knife and fork. Meanwhile, the huge Steak Bomb burrito Pepé ordered was something the Georgia PI could eat with one hand while holding his Diet Coke in the other, with no silverware required.

The two investigators didn't talk for a bit, concentrating on their food. Despite the omelet Jimmy had consumed less than two hours earlier, he inhaled the biscuits and gravy; they were just that good. However, he was glad he had the foresight to get a single order rather than a double or triple. One biscuit, split in half and drowned in white peppered gravy with sausage, was plenty for him; two or three would have bordered on pure gluttony.

When Jimmy was done with his biscuits and had employed his spoon to avoid leaving any gravy behind, he sat back in his chair and told Pepé, "You said you had a case to discuss. When you're ready to talk, I'm ready to listen." He didn't want to hurry Pepé along.

Pepé waved the hand with the steak burrito at Jimmy. "I caught a case the other day, and you might be interested in helping me. It's kind of a missing persons case, but with a twist." He took a drink of his Diet Coke before continuing.

"I got a call from the Glynn County Sheriff's Office. They didn't have anyone to put on this one, so they farmed it out to me. I'm more than happy to pick up their slack. The woman – a Mrs. Charlotte Epps – wants someone to find her husband. He's been missing for six years, and she's pretty sure he's not coming back. She hasn't heard a peep from him in all that time and wants to get on with her life. It could be that someone on the side wants to help her change her last name again, but she can't as long as she's married. She doesn't want to get divorced; she wants her husband declared dead. Then she can collect his insurance benefits and all that fun stuff before she gets married again. That's why I think someone is pushing her to do it – she'll bring a lot more money to the marriage if her first husband is declared dead. And they say love is blind."

Pepé took another bite of his steak bomb and another slurp of his Diet Coke to wash it down, then declared, "I think someone sees quite clearly what he wants to charge for his love." Pepé filled their corner of the restaurant with his laughter.

"So, where do I come in?" Jimmy asked. He took another sip of his coffee, which was getting cold now. That was the only bad thing about the classic diner cups: they tended to get cold if you didn't drink the coffee fast enough. Whatever material they were crafted from didn't always hold the heat in very well.

"You can do the fun stuff," Pepé said. "You can do that interweb searching stuff you like to do, like looking for signs that this guy has been lying low rather than being dead. The tricky part is that you have to go back six years to see if he took it on the hoof. It's a lot easier to check on somebody if they've only just disappeared recently, I know, but that's not what Mrs. Epps is asking me to do, and by 'me,' I mean us."

"Couldn't the Glynn County Sheriff's Office do that stuff?" Jimmy asked, pushing his coffee cup away. Having consumed two breakfasts, he had had enough coffee.

"Like I said, Jimmy, they don't have anyone they can put on it. Besides, it's not really their kind of thing. It's much more of a private investigator case. You'll want to find out if Mrs. E. made a missing person report six years ago, and if not, why not? You know? Things like that."

"So, what are we talking about here? Six years ago … 2016, this guy goes missing? And Mrs. … Epps, you said? Mrs. Epps waits until now to find out if he's dead or just got tired of her? Maybe he's the one who found someone else and decided it was easier to skedaddle. Is there a sizeable estate involved, and that's why he skated? He didn't want the graciousness of the divorce courts to give his wife half of what he had accumulated?"

"It could be," said Pepé. "But there's something else, too. I've been meaning to check since the Glynn County Sheriff's Office contacted me: is it seven years you gotta be gone before they can say you're dead?"

Jimmy was already applying his thumbs to his phone to yield up the answer. In a few seconds, he shared what he had found.

"According to the Georgia Code, Article 1: Administration of Estate, 53-9-1 from 2020. 'A domiciliary of this state who has been missing from the last known place of domicile for a continuous period of four years shall be presumed to have died; provided, however, that such presumption of death may be rebutted by proof. The date of death is presumed to be the end of the four-year period unless it is proved by a preponderance of the evidence that death occurred earlier.' In other words, unless someone can prove otherwise, anybody that disappears for four years can be presumed dead. Tell me again why we always think it's seven years?"

Pepé loudly slurped the last of his Diet Coke, flushing down the remains of his breakfast burrito, and said, "It's because of that movie. It comes on TCM every once in a while. *My Favorite Wife*, with Cary Grant and Irene Dunn. Irene Dunne plays this woman who, after being shipwrecked on a tropical island for seven years, is declared legally dead by her husband, Cary Grant. But then, she returns home to her husband and their children just as he's about to leave with his new wife on his honeymoon."

"So, the old wife comes back just as he's taking off with his new wife?" Jimmy asked. "Which one was better looking?"

"I dunno. It's kind of a toss-up. It depends on whether you like brunettes or blondes. It all depends on personal preference, you know?"

"So, does Cary Grant go on his honeymoon? Or should I say his second honeymoon?"

"No, and that really ticks off the new wife, as I'm sure you can imagine."

"Completely understandable."

"Then Cary Grant finds out his first wife wasn't alone on the deserted island. It turns out she was marooned there with Randolph Scott, who's almost as good-looking as Cary Grant. So, Cary Grant gets jealous, and – long story short – he gets arrested for bigamy and ends up before the judge—the same judge who declared Irene Dunne dead and the same one who married Cary Grant to his new wife. The judge annuls the second marriage, and Cary Grant and Irene Dunne make up and live happily ever after."

"And what is this movie called again?" Jimmy asked.

"*My Favorite Wife.* Whenever it comes on, <u>my</u> favorite wife watches it. That woman loves Cary Grant movies. Especially Father Goose with him and Leslie Caron on that South Seas island with all the schoolgirls."

Jimmy asked his friend and partner, "Is there anything in the movie that might help us find out if this Epps guy is dead or alive?"

"Not in the movie, but I think you already found something: Mrs. E. doesn't have to wait seven years. Georgia is only four years. That's good information to have, not that I would ever pull a Houdini on my missus."

"I think that would be a David Copperfield now, Pepé. You need to keep up with the times."

"Yeah, whatever."

"What's Mr. E's name? It's always helpful to have more than just a last name for searching."

"His name is—or was—John Epps. Born in Dess Moyness, Iowa." Pepé pronounced all the s's.

"The s's are silent, Pepé. Duh Moyn."

"Yeah, I know. I'm just having fun." The former cop leaned back in his chair, patted his belly, and belched. "That was a good steak bomb. Anything you can put in a tortilla is usually good, though. You know?"

"I'm right there with you."

"Anything else in that stuff on the Georgia Code for declaring somebody dead?" asked Pepé.

"Actually, yes. Get this: if someone has been missing for twelve months continuously, you can have them declared dead by a 'preponderance of the evidence.' So, Mrs. Epps didn't have to wait seven or even four years. She could have had him declared dead after only one year if she had overwhelming evidence. Maybe she didn't have enough evidence. It's possible she was letting some investments grow before having him declared legally dead. Or – think about this – maybe she loves the guy and actually wants him back." Now Jimmy wished his coffee was still hot, or at least warm, but he left his cup where he had moved it before asking his friend, "Riddle me this, Batman. If there's legally dead, what's *illegally* dead?"

"That's when someone whacks you without your permission," Pepé answered. His eyes crinkled, and their corner of the restaurant was again filled with his laughter.

Chapter 3

THEY STOOD OUTSIDE STEFFENS IN the cool November air. It felt refreshing after their recent extended stretch of summer. Still, Jimmy would take the heat and humidity over Minnesota's drastically abbreviated summers and overly-exaggerated winters any time.

"Let me make sure I know what I'm doing," Jimmy said. "I'm trying to track down a guy who's been missing for six years because his wife didn't know she could have him declared dead after one year – four on the outside, right?"

Pepé nodded.

"You said Glynn County contacted you about the case, so I'll assume Mrs. Epps lives somewhere near Brunswick."

"Jekyll Island," Pepé responded.

"Nice," Jimmy replied. "And the occupation of the possibly deceased John Epps?"

"A doctor. Family practitioner. He was part of a group. They just absorbed his patients at first, then got a new partner when it became obvious that he wasn't coming back."

"I imagine that with him being a doctor, they lived pretty well."

"Not all do. Malpractice insurance can be a real bugger, you know? From what the Sheriff's Office tells me, Epps was in the middle, not rich, not poor. You could say he was comfortable."

"Okay. So, a comfortable doctor just disappears one day. Gets up in the morning, kisses his wife goodbye, leaves for work, and then takes a detour and is never heard from again. Is that about it?"

"I don't know if he kissed his wife before leaving, but that's close enough," Pepé said, grinning around a toothpick poking out from the corner of his mouth.

"I assume you have not yet met the aforementioned Mrs. Epps, correct?"

"You are correct. I plan to see Mrs. E. early this afternoon. I should be able to get you a picture of the doctor and a snapshot of their financial information. Neither she nor the police volunteered that Dr. Epps's credit or bank cards have had any activity since his disappearance. He either had cash squirreled away, a partner he had funneled money to, or, as she maintains: he's dead."

"There may be another possibility, Pepé."

"Oh, yeah? Enlighten me."

"He could still be alive, living either very frugally or off someone else. He could have changed his identity, too. And one other thing ..." Jimmy paused.

"Yeah?"

"Does she want him dead or alive again? If we find out he's alive, does his wife want him back? Or does she prefer him dead?"

The former cop's eyes widened for a second, then narrowed. He leaned back and stared at Jimmy. "What you talkin' 'bout, Willis?"

"Hear me out, Pepé. You know I abhor violence and don't even carry a gun. I'm just thinking about the code for getting someone declared dead. It said ..."

Jimmy pulled out his phone and swiped across it to bring up the screen he wanted.

"Any person 'missing from the last known place of domicile for a continuous period of four years shall be presumed to have died; provided, however, that such presumption of death may be rebutted by proof.' To the state of Georgia, he's already presumed dead. If his wife is considering getting a replacement for the doc, she's already assumed he's not returning, too. But he may want to stay that way even if he's *not* dead. He may like his new dead lifestyle. Gratefully dead, you might say."

"So, if he's alive, we don't tell her we found him?"

Jimmy replied, "Or we tell her we found a preponderance of proof that he's dead. Part of that depends on him. And we haven't met the missus yet. She may not be the most pleasant person in the world. Obviously, the guy had reasons for making himself absent from the home and clinic. You and I both know that his reasons could include a younger version of his wife – that's always popular – or that the pressure of his work and marriage became too much for him. He Just. Wanted. Out. Haven't you ever felt that way, Pepé?"

"Not badly enough to want to leave Gwynn behind."

"That's because you have a good one, Pepé, and I mean that. But we don't know about Mrs. Epps. She and her potential Mister Number Two may *both* want Dr. Epps to stay dead. She may only want the state's official seal so she can finish her plan, and she just wants us to make sure the road is clear. Have you ever thought about that?"

"There was a time, you know," Pepé said, leaning back against his pickup as cars drove past them on Highway 17, and Jimmy knew his partner was going to wax nostalgic.

"There was a time when people got married for life, you know? For better or worse, for richer or poorer, in sickness and health. A time when people didn't view their spouses as disposable. People today don't get married so much as they take out a *lease* – like on a car. At the end of the lease, you can either turn the car in for a new one or buy the one you've been driving. People turn their spouses in for new ones when they get tired of them. It's not a no-fault divorce; it's a no-work marriage. They seem to think, 'I'll stick around as long as it's all sunshine, roses, and unicorns. But if it isn't fun anymore, I'm outta here.' You know?"

Jimmy had assumed a similar posture to Pepé's, leaning against his white Nissan SUV. Cars cruised by fifty feet away, some going south toward Jimmy's house, some headed north.

Jimmy had his phone in his hand when it suddenly rang. He jumped a little in surprise, then looked at the number. No clues. He held it out to Pepé. "Any idea whose number that is?"

Pepé looked at it and shook his head.

Jimmy answered the device, "This is Jimmy Favreaux. Hold, please."

He put the phone down at his side and whispered, "I'll catch you later, Pepé. Let me know what you find out after meeting with Mrs. Epps."

Pepé gave him a thumbs up and got in his pickup. As Pepé drove away, Jimmy resumed his call.

"Thank you for holding. This is Jimmy. What can I help you with?"

"Mr. Favreaux, this is Hillary Lyst's personal secretary. We would like to meet with you today if that's possible."

From hearing just that tiny snippet of the woman's voice, Jimmy's mind's eye pictured the secretary as five-four, slender, with nice legs, a pleasing shape, blonde hair, about thirty-five years old, and very single. Someone who also wasn't opposed to "older" men. Jimmy thought, *Let me be right for a change!*

"Well," he replied to Hillary Lyst's personal secretary, "that depends."

"On?" she asked.

"On where I'm supposed to meet him or her and whether you'll be there."

A little giggle. *Good sign!*

"Hillary Lyst is a man, just so you know. I understand it's hard to tell these days with all the unisex names, but he's definitely a man. He's the owner of Lyst Publishing in Fernandina Beach. We maintain a small office on Sadler Avenue, near Starbucks. Do you know where that is?"

"Indeed, I do," Jimmy answered cheerfully. "I was there just yesterday, as a matter of fact."

He was telling the truth. He and Daani had stopped in at the coffee house with the mermaid logo. They were on their way to the beach, and they both wanted a latté to drink in the car or while wading in the morning waves at American Beach.

"Did you see Staples when you were at Starbucks?" she asked.

"I was busy looking elsewhere," Jimmy answered honestly, "but I know where the Staples is."

"We're located just east of Staples. I promise you'll find me if you turn right at Staples."

And if I find you, do I get to claim the prize? Jimmy thought, but he kept that happy thought to himself. Instead, he answered, "Is there a time that's best for you?"

"Would one o'clock work for you, Mr. Favreaux?" the secretary asked.

"Please. Call me Jimmy. Mr. Favreaux is my dad." Another giggle. Another good sign!

"All right, Jimmy. Would one o'clock be all right for you to meet with Mr. Lyst?"

"I think one o'clock would be wonderful," Jimmy answered. "Tell Mr. Lyst that I'll see him then."

"Thank you. I have you penned in."

And if you're as cute as your voice and personality, I'll let you pen me in and close the gate! Jimmy answered in his head.

"May I ask you a question, Miss…?" Jimmy waited.

"Yes?" She hadn't taken the bait. He'd have to be more direct. He'd have to figure out another query to uncover the woman's marital status. Jimmy felt he had been good enough for long enough that God should give him this one. *Just once.*

"May I ask what this meeting is regarding?" Jimmy asked.

"I'm not at liberty to offer you specifics, but we hope you might be willing to take our company on as a client."

Work is good, Jimmy thought. And Mr. Lyst's personal secretary might help Jimmy forget about Daani calling him Uncle Jimmy.

"I hope we can arrange to take you on, too," Jimmy said. "Are you going to be at the meeting with us?"

"Oh, yes. I'll be there. Most definitely."

"That's great. I, uh, I didn't catch your name, though."

"It's Wendi … with an 'i,'" she said. "Wendi Lyst."

Jimmy paused, holding the phone down at his side, wishing she had said any other name than that.

"Daughter?" he asked, fingers crossed.

"No," she giggled.

"Well, you can't be his son, so I'm really hoping you're his sister." Jimmy saw his afternoon of idling away his time with a pleasant young blonde thing fading away.

More giggling. "No, Jimmy. I'm Mrs. Lyst. We'll see you at one o'clock."

By her voice, she could have been a dead ringer for Marilyn Monroe. Then, in the sexiest voice to whisper in Jimmy's ear in a very, very long time, she breathed into the phone, "We'll *both* see you at one o'clock. I'm really, really looking forward to meeting you, Jimmy. Buh-bye."

Mrs. Lyst. At least she hadn't said she was Mr. Lyst's mother! Jimmy would have had to swear off women for the foreseeable future if she had.

Jimmy stared at his cell phone for a minute before fully comprehending that she had hung up. He gave himself a little shake, hiked his shoulders northward toward his ears until they crunched, cracked his neck on each side, walked around his vehicle, and climbed in.

✳✳✳

Less than ten minutes later, Jimmy googled Lyst Publishing from his home office. He was glad to discover the client did, indeed, exist. It's always much easier to be paid by a company that exists.

Unfortunately, there were no pictures of the disembodied voice of Wendi Lyst. Jimmy would have to wait for the real thing.

Mr. Hillary Lyst had been a newspaper editor in his younger days, but in his early thirties, he had abandoned his career to launch a small book publishing company. Some might say he was a visionary, disembarking from a sinking ship before even the captain knew the situation. Print newspapers – especially small-town papers – were becoming dinosaurs, and the internet was the giant meteor spelling their demise. Maybe Lyst had seen the hieroglyphics on the wall and decided to take his publishing skills and use them differently. Books and newspapers perform similar jobs, telling stories and educating the masses. In the early days of the internet—thirty-plus years ago—a skilled editor could make the sort of transition Lyst had. He had probably done much of the book editing himself, if not all. Meanwhile, newspapers began closing their doors as the internet replaced them.

It turned out that Hillary Lyst was sixty-nine, a native of southwest Georgia, born in 1953. When he was thirty-two, in 1985, he started Lyst Publishing, something Jimmy found impressive for two reasons. First, a relatively young man with no experience in the book publishing world had successfully launched a company that was still around nearly forty years later. Second, Lyst had seen the inevitable death of print media and acted on his farsighted belief. Jimmy decided he would need to ask the man how he had done that and if he could pass along any stock tips to Jimmy.

There wasn't a lot of information about the publishing company. Its website was down due to "technical issues," but it had a banner that said they weren't taking submissions at this time, and they would let aspiring authors know when they were open for submissions again. Jimmy wondered how the company could be closed for submissions when publishing for new and unknown writers kept their doors open. They published for those who envisioned themselves as the next Ernest Hemingway, David Baldacci, or William Kent Krueger. By Jimmy's reckoning, a publishing company that wasn't taking author submissions was akin to a dairy being closed for milk deliveries from dairy farms. It would be hard to make ends meet.

Perhaps the delightful-sounding Wendi Lyst could enlighten Jimmy about how a book publisher can make money without submissions.

Thoughts of Wendi Lyst caused Jimmy to wonder if she was Hillary Lyst's second or third wife. Perhaps he's so married to his work that he has no time for a wife. Jimmy was full of questions, but they would need to wait. He just needed to be patient. It was still two hours until he had to leave to make his one o'clock appointment.

In the meantime, he opted to do a little digging on his partner's new case, checking into the background of the missing-and-presumed-dead Dr. John Epps, formerly of Des Moines, Iowa. Pepé had a meeting scheduled with Mrs. Epps at her home on Jekyll Island, Georgia, about the same time Jimmy would be at Lyst Publishing in Fernandina Beach, Florida.

As Jimmy typed the good doctor's name into a search engine, he thought, *Jekyll Island is a long way from Des Moines, Dr. Epps.*

Chapter 4

JIMMY SOON DISCOVERED THAT THE missing Dr. Epps was not the first Dr. John Epps from Des Moines. And while Jimmy had not located a distinct family line that connected them, he was just getting started.

Jimmy knew that many family generations carried on a family business, whether that was steel production, oil, cyber technology, or medicine. Names also tended to be an item that was frequently handed down. There were at least three James Favreaux's in Jimmy's family tree.

Just typing John Epps into Google produced far too many results. Adding "Dr." to the search helped, but it was still unwieldly. Unfortunately, Jimmy had no idea how old Dr. Epps was, so he switched over from Google to ancestry.com. Most of the top results from Google pointed to Ancestry anyway. Jimmy figured Ancestry paid a premium price to Google to appear at the top of results.

Jimmy accessed the Des Moines census information section. Some states, including Iowa, used to do their own censuses in addition to the federal ones. Still, Jimmy knew the chances of finding Dr. Epps in a census were slim since the most recent data available to the public was 1940.

Jimmy received a pleasant surprise at Ancestry: the 1950 census had recently been opened for public consumption. A birthdate from 1950 would only make John seventy-two, a viable candidate for a doctor on Jekyll. Jimmy would have a better idea of how to fine-tune his search after Pepé reported back from his meeting with Mrs. Epps. Jimmy began digging. He found other Epps in the search—even a Christopher Columbus Epps—but not a John. He had known it was a long shot, but you don't know until you try.

Suddenly, a list of suggestions on the side of the Ancestry screen snatched Jimmy's attention away from the 1950 census. A link simply said "**Dr. John Epps**," but it was from the Criminal Matters section of the July 26, 1881, Burlington, Iowa, Daily Hawkeye newspaper. Jimmy couldn't resist clicking on it.

> *"A shooting affray on Sunday evening between*
> *F. W. George and John Epps, one a printing press*
> *engraver and the other a quack doctor and*
> *barber, was over a frail girl to whom both had*
> *been paying attention. Epps declared in his*
> *statement that (he) was endeavoring to procure a*
> *divorce from his wife to marry the girl. George was*
> *allegedly endeavoring to procure a divorce from*
> *his wife to marry the girl. George, who was forty*

years old, claims Epps was trying to procure an
abortion for the girl, and he killed him as a friend
of the girl's parents."

Jimmy couldn't resist checking to see how far Burlington was from Des Moines. A little over 150 miles.

The murdered John Epps from the news item could be a relative of the Jekyll Island Epps, possibly a namesake. Jimmy went back to the Ancestry page, tweaked the filters, and searched again. This time there were several other results, including one from the Le Mars Daily Liberal dated August 1, 1881.

"A deliberate and cold-blooded murder occurred in
Des Moines on Sunday, July 24. The murderer was
F. W. George, an engineer, and his victim was Dr.
John Epps. The trouble between the two men had
its origin about a girl and appears to have been the
result of jealousy. The murderer, who met and shot
his victim dead in the street, is a man of about forty
years of age and has a family. Dr. Epps was about
53 years of age and was a widower."

The two newspaper accounts agreed the murder occurred on Sunday, July 24, 1881, and the Burlington story narrowed it to the evening. The Le Mars story added that Epps was 53 years old and a widower, which meant there might be children. Jimmy was getting excited. Another promising lead, but probably for another time. For now, he could see no connection to their current case other than the name.

Jimmy figured a murder in the big city of Des Moines would be of interest across most of Iowa. He checked and discovered that Le Mars was in northwestern Iowa, about 200 miles north of Des Moines, as the crow flies.

Something about the town's name rang a bell in Jimmy's head. He knew he shouldn't get sidetracked like this—*sidetracked from a sidetrack?*—but there was still plenty of time until he had to leave for his meeting with Wendi Lyst.

And her husband! he reminded himself.

Jimmy pulled up another window to hunt down Le Mars, Iowa. With a few keystrokes, he brought up the Le Mars bio.

> *Le Mars is recognized as "The Ice Cream Capital of the World" because more ice cream is made here by a single privately held, family-owned company (Wells' Enterprises, Inc., makers of Blue Bunny Ice Cream) than in any other city in the world!*

Wells Blue Bunny ice cream and ice cream treats. That's why the name had nagged him. He had seen it on the containers.

With one itch relieved, Jimmy returned to his search for John Epps, murdered in Des Moines in 1881. He found a few lines in the Waterloo Iowa State Reporter from August 3, 1881.

> *"A shooting affray occurred at Des Moines last Sunday week between F. W. George and John Epps, one a printing press engineer and the other a quack doctor and barber, about a frail girl to whom*

both had been paying attention. Epp's death was instantaneous."

This new report said Epps's death was instantaneous, whereas the Hawkeye said he gave a statement to the police. "*Epps declared in his statement that (he) was endeavoring to procure a divorce from his wife to marry the girl.*"

Pepé had often said that one thing that never changes is that whenever a pretty girl is involved, men become increasingly stupid.

If Epps was killed instantly, who gave the police a statement? The girl? It sounded like something a girl kept on the side might say: "He was going to divorce his wife to marry me." Most often, that was a lie men used to keep sneaking into a girl's bedroom. The goal was to have a traditional wife for public occasions and a side chick for fun.

Jimmy recalled a case where a wife confronted her husband's "side chick," a much-younger woman who boasted to the wife's face about the man's promise to divorce his wife.

The wife responded, "Oh, honey. If it were only that easy. But you see, darling, he likes money and material wealth and pretty young things like you. And if he divorces me, he will lose <u>at least</u> half his money and <u>most</u> of his nice things, including the house, his fancy car, and his children. Girl, you can't make up for that, no matter how inventive you are in the bedroom. That man's not going anywhere until *I* decide he's leaving. In the meantime, he and I both enjoy his money and the things it buys, he enjoys you, and—best of all—I don't have to entertain him like you do. I call that a win-win."

Jimmy wondered if the John Epps of 1881 had a similarly pragmatic wife before F.W. George cut short his medical practice and hair-cutting business. Jimmy kept looking at the results from Ancestry.

The Algona, Iowa Republican published a blurb that said Epps was shot twice, the second shot being the fatal one, and included the line: *"A woman was at the bottom of the trouble."*

The Palo Alto Recorder from Emmetsburg, Iowa, gave it one sentence on August 6, 1881.

> *"F. W. George, a machinist from Des Moines, irritated over some words about a girl, killed a barber named John Epps, who called himself the Indian doctor."*

Jimmy doubted the history lesson had any bearing on the currently missing Dr. John Epps, but he found it fascinating. Late nineteenth-century drama – murder in the street, as the newspapers of the time had reported. How similar and yet unlike today, when everyone's cellphone videos of a police stop or arrest go viral in hours, spreading worldwide at the speed of broadband. In 1881, information crept along, taking two weeks to spread a couple of hundred miles from the origin.

Jimmy couldn't find anything about the trial or sentencing of F.W. George. *There ought to be something,* he thought. The man had ended another man's life over an argument about a young girl. She may have been a runaway, a hooker, or a Native American—an Indian in the parlance of the time. Regardless, the newspapers were correct: *"A woman was at the bottom of the trouble."*

One paper quoted George saying Epps was trying to procure an abortion for the girl but not whose child she was carrying. Had George killed Epps to prevent an abortion or because the girl had been playing doctor with Epps? If George was trying to protect her honor, Jimmy was confident it had already been tarnished.

Jimmy bookmarked the search so he could return to it later. If a story about a murder had been picked up by five newspapers, there should be some follow-up about the man accused of the killing. Jimmy was sure with enough time to poke around, he could dig up something.

He still wanted to see if the 1881 Dr. Epps was a direct or indirect ancestor of the currently missing Dr. Epps, if for no other reason than to satisfy his curiosity. As he shut down his computer, the phrase from the Algona State Reporter echoed in his mind: *"A woman was at the bottom of the trouble."*

Like great-great-grandfather like son? Perhaps. Would further research reveal any familial traits? Who knew? Jimmy didn't have time right now to see if Dr. John Epps – an 1881 murder victim – had any children and if any followed him into medicine. Or grandchildren. Or if it was all just coincidental that the two men had the same name and title and hailed from the same city.

But right now, it was time to leave for his meeting with Wendi Lyst.

And her husband, of course!

Chapter 5

JIMMY HAD DRIVEN TO FERNANDINA more times than he could remember since moving to Florida. He liked the town, but not enough to move there. It was a great place to visit, though.

It had great beaches – the Main Beach, Peter's Point, American Beach, and the public beach access down at the southern point near Amelia Island State Park. You could always find a delightful stretch of beach for walking or lounging, something Jimmy appreciated most about Fernandina. Another bonus was they were never inundated with thousands of college students for Spring Break.

Coming from landlocked Minnesota (and the even-more-landlocked Winnipeg before that), Jimmy loved the beaches' sights, smells, and sounds. He decided it was what northern Minnesota's lakes lacked – proper beaches. The diversity of shells, crustaceans, and shark teeth placed Fernandina head and shoulders above freshwater beaches.

The mere fact that the water didn't numb your feet to the bone raised Florida beaches to the pinnacle in Jimmy's mind. Lake Superior seemed to never warm above forty degrees. Jimmy had waded in it a few times, but it made his feet ache almost immediately after stepping in. His ankles and feet turned red from the frigid cold. And it was a pebbly rock bottom at Superior, not the sugar sand he enjoyed now.

From thoughts like that, one might get a false impression that Jimmy didn't like the Northland he had left, but the truth was, he loved both the North and the South, just in different ways. Jimmy wished he could find a perfect blend of clean air and crystal-clear water from northern Minnesota mixed with the warm ocean surf and gentle breezes of Georgia's Golden Isles. He was looking for a place that incorporated the best of both worlds. A place with the gentleness of Minnesota's outdoors and the determined tenacity of the marshes, lakes, and forests of Georgia's coastal plains.

Nothing compared to the soft grass of Minnesota under your bare feet, Jimmy often thought. The grass near the coast was coarse, almost brittle, and it was more like walking on straw than a green carpet. Nearly everything native to Florida and Georgia was out to kill you: Spanish Bayonet plants, Century Plants with giant spikes on the tips of the leaves, Saw Palmettos with sharp sawblade shafts, and Sago Palms with feathery-looking fronds as soft as shoe leather baked under a Death Valley sun.

Growing up, Jimmy had never needed to watch for poisonous snakes while hiking in the woods. These days, he had a dozen varieties in the half-acre around his house, from cottonmouths to rattlers to copperheads. Black and Brown Widow spiders and Brown Recluses loved to fling their messy webs around his house and carport, depositing egg sacs that could produce hundreds of new recruits. Walking around the edge of a small lake or creek could bring about a face-to-face encounter with an alligator, a prehistoric-looking creature that barely looked real. Until they blinked or opened their mouths, that is.

Despite the increase in threats to his life, Jimmy loved his new home.

Driving down Highway 17 to Yulee, Jimmy soaked in the palm trees, Spanish moss-draped live oaks, the rows of straight, tall pines planted by wood product companies, and ditches dappled and flecked with wildflowers.

Jimmy hung a left turn in Yulee, merging onto another historic highway, A1A, 72 miles of officially designated American Byway. Primarily a two-lane roadway, A1A navigates through Florida's serene beauty and history. The land and waters on either side have been part of the sweep of nature, archaeology, and recreation for nearly 500 years and American history since before 1776.

Today, though, Jimmy was noticing how built up the stretch of road from Yulee to Fernandina had become. The ribbon of road lined with businesses from Yulee to Fernandina was like a new unnamed city. It felt as though Jacksonville was swallowing the smaller town, making it just another extension of Jacksonville, which was already the second-largest city (by area) in the U.S.

In many respects, it was unofficially annexing Yulee and Fernandina. It was essentially a bedroom community, a place near enough to Jacksonville to justify the commute but still far enough away to enjoy a little taste of solitude.

After Jimmy crossed the causeway onto Amelia Island and into Fernandina, he let his thoughts of out-of-control expansion drift away. He considered making a quick stop at the beach, even if it made him late for his meeting. The investigator could always claim he couldn't find their office. Except that Wendi had said if he went to Staples and turned right, he'd find her.

Jimmy didn't know what it was about the woman's voice, but he really wanted to unveil the face connected with that sexy voice. He imagined the rest of her was as coordinated as an expensive French outfit.

He wondered if it would be in bad form to pray that she might be exactly as he envisioned her in his mind. *Yeah, probably, but what the heck — you only live once.*

****

Jimmy saw the Starbucks where he and Daani had stopped a couple of days earlier on their way to the beach. He should have asked Daani to let him know when she made it back to Turtle Lake, but he didn't want to make it weird for her. It was already weird enough for him. *Uncle Jimmy!*

Just past the Starbucks and its mermaid logo, Jimmy turned his car into the parking lot that serviced a plethora of businesses, including the Publix grocery, Staples, and Bealls.

Wendi had said they were just east of Staples. Her exact words were, "I promise you'll find me if you go to Staples and turn right." Not you'll find *us*, but you'll find *me*.

As Jimmy pulled his vehicle into a spot in front of Staples, he realized his hands were sweating. *What is wrong with me?* he thought. She was a potential client, not a date to the junior high mixer. And *she* wasn't even the client; Mr. Lyst was!

Jimmy wondered how Pepé dealt with clients like this. No, he knew how Pepé handled it: he was happily married. Pepé had a beautiful wife waiting at home for him every night. Since semi-retiring, Pepé saw Gwynn more than he ever did when he was young, working for the Charleston Police Department (CPD) and as a Navy Watch Commander. Now, as a freelance investigator, Pepé chose which cases and clients to take, unlike previous stints when someone else gave him his assignments.

Maybe someday Jimmy would settle down with a woman to share his time with, but that woman had not come into this life yet. But you never know. Maybe the Lysts had a daughter who sounded like Wendi. If so, Jimmy would let her call him up all the time just so she could talk to him in that sexy voice.

> *"Honey? Can you swing by the Winn Dixie to pick me up some peaches? I would soo appreciate it if you would do that for me. You just have no idea how happy it would make me. And you know that if I'm happy, you're happy."*

Jimmy checked his hair in the vanity mirror of his vehicle then checked his teeth for unexpected surprises that could make his clients wrinkle their noses and show him to the door. He tossed a couple of mints in his mouth for insurance. *Happy wife, happy life.* He imagined Mr. Lyst was also happy.

***

Jimmy had a difficult time finding the place, which is not a great thing to happen to a finder of people, places, and things. It was good that he was a few minutes early because he roamed around outside unsuccessfully, looking for the elusive Lyst Publishing. Finally, a Staples employee leaving work asked him if he needed help.

"Yeah," Jimmy replied. "Do you still sell those 'That was Easy' buttons?"

The employee, a college-age girl in jeans and a polo shirt, smiled politely at his remark but didn't laugh. No surprise.

"I actually *do* need your help," Jimmy said before she could abandon him to his own devices again. "Do you know where Lyst Publishing is? The lady on the phone said to go to Staples and turn right. I did, but I haven't found their office yet."

"Let me help. C'mon with me," the girl answered, as though she was still working and taking someone to find paper clips and gel pens.

They walked past where Jimmy had looked before, finally stopping a couple of stores further down the sidewalk. A single door was flanked by two storefronts. A small sign on the door quietly proclaimed Lyst Publishing.

"Here you go," Jimmy's personal guide said.

"Thank you very much, um, Allyson," Jimmy responded, reading her name from the nametag still attached to her shirt.

She said, "Good luck," and returned the way she had come, leaving Jimmy standing alone in front of the door.

He walked back and forth on the sidewalk in front of the door for a few minutes. He didn't want to be too early, but he didn't want to be late, either. On the other hand, some clients held tightly to the concept that if you're fifteen minutes early, you're on time, and if you're on time, you're late. Jimmy had no idea which way Hillary Lyst swung on that playground, but he was about to find out.

The conditioned air hit Jimmy in the face, cold, crisp, and artificial. There was a hallway in front of him, lit by fluorescent fixtures giving off a faint buzz. Jimmy stood just inside the door for a moment, looking down the hallway. He could see another door at the end of the hallway. He felt like someone had miscalculated when building the two buildings, leaving a narrow, unused space between the two. Not wanting it to go to waste, the owner made a small office in the back and used the gap between the buildings as a hallway.

Jimmy's footsteps didn't echo in the narrow space because he wore soft-soled shoes. His shoes were a throwback to an earlier era when private investigators were called gumshoes because of their soft-soled shoes. *The better to sneak up on you with, my dear.*

Reaching the door, Jimmy didn't know if he should knock or simply go in until he saw the little plate on the door that said, "Lyst Publishing. Please come in."

In for a penny… he thought. Jimmy opened the door and walked in.

A wooden desk was situated almost in the middle of the room, just slightly off to the right. He assumed the space on the left was to get past the desk and into the boss's office. The desk had a sheet of glass on top with notes and pictures under the glass. It was like the office version of a refrigerator; it was where personal touches went. There were pictures with multiple people standing together, but from Jimmy's perspective, they were all upside down. Obviously, they were for the enjoyment of the person who sat at this desk: Wendi Lyst. Unfortunately for Jimmy, he couldn't see the pictures without walking around the desk to examine them right-side up. He leaned on the front left corner and tried to bend over the desk while tilting his head to one side to see what he could make out in the pictures. Maybe Wendi was in the photos, and he'd get a preview before she ushered him into Hillary's office.

"May I help you?"

It was *that* voice, and it sounded even sexier in person. Jimmy straightened up and turned to where he thought the voice had originated.

"I was just looking at your pictures … trying to, anyway. I'm a nosy guy, sorry. It comes with the job. I'm Jimmy Favreaux." As he spoke, she stepped out from a doorway hidden by filing cabinets. Jimmy hadn't even noticed the door.

She was everything he had imagined. Blonde, just the right amount of curves, heels that made her legs look spectacular, perfectly done makeup, and a smile that said she already knew who he was. She wore a black skirt with a tasteful white blouse, a combination every personal secretary with a nice figure should wear. If Jimmy was Hillary Lyst, he'd make sure she had a closet full of this exact outfit, one for each day of work. Her earrings were silver, a nice contrast to her blonde hair and a perfect complement to her black and white outfit. Her age was a complete mystery, tucked right into that sweet spot between her mid-thirties and mid-forties, the age Jimmy felt every woman should be.

He had always believed it was the stage in every woman's life when they truly came into their own. Marilyn Monroe had been all of thirty-six when she died.

Her walk was smooth and graceful as she came over to her desk, not exaggerated like a runway model but not plodding like a farmer. Jimmy was afraid he was probably staring and gave his head a little shake to snap himself out of it.

She slipped out a hand toward him, complete with perfectly manicured nails. Jimmy extended his hand, and she placed her delicate hand on his. Instead of the usual way of shaking hands, though, she just let her hand rest on his, the way royalty and famous women tended to do. He noticed that her left hand sported a diamond wedding ring, its stone a size he could never afford. Jimmy had a mental picture of his hopes, like waves, crashing on jagged rocks. Apparently, she really was Mrs. Lyst.

"Hi, Jimmy. I'm Wendi Lyst. We spoke on the phone. I'm so glad you could meet with us today."

Too Jimmy's ears, Wendi's voice was even better than Marilyn Monroe's, and only partly because Wendi was alive.

"Did you have any trouble finding our office," she asked, releasing his hand.

"What do you think? I'm a professional. I'm a finder."

"Mmm-mm. I'll bet you are." Her voice had overtones of Eartha Kitt when she played Catwoman. "It's just ... I thought maybe I saw you walking back and forth outside before you came in."

Uh-oh. "Well, ah, you know, I didn't want to be too early," Jimmy stammered. "Especially since I didn't have any trouble finding your place."

"Uh-huh," she replied with a knowing smile. She was enjoying this, Jimmy knew.

"Well, you know what they say, if you're fifteen minutes early, you're on time, and if you're on time, you're late. I like to arrive somewhere in between," Jimmy responded with a smile of his own.

"Well," she said, "since you're on time, let's go meet Mr. Lyst."

"That's why I'm here," Jimmy said. "Lead the way." He had watched Wendi walk toward him when she came into the room, and he had a sneaking suspicion that she looked just as good walking away.

Instead, Wendi stepped aside to let Jimmy go first as they crossed the ten feet to Mr. Lyst's office door.

Chapter 6

WALKING PAST THE DOOR HIDDEN on the left by the file cabinets, Jimmy saw that its doorplate said RESTROOM. A few more feet brought him to a door that read HILLARY J. LYST: PUBLISHER.

Wendi stepped past Jimmy, tapped on the door lightly, and opened it without waiting for a response from inside. She stepped in and turned, holding the door open for Jimmy.

The entire office was lined with bookshelves from floor to ceiling, and each shelf was full. A ladder hung off the shelves on one wall to allow access to the shelves near the top. Jimmy had seen some old, big-city libraries that used ladders like that.

Jimmy thought, *I guess in nearly forty years of publishing, you probably accumulate some books.*

As though reading his thoughts, Wendi said, "Yes, you *do* assemble quite a collection of books in this business."

Jimmy stared at her, wondering what other thoughts she could read.

"What?" she said with a little laugh. "That's what everybody thinks when they come in here for the first time."

Jimmy stood in one place and slowly rotated, taking in the spectacle of the hundreds of books. It was easy to forget he wasn't in a public library; this was a personal library. He could make out biographies, memoirs, mysteries, and histories from the book titles closest to him. Jimmy was sure the collection included many other genres as well.

"People have been writing about history for ... well, all of history," a voice said behind Jimmy. He turned to discover a short man with thinning white hair, a goatee needing trimming, and gold-colored glasses with round rims perched on a substantial nose. The man looked over the top of the glasses, not through the lenses, his eyes an indistinct greyish color. He was about Jimmy's height and wearing a white shirt with a button-down collar and black trousers. Tasseled black loafers poked out from beneath the cuffs of his slacks. His outfit was like the male version of Mrs. Lyst's, although hers complemented her figure much more nicely. Jimmy realized that opinion could just be a personal preference.

"Mr. Lyst?" Jimmy asked, reasonably confident of the man's identity since this *was* Lyst publishing, and Jimmy was standing in Hillary Lyst's office surrounded by books the man had published over the last nearly forty years.

"What gave it away?" the man said with a genuine twinkle in his eye. His sleeves were rolled up to his elbows, and he extended a hand to greet the private investigator. As they shook hands, Lyst placed his other hand over their clasped hands and said, "If you had not guessed my identity, I would have been quite trepidatious about enlisting your aid for our little project."

Releasing Jimmy's hand, Lyst stepped past him to take his place at his desk. Settling into his chair, the publisher said, "Now, there's a word we don't hear very often anymore: trepidatious." Lyst looked like he was tasting the word as he repeated it.

He asked, "What do you think of it, Mr. Favreaux?"

Jimmy was continuing to examine the books on the shelves. He realized Mr. Lyst's question could be part of the vetting process, so he decided to tone down his customary wise guy response system. His decision came too late, though, as automation overrode self-preservation.

Jimmy heard himself say, "It doesn't make me trepidatious if that's what you're asking."

Hillary Lyst sat forward in his chair, looked at Jimmy over the top of his glasses, and burst into a high-pitched noise, a sort of cross between an asthma attack and a pig squeal. It took Jimmy a second before he realized it was laughter or, at least, something that passed for laughter.

"Well, I'm pleased it doesn't make you too trepidatious," the publisher said. Then he added, "You're two for two so far. Let's see if you can win the big prize." He gave Jimmy a quick wink.

Jimmy was now paying full attention to the small, older man sitting behind the desk.

"If you are as astute as I perceive you to be, you will have already reconnoitered our company and certainly perused our website. Am I correct, Mr. Favreaux?"

"Please, call me Jimmy."

"Fine, Jimmy. And you can call me Mr. Lyst." Jimmy saw the twinkle in the older gentleman's eye again and knew he had best listen carefully. The guy liked to play the eccentric card, but Jimmy had a gut feeling that he was as sharp as a razor.

"Did you happen to notice anything unusual, offbeat, or unexpected about our website, Jimmy? Something that piqued your sense of inquisitiveness?" Lyst asked, still looking over his glasses at Jimmy.

"No, sir," Jimmy replied. "Nothing *that* unusual … except I noticed that you aren't accepting new manuscripts right now."

"Bingo!" The man raised both hands in the air over his head like he was at Our Lady of Perpetual Winnings on a Friday night. He quickly lowered his arms again, putting one hand in his lap and resting his other arm on the desk. He leaned forward on his arm, focusing on Jimmy.

Fastening his eyes on Jimmy, he asked, "How can a business that earns its remuneration and compensation from publishing books keep its doors open when it's not accepting novels, novellas, histories, and – the latest craze – self-help e-books?"

"That does sound like a conundrum," Jimmy replied, and Lyst's face broke into a grin that Jimmy thought was as bright as the sun's first appearance over the horizon at dawn. Jimmy recognized it because he had seen the sunrise several times after cases that kept him up all night.

"Yes!" Lyst crowed. "As Sir Winston Churchill said, 'It is a riddle, wrapped in a mystery, inside an enigma.'"

"Kind of like a dairy that isn't accepting deliveries from dairy farms."

"Exactly. Wonderful metaphor, Jimmy."

"I could come up with another about bees and honey and the beekeeper if you'd like."

"Unnecessary at this juncture," the older man said. "But keep it in your back pocket in case we need it later. Let me ask you this: have you any inkling why we had to stop taking submissions?"

"Well, sir, that was going to be one of my first queries, but you beat me to the punch." Jimmy was enjoying the man's erudite vocabulary, mainly since it allowed him to use words he usually kept in reserve. He was always on the lookout for new five-dollar words for future occasions.

"Do you know much about the publishing industry, Jimmy?" Lyst asked.

"I would be remiss if I said I did, but I would also be remiss if I said I knew nothing. Suffice it to say that I have a working knowledge of the publishing industry related to newspapers and their publication, but that is the extent of my knowledge. In a previous life, in a frigid, faraway land, I worked for a chain of newspapers. Not as a writer, editor, or publisher but in their information technology department. Even my experience from that arena has become quite antiquated in the dozen years I have been away."

"Indeed. Technology travels at a far quicker pace than many people realize. I imagine we could go on at length about the differences that have transpired between the years I toiled in the galleys and your tenure. Computers as we know them today did not yet exist when I was in the paper business. We had cathode ray tube terminals. Sounds like they're going to die, doesn't it? Terminals. Well, they did, eventually. We typed our articles on word processing terminals and fed them to another machine that converted the stories into paper spools with holes punched in them. Another machine read the punched holes in the spools and produced lead type that would eventually be machined to make curved aluminum plates. Those plates would go in big drums on the press to print the newspapers. It was a fascinating process. I always loved being serenaded by the pulsing rhythm of the running presses."

"Yes, sir, Mr. Lyst. My boss at the newspaper chain said he could sleep like a baby with the 'music' of the presses for a lullaby."

"I can appreciate his sentiments." Lyst sat back in his chair and folded his hands across his lap. A faint smile crossed his face, and a faraway look settled in his eyes. It was the same expression the newspaper chain CEO would get when the press was running on the other side of the wall from his office. Jimmy knew Lyst was hearing the rhythm of the running presses in his memory as they produced miles and miles of daily newsprint.

After a moment, the publisher's expression shifted and took on a tighter look. Jimmy could tell he was back in the present. Mr. Lyst's next question caught Jimmy flatfooted.

"How many of these books do you suppose are first-editions?" Lyst asked, then answered his own question before Jimmy could open his mouth. "All of them. Each one is the first edition. And most don't have any subsequent editions, either. Do you have any idea what all of them together are worth?"

Jimmy shook his head.

"They're enough to last me the rest of my life." Lyst let the information float between them for a moment, then continued. "Mind you, Jimmy, that doesn't mean they're worth much at all." Jimmy blinked, slightly confused, but waited for more.

Lyst went on. "As the late great philosopher Jackie Mason used to say, 'I have enough money to last me the rest of my life *unless I buy something*.' In other words, none of these are worthy of bestseller status, so I had best not go out and purchase something frivolous. These shelves contain some fine books, many actually, but none on the order of *War and Peace*, *A Tale of Two Cities*, or even *A Tree Grows in Brooklyn*. They have kept me busy, and they have kept me clothed and fed, but they have not made me rich."

"Did the prospect of great wealth precipitate your departure from the newspaper business and the launch of Lyst Publishing?" Jimmy asked.

"Excellent question. Thank you, Jimmy!" Lyst responded to Jimmy's queries like he had been marooned on a desert island for years with no one to talk to. "No, Jimmy, I did it because not everyone is a Hemingway, Steinbeck, Dickens, or a Samuel Clemens. Does that mean their stories and contributions to literature don't deserve to be printed? No, it does not. Therefore, I made it my purpose to offer an avenue for the average man to see his words—his story—on the printed page."

Jimmy had been standing the entire time he had been in Lyst's office. As if suddenly realizing his faux pas, Lyst stood up and motioned to the two chairs opposite the desk from him. "Please, have a seat. I don't know where my manners have disappeared to today."

Jimmy sat in the right-hand chair. Wendi came around and took the one on the left. Jimmy tried to keep his attention on Mr. Lyst, not Mrs.

"Do you have children, Jimmy?" The PI was startled by the sudden swings in the conversation but tried not to show it.

Shaking his head, Jimmy responded, "No, Mr. Lyst. I've never been married."

"Well, neither have many other people, but that hasn't stopped them from producing offspring." He began to emit the high-pitched sound he had made earlier but glanced briefly at Wendi and stopped abruptly, clearing his throat before speaking again.

Turning his full attention toward her, Lyst said, "Wendi, my dear. Would you be so good as to bring us some fresh coffee? I'm sure Mr. Favreaux would like a little pick-me-up, wouldn't you, Jimmy?"

Jimmy nodded his agreement, mumbling a noncommittal, "Whatever you say."

Wendi looked back and forth between the two men for a moment, then stood, smoothed her skirt, and left the room without a word, closing the door behind her.

Lyst leaned forward, placing his right arm on his desk, and in a conspiratorial voice said, "You likely were surprised by my question about children, Jimmy. I apologize for catching you unawares. My ramblings do have a rationale, however. Did Wendi tell you anything about our relationship?"

Relationship? Jimmy groaned inwardly. "No, not exactly," he replied. "She did *tell* me that she is *not* your daughter."

"Indeed? What *specifically* did she tell you?"

"After she told me her last name was the same as yours, I – um, I asked her if she was your daughter or your sister. She said she was *Mrs.* Lyst." Jimmy squirmed internally, feeling like he was in a police interrogation room under four bright lights.

Lyst Publishing's founder and namesake sat back in his chair again, meshed his fingers together over his stomach, frowned, and then ... grinned ever-so-slightly. It was a grin combined with mischief or shenanigans or perhaps both, Jimmy thought.

Lyst suddenly sat up straight, saying, "I'm glad she explained her role. She has spoken fitly and truthfully." Without another word, the older gentleman stood and walked over to one of the walls of books behind his desk. He hooked his hands behind his back, staring at the books before him on the shelves.

But not seeing them, Jimmy thought. The publisher was silent for several long moments before suddenly speaking again.

"I had a child," Lyst began, not speaking in Jimmy's direction. "A son. Charles Jefferson. He was born five years before I began this publishing company. He would be forty-three now." He paused and cleared his throat. "I lost him three years ago. He was killed in a collision on a rainy night on I95 with a semi. He was returning home and hydroplaned. He crossed three lanes of traffic and the center median before being broadsided by the semi-truck. He was killed instantly." He paused briefly, looked down, then said softly, "As was his mother."

Jimmy was glad Lyst had his back to him so that he couldn't see the look of shock and surprise on Jimmy's face. The investigator tried to compose himself in case his client turned around.

Lyst took a book from the shelf directly in front of him, but Jimmy knew he wasn't truly looking for some light reading while sharing a story of personal tragedy and loss. Lyst closed the book and held it briefly to his chest in a soft hug before reshelving it. The older man turned around and placed his hands on the back of his chair. "So," he said. "Wendi explained that she is Mrs. Lyst? And you were unconvinced? Perhaps because of her young age? Allow me to put your mind at rest, Mr. Favreaux. She is. And she has been invaluable these past several years in helping me to recover from my grief."

The office door opened quietly, and Mrs. Lyst reappeared with a silver tray holding two cups of coffee and a small bowl with sweeteners and creamers.

She smiled broadly at Jimmy, leaned down with the tray, and purred quietly so only Jimmy could hear. It was the same voice he had first heard on the phone.

"Coffee, tea, or … me?"

Chapter 7

LYST HAD RETAKEN HIS PLACE behind his desk. Wendi placed a cup of coffee on a matching saucer in front of him. He gave her a brief nod of thanks. "Now that we've cleared that up," Hillary Lyst said, "let's get back to the purpose of our meeting, the wherefore of your presence among us, Jimmy."

Wendi retook her chair on the left. Despite her presence, she had spoken very little during their meeting.

Lyst continued. "When my son and wife were killed in that accident, there was eventually an insurance payout, but not what the average person would consider a life-changing amount. Still, I had an idea of how to use it to change someone else's life, maybe several people's lives. I decided to hold a contest for potential authors. The winner would receive fifty-thousand dollars, and the runner-up would garner ten thousand. The runner-up's prize would allow him or her the freedom to have their novel professionally edited and published yet retain a sufficient amount for rudimentary promotion and marketing."

He paused in his story to take a sip of the coffee Wendi had set before him. "This is excellent coffee, Wendi. Thank you for making it for us. How is yours, Jimmy?"

Jimmy was sitting quietly, his saucer in his left hand, his cup in the right, facing the publisher's desk. His position kept Wendi in his field of vision.

"It's very lovely, sir," Jimmy responded. "I mean, the *coffee* is delicious; it's just what I needed."

Jimmy wondered if there was enough room under his chair to hide in. But instead of attempting to disappear, he took another sip of the hot liquid. He caught a glimpse of Wendi smirking. Mr. Lyst seemed oblivious to Jimmy's discomfort as he continued to share the details of the contest he had created from the insurance money.

"First, let me tell you about the runner-up since there's less to tell. His name is Oscar Metz. He lives in a mobile home park here on Amelia Island. He was ecstatic to receive the news that he had won second place. He's a freelance short-story writer who has had minor success seeing his stories in magazines and online e-mags. But he did remarkably well in the long form, and our panel awarded him runner-up status for his romantic comedy *Three Devils and An Angel.*"

"I'm sure," Jimmy replied. "Even ten thousand is a huge bump for a freelancer."

Lyst continued. "Oscar lived—past tense—with his widowed mother in an old trailer. I'm afraid she passed away several years ago, shortly before the COVID pandemic struck. I believe her benefits passed to him, so coupled with his freelance writing income, he's not destitute. And yes, the second-prize premium represents a tidy windfall for him."

Lyst opened a drawer on his desk and pulled out a slightly-faded, worn paperback. He looked at it briefly, turning it over to read the back cover.

"Have you ever heard of Trevor Mcintosh, Jimmy?" Lyst asked him.

"No, I can't say that I have."

"He's an author. He is not a first-time author, but it's been more than a few years since he wrote anything. He had a single big splash about thirty-five years ago in the pool of writers on the bestseller list, but after the ripples died away, he disappeared. He was twenty years old at the time. He wrote the book you see here in my hand. And no, we didn't publish it. It's called *Growing Up Southern*. It did well for a while, but then the buzz died down."

He laid the book down on his desktop, looking at the cover again before turning his attention back to Jimmy.

"Big publishing houses are always looking down the road. They want to know the title of your next book and what it's about. Their first question when an author turns in a manuscript is not, 'What are you going to do with your free time and money now that you've finished this book?' You should always have a skeleton outline of your next book ready to submit with your final manuscript. An outline containing several completed sample chapters is even better. I'm afraid Mcintosh did not follow protocol when he wrote his first book, which contributed to his fall from grace in the publishing world. He just wanted his royalties check and for his publisher to leave him alone. He's rather odd in other ways, too."

"Odd? How so?" Jimmy asked, deciding he needed to focus on what Lyst was saying. While he appreciated Wendi's feminine features, that wasn't why he was here or what he was being paid to investigate.

"You remember when we talked about the newsroom from my day and how it differed from your time in that field?" Jimmy nodded. "I told you that we used CRT workstations, not computers, to produce our stories. CRTs were lightyears beyond typewriters and Linotype operators, but they were akin to the Stone Age compared to today's computers and direct-to-plate operations."

Jimmy grunted in agreement, indicating he was following the track of Lyst's story, but he had nothing enlightening or pertinent to contribute, so he kept quiet.

Lyst pushed onward. "Mcintosh is a bit of an eccentric, shall we say. Rather than advancing with technology, he went backward. Mcintosh wrote his new novel on a manual typewriter. He said he isolated himself for six years and banged it out slowly and carefully, like authors from years past. It was nearly a thousand typewritten pages, and he titled it *Where the Ocean Swallows the Moon*, subtitled *Five Years on a Freighter*."

Jimmy held up a finger for a question and asked, "Is it autobiographical?"

Lyst looked over his glasses and smiled at the PI. Jimmy felt like he had just racked up a few points for asking the correct question.

"Maybe yes and perhaps no," Lyst answered. "He said it was a work of fiction, but it reads like an autobiography."

"So Mcintosh crewed out on a container ship and wrote about it. Is that what you believe, or is that what he *wants* you to believe?"

Lyst placed his index finger on the tip of his round nose, indicating Jimmy was right on the mark. "I believe that's the man's desire. He wishes us to accept it as his story, clothed in a fictional setting."

"But you aren't biting?" Jimmy asked.

"Wendi and I went to his house – if you can call it that – to pick up the manuscript. I feel confident that man has never been on a shrimp boat, let alone a container ship. Personally, I doubt he's ever worked a day in his life. If and when you go to interview him … well, Jimmy, I'll be very interested to hear *your* impressions of Mr. Trevor Mcintosh."

Lyst stopped and waited for Jimmy to ask questions.

"But you said Mcintosh was the winner of the contest? And he won fifty thousand dollars? Were there other sundries included with his prize?"

"He was, and he did. Mcintosh's award includes full editing, professionally designed cover artwork, and a complete publishing package in hardcover, paperback, and e-book versions. On top of that, he will receive advertising in newspapers in major cities, placement in brick-and-mortar bookstores, and a publicity book-signing tour to initiate the book's release. All that is over and above the fifty-thousand dollar cash prize."

Jimmy whistled his appreciation of the total prize. "Okay. So, what's the issue?" he asked, trying to tease the problem to the surface.

Wendi spoke for the first time since bringing in the coffee. "Mcintosh turned in his manuscript the old-fashioned way, a double-spaced typewritten document. The manuscript was in Mr. Lyst's desk."

"Was?" Jimmy asked, starting to realize where this was headed.

"It was, yes," Lyst responded. "As in, it *was* there, but it *is* no longer." As though to punctuate his statement, Lyst pulled open the drawer and looked briefly in its direction before sliding it shut again.

"I'm not following. What's the problem?" Jimmy asked. "You print another copy, and life continues. Am I missing something?"

"Unfortunately, yes, you are. So are we. Trevor wrote it like authors did before computers, electric typewriters, and carbon paper. It was written on a manual typewriter. Before you ask, it was definitely not printed on a laser printer. You could feel the irregularities in the paper from the impact of the typewriter keys. Also, laser printers make all the letters uniform in color. In contrast, letters typed on a manual typewriter vary in color because some letters get pressed harder than others. And as the ribbon gets used, rewound, and used again for economy's sake, the words become lighter and lighter each time the ribbon is reused. So, we know without a doubt that it was done on a manual typewriter. And no carbon paper was used, so no copy exists."

The publisher let the statement hang in the air like a lure on the surface of a bass pond. Jimmy bit.

"Wait. This guy gave you his only copy of his book? Is he nuts?"

"It is quite possible that he is indeed, as you say, nuts. Still, it is also possible that *we* are just as nuts because we didn't make a copy," Lyst explained, fiddling with his now-empty coffee cup.

Jimmy was unsure what to say. He was good, but he was not God, who created an entire universe from nothing, *ex nihilo*. There was no backup software he could run to recover the document, no drive tools to resurrect the lost file. There was no way Jimmy could perform a Creation-esque miracle and create an award-winning manuscript out of thin air. So that's exactly what he told Hillary and Wendi.

"Of course, you can't," Lyst responded. "I'm not an unreasonable man. The onus for this rests entirely on me for not having Wendi make a copy in the first place, locking it up offsite, scanning it into a digital copy, or all of the above. It's on me, and I can't expect you to retroactively do what I didn't. *Mea culpa*, Jimmy. But I have seen your business card, Mr. Favreaux, and I believe it says 'Finder of people, places, and things.' Is that correct?"

"It is," Jimmy said, sitting up in his chair, suddenly nervous about where this was headed.

"I believe *Where the Ocean Swallows the Moon* falls into the category of a thing, don't you agree?"

Jimmy looked across the desk at the older man, who was again regarding Jimmy over his round, gold glasses. Neither man blinked for a few seconds before Jimmy broke contact, lowering his eyes.

"I agree. It does," he said quietly.

"Outstanding," the older man responded, his eyes crinkling with glee.

Wendi interrupted to add, "I checked up on you, too, Jimmy. I talked to other clients you have worked for, and they all said the same thing."

That I'm a flake? Jimmy thought.

"They all said you do whatever you need to get the job done. Not just that, but you go above and beyond to make the client satisfied, even if it means placing yourself – and your fee – at risk. For those reasons and others, we believe you are the perfect investigator for our job. We have *complete* faith in your ability to locate Trevor Mcintosh's manuscript and return it to us." As she finished, she placed a hand lightly on Jimmy's arm.

Jimmy knew if he was going to take on the impossible, he needed to be well compensated.

"What kind of money are we talking about for my work – assuming I *take* the job *and* assuming I'm successful?" he asked, feeling uncomfortable pressure from her hand on his arm. He was afraid Mr. Lyst would notice steam escaping from his shirt collar.

"We're prepared to offer you ten thousand dollars for the return of the original manuscript. Plus, expenses," Mr. Lyst answered.

"T-ten t-thousand? Dollars?" Jimmy stammered. Wendi smiled, patted his arm lightly, and removed her hand.

"Yes, Jimmy," Lyst continued. "We anticipate the book will bring in approximately ten times that amount, quite possibly much more. And then there are the movie rights that we have secured on top of that. So, we believe ten thousand is an adequate inducement. Plus, expenses."

Jimmy swallowed hard. He thought about pinching himself to see if he was dreaming. Instead, he asked, "Where, exactly, can I find this Trevor Mcintosh?"

"Wendi will provide his address. He lives north of here. It's up in Georgia, on one of the other coastal islands, like Amelia Island. It's the one that was a playground for captains of industry a few generations ago: Jekyll Island."

Wendi stood, collected the cups and saucers, and exited the office. Jimmy was still trying to wrap his head around a single payday equal to more than two months of his annual income.

Lyst answered another question Jimmy had not asked. "Remember when I told you all these books are first editions?" Jimmy nodded.

"And I told you that none of them made me rich?" Lyst asked. Jimmy simply met his eyes to acknowledge the question.

"I'm still not rich, but I have a little money set aside from the insurance beneficiary benefits. I need you to understand that I had to lose my wife and my son to make this little contest possible." He looked away and said, "I would give away *everything* I have to bring them back. No one and nothing can fill the hole in my heart their losses left behind."

Not even Wendi? Jimmy thought. He noticed that Lyst said only things like this when Wendi was out of the room. *Probably doesn't want to hurt her feelings,* he assumed.

"Wendi will give you everything you need to begin finding our stolen manuscript," Lyst told the investigator.

Hillary Lyst stood and extended his hand toward Jimmy, who hastily stood and shook the older man's hand. The publisher sat down, swiveled around to his computer, and began typing. Jimmy realized their meeting was over.

***

"I've got *your* number, Jimmy Favreaux," Wendi cooed as Jimmy departed Lyst's office and walked over to her desk.

What the …? Unsure how to respond, he stammered, "Y-you do?"

"Of course," she replied and cheerfully added, "I called you to set up our meeting this afternoon, so I already have your cell number."

Phew! Jimmy breathed a tiny sigh of relief.

"Did you think I meant *something else?*" she asked in her sexy voice, the one that made him forget everything else happening around him.

"What? Pssh. No. I knew exactly what you meant." He hoped she bought his response.

"If it's okay, I'll just text you Mcintosh's address. Then you can use your phone's GPS to locate him. I'm sure you'll want to interview him and uncover any information he might have about this."

"Can you give me the address for the second-place winner, too?" Jimmy asked.

"Absolutely. I'll text it at the same time I send Trevor's."

"Has Mcintosh been told the manuscript was stolen?"

"Oh, yes. Mr. Lyst called him the next day."

"And what was his response?"

"He seemed surprised, then became quite angry. But he settled down quickly after we told him he would be allowed to keep the fifty-thousand dollars."

"Who wouldn't?" Jimmy answered.

"Exactly," she replied. "Mcintosh wouldn't lose much, at least not compared to our estimated loss. The book sales and the movie rights …"

"And the publicity," Jimmy added. This book deal could put Lyst Publishing on the radar for upcoming new authors – paying customers.

"Precisely," Wendi responded. "And that's a loss for both the author *and* us."

"Although …" Jimmy considered. "Mcintosh gets notoriety *and* mystique. Everyone will know he wrote an award-winning book that no one will ever see."

"Except," Wendi said, and she started purring again, "*you're* going to get it back for *me*, aren't you?" Jimmy noticed her use of *me*, not *us*.

"I'll do my best," was his verbal answer.

Jimmy was sure he was being manipulated, but what flitted through his brain was, *Anything you want. Anything at all.*

"I'm sure you'll be successful," she responded. "You wouldn't want to disappoint me, *would* you?"

"Not in a million years," came his reply.

"I thought so." She smiled her big, beautiful smile at him.

Jimmy turned to depart, then turned around when one last thing occurred to him, à la Columbo.

"Has Oscar Metz been told the winner's manuscript was stolen?" Jimmy asked.

"I haven't told him. Mr. Lyst and I agreed that it would be best to wait until you retrieve the missing manuscript. We don't want Mr. Metz to cause a ruckus and demand to be moved to the head of the class."

Jimmy replied, "A manuscript in the hand versus two in the typewriter sort of thing, right?"

Wendi nodded and gave Jimmy a four-finger wave.

Jimmy got a text from Wendi with Trevor Mcintosh's address right after getting in his car. His phone pinged again with another text from Wendi.

Have a lovely afternoon. "Mrs. Lyst"

Jimmy sighed, then smiled as he put the vehicle in gear.

Chapter 8

JIMMY WAITED UNTIL THE NEXT day before driving to Jekyll Island to see Mcintosh. He anticipated pondering the nuances of the case for an hour and a half while driving. He tried to focus on Trevor Mcintosh, the oddball author who used a typewriter and no carbon paper. Instead, he was distracted by thoughts of Wendi Lyst, which may have been why the trip took longer than he expected.

Jimmy had trouble finding the author's house. It turned out the street was one of the rare streets and roads not mapped by Google. His GPS app got him close enough that he could finish the old-fashioned way: driving slowly down the road, checking the names and numbers on the mailboxes. He finally found it: 132 Claflin Road, T. Mcintosh.

The house didn't look like something an award-winning author would live in. Or maybe it did. Jimmy didn't know any award-winning authors, so he didn't have much to base his assumptions on. He knew artists needed to suffer for their art, so perhaps the house was part of Mcintosh's suffering.

The house was one-story with chipped siding and a nearly flat roof. The part of the siding that still had paint was a light putty color, barely distinguishable from the pieces with no paint. It may have all been a dirty white, too. *Hard to tell,* Jimmy thought. The word hovel came to mind.

There was a carport to the right of the front door, but Jimmy would never trust *that* carport to park his Nissan under. Not in a million years. There was no car there at the moment, but there was no room for one. A couple of rusted patio chairs took up the space normally allotted for a vehicle. They had definitely seen better days, but those days were not recent. The chairs were all metal—or had been when new, probably back in the 1950s. Rust encrusted them where people's thighs never touched. The chairs faced an ancient Weber-style charcoal grill coated with dust and pollen on top. The underside of the grill's bowl was rusted and burned out, the ashes from the last cookout resting in the "ash-catcher" below.

The house was surrounded by giant live oaks with Spanish moss trailing from the branches and palmetto bushes sprouting from the trees' foundations. There was no actual grass you could call a lawn. The ground was primarily sandy dirt or dirty sand, with thousands of acorns scattered over most of it. The parts not covered with acorns were obscured by leather-like oak leaves unraked from previous seasons.

Jimmy knew from past experience to watch his step as he approached the house. Like magnolia leaves, oak leaves refused to disintegrate and—combined with the marble-like acorns—could put a man on his back before he knew he was in trouble. As if falling weren't bad enough, Jimmy knew those leaves could also camouflage a rattlesnake, cottonmouth, or copperhead with its skin nearly the same color as the fallen leaves. Jimmy disliked snakes strongly, and had never learned the rhymes about white, black, red, and yellow.

In Jimmy's mind, snakes were not happy fellows, but he knew they had a niche in the ecosystem, so he opted for a live-and-let-live option. However, he wasn't sure the snakes knew, so Jimmy always watched his feet when walking through brush and leaves in case he encountered a snake that didn't understand Jimmy's brand of compromise.

Pulling up next to the house to the left of the front door and the sketchy-looking car port, Jimmy turned off his vehicle and climbed out. He stretched out his back, accompanied by several satisfying crunches and pops that were both felt and heard. He mounted the wooden steps leading to the front door. There was no doorbell or visible security cameras. No surprise.

Jimmy looked at the surrounding property and then up the visible road to the right and left to see if any other cars were approaching. He couldn't see the next house, but he knew there were several other prime real estate beauties just like this one on the same dirt road. Spanish moss and palmettos helped mask their presence.

Jimmy decided against his cop knock for this visit, opting for his Southern Baptist deacon visitation knock instead. He rapped three times on the door with its flaking paint and stepped back to wait.

When Jimmy had begun visiting churches several years before, he discovered that Tuesday nights were usually visitation. Whichever church he went to on Sunday morning would send a visitation team with a deacon out to his house on Tuesday night to welcome him and ask how his visit had been. Jimmy quickly learned the way to avoid the visitations was to simply tell the greeters (and the visitor watchers in the church lobby) that he had been at the church before. It had just been a while, he would say, and "Gee, it's sure good to be back!" He was confident God was used to hearing much worse lies from the lips of the congregants.

Jimmy's first trio of knocks hadn't raised any sounds or response from inside. So, he tried a quick double-tap to let anyone within know he was still there. If no one answered the knock, he would wait a bit, then give a slow double tap. One … two. Someone waiting for a church squad to move on would understand that the last knock meant they conceded defeat.

Jimmy gave the one-two finale and went back to his SUV. He got in, started it up, turned the radio up loud, backed up, and swung out of the driveway. After just a few feet, Jimmy snapped off the radio, executed a quick three-point U-turn, and pulled back into the driveway. He slammed on the brakes, making the wheels slide on the gravel while he kept his eyes on the windows. He saw a set of curtains in a window at the far end of the house move slightly like someone was checking to see if a car had pulled in or left from the driveway.

Jumping out of the vehicle, Jimmy ran to the front door and gave his sharp cop knock, barking out loudly, "Trevor

Mcintosh! I need to have words with you. Now!" This was no deacon visitation.

Jimmy kept his eyes on the windows along the side of the house. Nothing.

He banged harder on the door, hard enough to rattle it in its frame.

"I said *now*, Trevor! Haul your butt outta there!"

He put a bit of Southern drawl into his speech, hoping he sounded enough like a Southern sheriff to cause an involuntary, instinctual response from Trevor.

A voice came from within the old house. "Fer crying out loud! Keep yer pants on. I'm comin'!"

Jimmy smiled to himself. Apparently, he was bilingual now, able to convince reprobates that he was the law.

Jimmy heard the muffled sound of feet stomping from one end of the house to the front, where he waited. Jimmy stepped away from the door, a few feet to the left side, feet firmly on the sandy ground.

Sure enough, the door opened, and Jimmy was blessed with the image of Trevor Mcintosh, author.

***

He was about four inches taller than Jimmy, which put him in the neighborhood of five-ten or five-eleven, a hair under six feet. He had on dirty white or cream-colored pants — it was impossible to tell which for sure — and a wife-beater t-shirt permanently stained with food and sweat.

Trevor's skin was pasty white and looked loose instead of firmly attached. His dark hair was thinning and stringy; it looked like it hadn't been washed in several days. The author's waxy complexion made Jimmy think the man had been hidden inside his house for weeks or months. From the look of his clothes, he hadn't changed them recently, either. His pants were unbuttoned in the front, allowing his belly breathing room.

Suspenders were attached at the waist of the pants, but they weren't in place over his shoulders; they drooped at his sides, hanging nearly to his knees. Jimmy hoped the suspenders were more for decoration and less for function.

"Yeah?" Mcintosh asked. *Not a very bookish opening,* Jimmy thought.

"Are you Trevor Mcintosh, the author?"

"Could be. It depends on who y'all are."

"I'm not a cop if that's what you're worried about. Lyst Publishing sent me," Jimmy said. He saw the faintest spark of animation in Trevor's face, almost a facial tic. Mcintosh gave a little shoulder roll, hooked one side of his suspenders over a shoulder, then repeated the action on the other side. The result was that his belly looked like a stop-action photo of a river about to leave its banks during a spring flood.

"Hillary sent you? Did he get my manuscript back?" (It came out "Hill-ry sent cha? Dee git muh manyascrip back?")

Jimmy said, "No, not yet, but we're working on it. Do you think we could go inside and discuss it?"

The writer looked over his shoulder through the door he had left ajar. Turning around and pulling the door closed, he said, "Why don't we set under the carport? There's a couple of chairs there we can use. I think we'd be more comfy out here in the fresh air, don't you?"

Jimmy looked at the rusted chairs. They looked pretty sketchy, but if they could hold Trevor, they could hold Jimmy.

"Okay. Fine. Let's have a seat." Jimmy walked past the front door and over to the chairs. He picked the one that looked less likely to dump him on the ground. He slowly lowered himself onto the seat, waiting to see whether his faith in the chair was deserved. When nothing broke under him, he relaxed somewhat.

Trevor Mcintosh had walked down the steps behind Jimmy and plodded over to the remaining empty chair. The author had no apparent qualms about the sturdiness of the chairs and sat down with none of Jimmy's apprehensions. Jimmy's suspicions when he heard Mcintosh walking in the house were born out: he was not wearing shoes, just socks. One sock had a hole by the big toe, and the other had a gap on the heel. Jimmy thought, *You could really use that award money, Mr. Mcintosh.*

Crossing one leg over the other, Mcintosh asked Jimmy, "You don't happen to have a cigarette on you, do you?" What he actually said was, "Y'ain't gotta cig-ret, d'ya?" but Jimmy filtered the man's words before responding.

"Sorry, no," Jimmy replied, shaking his head.

"That's okay," Mcintosh answered. "I don't really smoke."

Curious, Jimmy thought. Lyst was right: he is a bit eccentric.

"I'd like to ask you a few questions if that's all right," Jimmy began.

"I thought I answered all of Mr. Lyst's questions before. I still won the contest, didn't I? It's not my fault someone stole it."

"I assume so. I have nothing to do with that part of it."

Trevor Mcintosh was examining his cuticles, nibbling at his nails while the men sat under the carport-cum-lanai. Though his cuticles were ragged and his nails bit down to the nubs, his hands were reasonably clean, with no ground-in grease, oil, or dirt evident. Jimmy wondered about the man's ability to write a grocery list, let alone a thousand-page manuscript so impressive that Hillary Lyst had awarded him the top prize. Something was off here, but maybe the man just wasn't very good with people. Jimmy would have to ask carefully crafted questions to get Trevor to open up and share the truth with him. Mcintosh continued to scrutinize his cuticles and avoid direct eye contact with Jimmy.

"How long did it take you to write your book?" Jimmy asked, trying to get the other man to relax and open up.

"I think I told Mr. Lyst it took me five or six years."

You're not sure? he thought, filing the answer away. "That's a long time to work on a project. You must be very dedicated."

"Yeah. I guess."

Jimmy tried again. "Mr. Lyst said you had written another book some time ago."

"Uh-huh. That one only took me a year. It was only a couple hundred pages, though."

"Mr. Lyst also told me you typed your new book on a manual typewriter. Is that true?"

A silent nod. More fingernail chewing.

"You know, Trevor, I would really love to see that typewriter. Do you think I could see it? Maybe I could take a picture of you sitting at it. Like you were writing another book. I could use the camera on my phone to take a picture. We could use it in the publicity materials." Jimmy was playing a hunch. Trevor was quiet for a long minute.

"Naw. I don't think so."

"Oh, c'mon, Trevor. People would love to see you using the typewriter you used to write *Where the Ocean Swallows the Moon*. Why not? I know Mr. Lyst will want some publicity pictures for the promotional materials."

"Naw. I don't think so. I don't need anyone taking my picture. I'd have to get all cleaned up and put on a fresh shirt and pants. I don't feel up to it. I'm kinda tired and thinking about a nap before supper."

Supper? It wasn't even noon!

"You wouldn't have to get all cleaned up, Trevor. It would look more natural if you didn't, you know? Working for hours and hours, typing hundreds and thousands of words at a single sitting, chasing the muse that spurred you on to complete the book. That kind of thing, you know?"

"Naw. I don't think so. You sure you don't have a cigarette?"

"I don't smoke, Trevor, so I don't have any cigarettes. You shouldn't smoke, either. It's a nasty habit."

"My mee-maw smoked all her life, and she lived to be 102."

Jimmy stared at him for a second, then said the first thing that came into his head: "Well … think how much longer she would have lived if she hadn't smoked all those years."

Mcintosh ignored Jimmy's comment. He was concentrating on the fingernails and cuticles of his other hand now. He shifted in his seat, uncrossed his legs, and then re-crossed them, changing which leg was on top. Jimmy was reminded briefly of Wendi performing the same maneuver in Mr. Lyst's office the day before. He pushed the thought away to focus on his job.

Jimmy tried again. "How about if we go inside, and you just show me the typewriter, Trevor? I won't take any pictures of you. I just want to see the typewriter."

"Naw. I don't think so. Do you have any beer?"

"No, I'm afraid not. Are you thirsty?"

"Naw. I just like beer."

"Are you sure you don't have any copies of the manuscript, Trevor? Maybe one that you made changes on, and so you retyped it to have a clean one to turn in?"

Trevor stopped chewing on his nails. Jimmy saw the light come on behind the man's eyes for the first time. It was like an icy breeze blew between them, extinguishing any flicker of rapport Jimmy may have established. He could tell Trevor was definitely avoiding eye contact now.

"Why are you so worried about the manuscript and how I wrote it?" Trevor asked, taking the conversation in an even more adversarial direction. "I gave Mr. Lyst my story; he can read it anytime he wants. He's got the only copy."

"Well, that's the problem, Trevor. Mr. Lyst doesn't have your story anymore; he already told you that, remember?"

No response.

"Someone apparently broke into Lyst Publishing, and the only thing they took was *your* manuscript. Right out of Mr. Lyst's desk drawer."

"I still get the money, though, right?"

"That is what Mr. Lyst said, Trevor. He told you that. But I know that if Mr. Lyst doesn't have the manuscript, he can't print it. If he can't print it, he can't make any money from it, and then Mr. Lyst would be out all that money he paid you. So, it would be to your own advantage if you had another copy. Do you understand what I'm telling you?"

"Yeah. They're going to try and cheat me out of my award money by saying someone stole my book. Then they're going to change it a little bit and sell it as their own. That's what I think."

"Trevor," Jimmy replied. "Did you *meet* Mr. Lyst?"

"Uh-huh. He and that pretty lady that works for him came all the way here. I mailed part of the story to them, but I told them I couldn't take no chances with the post office losing the whole thing. So, they drove up here, and I gave it to them."

"So, you met Wendi?" Jimmy asked, wondering if he could use that to his advantage.

"The lady drove the car."

"Yes," Jimmy said slowly, "I imagine she probably did." Jimmy shooed away any thoughts of Wendi. "Did you show *them* the typewriter, Trevor?"

"Naw. I told them it wasn't here."

"It's not here?" Jimmy was getting tired of this little ride through Deception-Ville.

Trevor's personal grooming had moved from his fingernails and cuticles to examining the hole in the toe of his sock. After a moment, he shook his head and replied to Jimmy's question.

"Naw. I had to pawn it. After I get my award, I can get it back."

"Pawn it?" Jimmy asked. "Why did you have to pawn it?"

"Just needed money. That's all. I got things I need to get sometimes, and I don't use the typewriter that often, so I pawned it. I'll get it back afore I need it again."

"Couldn't you have borrowed money from someone else? Don't you have any family around here?" Jimmy probed the man's story for holes.

Trevor shrugged. "I got my ma, but she lives all the way over in Brunswick in a nursing home, and she doesn't have that much, neither. It's not a big deal."

"Okay, Trevor, whatever you say. I just wish you had another copy so we didn't have to spend time and money trying to track down the original, you know?"

Trevor sat back in his lawn chair and looked directly at Jimmy for the first time. "But I don't *have* another copy. I already told you that. I already told Mr. Lyst that. You'll just have to try harder to get my story back."

Jimmy decided to play another card he'd been holding back. "It would be a shame if we never find it and no one ever realizes what a great writer you are. It's been thirty-five years since you wrote *Growing Up Southern*, and a lot of people don't even know you wrote a book. I didn't know it. Mr. Lyst told me. This could be your big break and introduce you to a whole new generation of readers. They might even have to re-release *Growing Up Southern*. I'll bet you'd like that, wouldn't you, Trevor?"

Mcintosh continued to stare at Jimmy, saying nothing. Jimmy didn't know what he was hoping for, but he had figured on some kind of a reaction out of Trevor, not nothing. He decided to give it one more try.

"Just between you and me, Trevor, the guy who won second place is starting to make some noise about disqualifying your book and giving him the first prize. They still have *his* book, you know."

Mcintosh sat forward, and his expression turned dark and sour. His eyebrows furrowed, and he spat out his words like he had taken a bite of fruit that looked fine on the outside but was rotten inside. "They can't do that to me. They already tol' me I can keep my prize money. They tol' me! They can't give it to nobody else!"

Mcintosh stood up and stomped back into his house, slamming the door behind him. After a moment, Jimmy heard a click as the door was deadbolted from inside.

For the second time in as many days, Jimmy knew his interview was over and that he had been dismissed. Lyst had turned to his computer; Mcintosh had bolted the door. Both ways were effective.

Abandoned, Jimmy sat under the carport for a minute or two longer, thinking about the strange conversation he had just had. Then he got up, walked over to his SUV, climbed in, and drove away.

As he left behind the small, run-down home of a man who had written two more books than Jimmy had, he thought to himself that something was definitely off about Mcintosh and *Where the Ocean Swallows the Moon.*

It was a puzzle, and Jimmy wanted to put it together and figure it out.

As he got back on a paved road, his cell phone pinged. A quick glance told him it was Pepé. Jimmy pulled over into a driveway so he could read the text.

Hope your case is better than mine. Call me.

Chapter 9

JIMMY LEFT THE RANDOM DRIVEWAY he had pulled into and got back onto the road. He pressed the phone button on his steering wheel.

"Ready," the car cheerfully responded, ever helpful, never cranky or disrespectful.

"Call Pepé," Jimmy said.

"Calling Pee-Pee, mobile. Is that correct?"

Jimmy loved calling Pepé from his vehicle just to hear it call him Pee-Pee. "Yes," he replied, grinning broadly, even though he did this nearly once a day. It just never grew old.

He heard his partner's phone ring once, then Pepé answered. "Hola, dude. How you doin'?"

"Hey, Pepé. I'm doing fine. Where are you?"

"I'm driving on the causeway off Jekyll. I just finished meeting with Mrs. E."

"Well, turn around," Jimmy instructed his friend. "I'm on Jekyll, too. I'll meet you at the DQ, and you can buy me a Peanut Buster Parfait. Then I can catch you up on my case, and you can give me the backstory on yours. Sound good?"

"I'm turning around right now. I'll see you at the DQ." And Pepé was gone.

Jimmy had opted for the slightly longer drive along the northern coast rather than cutting through the middle of the island near the Jekyll Island Plantation and the Turtle Center. Seeing the Atlantic Ocean stretching away from him on his left was one of his favorite sights. Jimmy never tired of the ocean view. Every day at the ocean was different.

✳✳✳

Pepé was already at the Dairy Queen when Jimmy pulled up. Jimmy got out of his vehicle, stretched out the kinks from his back quickly, and went inside, waving as he got close. Pepé was sitting at a booth by the window, working on a Blizzard. Jimmy went to the counter and ordered a Reese's Pieces Blizzard. He took his treat and went to sit with Pepé.

"I thought you wanted a Peanut Buster Parfait?" Pepé said.

"This is better and bigger. Plus, I can afford it."

"Ooh! Maybe I should have waited for you so you could buy mine. You must have snared a good gig!"

Jimmy smiled, held up his palm, and flashed five fingers at Pepé twice.

"Ten? They're paying you a thousand? That's great! I know you can use the money. Things get tight sometimes—" Jimmy cut his partner off.

"—No, man, *ten thousand*. Plus, expenses. That means I don't even have to pay for this Blizzard, and I'm going to fill my tank outside at the gas station before I head back. I don't even need to check the price."

"Dude! I think you've moved up from the minor leagues. That's some serious money for a single job. Congratulations!"

"Thanks, man. It sure beats serving papers."

"Amen to that!" Pepé agreed, and they touched their paper Blizzard cups together in a muffled toast.

Jimmy took several spoonfuls, then set his Blizzard on the table and said, "I have to slow down, or I'll get a brain freeze, an ice cream headache."

"Oh, I know what you mean," his anti-crime partner agreed. He set his treat down and asked, "What's this new job that's paying you so well?"

Jimmy told him about Lyst Publishing, the contest, the loss of the manuscript, Trevor Mcintosh, and the Lysts' desire for Jimmy to retrieve the winning story. He chose not to reveal any details about Wendi. Not yet, anyway.

"So, the author who won the contest lives up here on Jekyll?" Pepé asked.

"Mm-hm. Up on the north end of the island," Jimmy replied. "He lives in a run-down shack under the live oaks and pines off a main road on a little dirt path. And the author is about as well-kept as his house. He had on a dirty wife-beater tee stretched over his belly, pants with suspenders around his hips, no shoes, socks with holes, and greasy hair. He gives slovenly a bad name. The guy's house makes my place look like the Taj Mahal. It's so bad that I wouldn't let *your* dog live there!"

"Don't speak too quickly, Jimmy. Pawley might like it. He comes from the barrier islands and marshes off the coast of South Carolina. He's a Boykin Spaniel from Pawleys Island."

"So, you named him after the place he was from? That's cool. Anyway, my point was that the guy lives in a shack, which is just a little surprising since he had a best-selling book, *Growing Up Southern.*"

"I remember hearing of that book, but it was a long time ago, at least twenty-five years ago," Pepé added.

"Thirty-five years, actually," Jimmy said. "The guy was just twenty years old back then, and he turned in his book to the publisher, took his money, and pulled a Howard Hughes. Like when someone goes off the grid to escape the mob. Mcintosh simply dropped out of sight until just recently. Suddenly, out of nowhere, this guy submitted a manuscript to the contest at Lyst Publishing. It's called *Where the Ocean Swallows the Moon, Five Years on a Freighter.* And the guy won, if you can believe it. It's nearly a thousand pages long, and get this: he typed it on a manual typewriter. But the best – or worst – part is: he didn't make another copy. And now their only copy has been stolen!"

"Dude!" Pepé drew out the word. It sounded like *"Dooooood!"*

"I know! My client said they expect to make well over ten times what they're paying me just from the book sales. And they own the movie rights, too. So, this is kind of big, and not just for me. It's a big deal for them, too. But I *have* to find that manuscript. That's the basis for the fee."

Jimmy thought about his casual promise to never disappoint Wendi. He smiled, imagining how grateful she would be when he strolled in and plopped the errant document on her desk.

"What are you smiling about, dude?" Pepé asked, working on his Blizzard again.

"Just burping from the Blizzard. Sorry." He brought his fist up, covered his mouth, and pretended to burp. He picked up his Blizzard and continued his treat and his story.

"I asked this Mcintosh guy if I could go inside his house, and he wouldn't let me in. I couldn't get past the front door."

Pepé asked, "He wouldn't talk with you?"

"Yeah, he did, but not in the house. We had to sit on some rusty chairs under the world's worst carport. I tried to get him to let me into his house by saying they needed a picture of him with the ancient typewriter he wrote his book on, but he wouldn't bite. He was very evasive about the manuscript and didn't seem to care whether it gets found or not as long as he gets the money the Lysts promised him. I kept trying to get in the house until he finally told me he had pawned the typewriter."

"What?" Pepé exclaimed, slurping up the last of his DQ treat. "He pawned it? Why?"

"He said he needed money for some 'things,' and since he didn't use it very often – like once every thirty-five years! – he felt he could let it go. He said he'd get it back after he got his prize money, Jimmy answered.

"Did you offer to go and get it out of hock?" Pepé asked.

Jimmy felt his face redden, heat rising from around the collar of his shirt. Shaking his head, he said, "No. It didn't occur to me. I guess I missed it."

"Could've caught him in the lie," Pepé said with a shrug.

"Yeah, I probably should have. Not that it would have made much difference. He barely made eye contact with me the whole time I was interviewing him. But get this—" Jimmy paused.

Pepé leaned forward conspiratorially in their booth.

"When I told him the second-place author was making noise about how *his* book should move up to the first place since they still have his manuscript and how *he* should get the top prize money, Mcintosh suddenly got mad. He said it was his prize money, and they couldn't do that to him. He said they were going to try and cheat him, he just knew it. He got up, stomped into this shack, slammed the door, and deadbolted it behind him. I took it as a sign the interview was over. What do you make of it?" Jimmy stirred up the pieces in his Blizzard and took another bite.

"Sounds like he already had the money spent. Did he have a lot of vices that you noticed? Drink? Smoke? Cars? Doesn't sound like women are part of the equation by your description of him. And pawning the typewriter to get some quick cash? He sounds like a real trophy. I think my first guess is probably on the mark: he's already got the money spent."

"Maybe he just wants to get out of his shack and into a nicer place, Pepé."

"I dunno. Maybe, but I doubt it."

"He asked me for a cigarette a couple of times, and one time he asked me if I had any beer. Weird. Huh? Wait, not weird. Mr. Lyst said he was 'an eccentric.' He was definitely eccentric, *weirdly* eccentric!"

Pepé started to laugh, but he kept it low. They weren't at one of their local, real Southern-cookin', everybody-knows-your-name diners, so he didn't let loose with his usual unrestrained laughter.

Jimmy changed the subject and asked Pepé, "How about your case? Mrs. E. with the lost husband? You gonna make any money on it?"

Pepé waved his hand through the air like he was shooing away a fly. "Nah. She can't afford much. I'm doing it more as a favor to Glynn County than anything. Besides, everybody deserves to have closure when something like this happens. My heart goes out to people whose loved ones have disappeared and they never find out what happened to them. They spend the rest of their lives not knowing if their wife or child – or husband – is dead or alive. They never know if they played a role in their disappearance and made them go away or if someone took them. It's not right. So, I'm doing it for expenses only."

"You're a good man, Pepé. A good man with a military pension!" Jimmy said, and they laughed and clicked their

Blizzard cups together again. But it was true. Without his pension from the Navy and his policeman's pension, Pepé couldn't take on a case like this where there was no money.

"Did you get a chance to do any of your interweb searchin' on her missing mister?" Pepé asked Jimmy.

Jimmy took one last slurp of his Blizzard with his straw, long and loud, making Pepé roll his eyes and chuckle. Jimmy smiled broadly, enjoying the companionship he shared with Pepé.

Pushing the empty Blizzard cup to one side of their table, Jimmy told Pepé about his earlier search for John Epps from Jekyll and discovering the murder of another John Epps in 1881 in Des Moines.

"I know it probably doesn't have anything to do with our John Epps, but it was intriguing – a little weird even – to be looking for someone from the 21st century and find the name popping up in a 19th-century murder. Two guys from Des Moines with the same first and last names, and both doctors? The 19th-century doc has to be our guy's great-great-great-something or other, you know? It made me want to search more and find out if they're related."

Pepé looked at Jimmy for a second, then moved his Blizzard cup over by Jimmy's, and his expression turned serious. "But to what end?" Jimmy's mentor asked. "What difference does it make if they're related? Directly or indirectly? What impact does it have on our finding my client's husband?"

Pepé continued. "Dead or alive, she just wants to know what happened. If you ask me, she's already given up on finding him alive. If she wants to be free to remarry, that tells me she's probably found a replacement for the good doctor. We need more intel on a possible trail left by our guy, and you can do your family tree research on his grandpappy some other time. Sound good?"

"That's fine, Pepé. I understand. With my current assignment from the Lysts and the fat paycheck waiting for me at the end, I can't afford to waste time chasing rabbits with no payoff."

Jimmy said what Pepé wanted to hear, but he also knew that he couldn't work 24/7, and Jimmy found hunting something down on the internet relaxing. Genealogy was usually a matter of pulling together all the puzzle pieces and turning them all right-side up so he could see the pattern they formed. It took his mind off the frustrations most cases produced as he tried to locate someone or something, especially when people were less than forthcoming with information, like Trevor.

Pepé stood up, and Jimmy followed suit.

"I have to head back to St. Marys. Gwynn is expecting me for supper, and you know I hate disappointing her. Especially on Tex-Mex meatloaf day."

"You don't want to be late," Jimmy answered. "You married way above your pay grade. I've always been impressed with how you caught her in a weak moment and convinced her to take you on as a makeover project."

Pepé started to laugh, but he didn't stifle it this time. Luckily, there were no customers in the DQ, but all the employees looked up as Pepé filled the place with his laughter.

****

On the drive back to Camden County, Jimmy's phone rang. He pushed a button on the steering and announced, "This is Jimmy."

"Jimmy!" It was Wendi. She sounded serious, with no flirtatious overtones. "Where are you?"

"Good afternoon to you, too, *Mrs.* Lyst. I just went by mile-marker seven, so I'm nearly at St. Marys."

"Can you come down to the office? It's important." She was all business. Jimmy decided he should pay attention.

"I can, but it'll be another forty-five minutes after I get to St. Marys. What's going on?"

"Mr. Lyst wants to meet with you again. Somebody called and told him they had *found* the manuscript! They said they're willing to make a deal."

"Money?" asked Jimmy, his Spidey-sense tingling.

"I think so," she answered. "I didn't ask yet. Mr. Lyst just told me to get ahold of you and tell you to come back to the office."

"Tell," not ask. I guess for 10K, that's expected, Jimmy thought.

"All right. I'm on my way. Let him know," Jimmy responded. "I'll push my speed up a bit. Everybody knows the speed limit is just a suggestion, right? Besides, my contract with Lyst Publishing includes expenses." Jimmy chuckled, knowing she was probably smiling at his chutzpah.

"Don't go too fast, Jimmy," Wendi replied. "If you had read that contract more carefully, you'd have noticed that it has a $100 a day limit on expenses."

Jimmy laughed nonchalantly. "Right. If I get stopped, I'll just charm my way out of it."

"Fine, but you saw how well that worked for Osama bin Laden with Seal Team Six," Wendi responded.

"Duly noted," Jimmy said and clicked off. Despite her warnings, he prodded the gas pedal with his foot, and his motorized steed dashed ahead.

Chapter 10

JIMMY AVOIDED INTERACTING WITH THE Florida State Patrol or the Nassau County Sheriff's Office, arriving at Lyst Publishing nearly ten minutes earlier than he promised Wendi.

This time, Jimmy knew how to get where he was going, and he walked in the front door, down the narrow hall, and into Lyst Publishing. Wendi was not at her desk, but Mr. Lyst came to the door of his office and waved for Jimmy to come in.

In Hillary Lyst's office, Jimmy sat in the same chair he had used the day before.

"I'm sorry Mrs. Lyst isn't in, Jimmy. She's running an errand for me, and it's time-sensitive."

"That's fine. When she called me, she said this was a bit of a command performance."

"Indeed," Mr. Lyst said, looking over his glasses at Jimmy, his brow furrowed. "What else did she tell you about the situation?

"Wendi – Mrs. Lyst – said someone had contacted you and wants to return the manuscript. But from what I gather, this is not an altogether altruistic offer."

"That it is not. Not meaning to get too far off the path, let me commend your use of the word altruistic. It's another word that has, unfortunately, fallen out of the average citizen's standard lexicon." Jimmy smiled, basking in the compliment, like a teacher's pet getting an A on a quiz.

Lyst continued. "Amusements aside, we received the phone call about two hours ago. The caller asked for me personally. He or she would not speak with Wendi except to ask for me."

"He or she?"

"Their voice sounded robotic, mechanical, neither male nor female. There was something familiar about it, though, but I can't seem to place my finger on what was recognizable about it."

"They probably used an electronic voice modulator to disguise their voice. I've seen them as low as ten dollars on Amazon, and there are even phone apps that do it. No extra machinery involved, and you can do it wherever you are with your phone. People don't know you're doing anything other than making a regular phone call."

"Yes, that's a possibility," Lyst said, rubbing his temples. Jimmy realized the man was quite stressed. Despite his usually perky demeanor, the loss of the manuscript and potential income was a drag on his system. "I've heard them used on television on shows about kidnappings and bomb threats and such."

"I'm sure it's because we've heard it on tv and in the movies so often," Jimmy offered.

Lyst shook his head in frustration. "Hmm. Could be. Let me tell you what the caller said. When I answered the phone, they told me they had the manuscript and were willing to make a deal to return it to us here. They said it was safe for now, but they couldn't guarantee it if we did not agree to their terms."

"Which are …?" Jimmy pressed, sitting forward in his chair.

"They were fairly straightforward. They want you to meet them at 5:30 this afternoon at a small drinking establishment near the interstate on Highway 17. It's called Mickey's Tap Room. Do you know it?"

Jimmy stared dumbly at Hillary Lyst. *Know it? It's about a stone's throw from my house! I drive by it every single day!* But what he told Lyst was, "Yeah, I know where it is. I've been by it a time or two."

Mickey's Tap Room was about a quarter-mile from Jimmy's house on his way to the interstate. It wasn't much, just a place to stop and get drunk if you lived within a mile or two of the state border and didn't care about the décor of the place where you drank. If Jimmy had been a drinker, it would have been ideal. He could have walked home every night if he had more to drink than he should. But Jimmy detested beer and referred to most mixed-drink cocktails as "gasoline drinks." He counted himself lucky that he had never developed a taste for alcohol.

"Splendid," Lyst continued. "Are you carrying a weapon?"

"I don't, as a rule," Jimmy replied, hoping it wouldn't cause the publisher to reconsider putting Jimmy under contract.

"Just as well. Loud, dangerous things. Besides, the voice on the phone said to come unarmed."

"I'm assuming they want something in exchange for the return of the *Where the Ocean Swallows the Moon*."

"Yes, but luckily for us, I had the amount available in the bank. I had to dip into my personal savings, but it was not a hardship. If we recover the manuscript intact, we'll be able to secure it, copy it, print it, and publish it. We'll recoup my money in no time. I have faith in that manuscript's marketability. And I have faith in you, Jimmy."

Jimmy felt a flush of warmth and guessed that his face had probably reddened a tad from the compliment.

"How much are they demanding for the document's return?" Jimmy asked.

"Only five thousand dollars."

Jimmy sat up and leaned forward in his chair. "Five thousand? You told me you expect to make ten times what you're paying me, which would be at least a hundred thousand dollars plus the movie rights, and this guy is asking for only five grand? Is this some kid who accidentally stumbled in here looking for comic books and found the manuscript instead?"

"That's not something I am conversant with, Jimmy. I know comic books can be quite valuable, but I have never published any, nor graphic novels – the comic book's big brother, if you will. I only know that I was pleased to send Mrs. Lyst to the bank to pick up the money for the handoff. Is that what you call it? A handoff? Or a drop-off?"

"It's a *payoff*. Mr. Lyst, she's not going to Mickey's, right? She's got no good reason to go in there." Jimmy suddenly envisioned scenes from one of those graphic novels Hillary Lyst had never published playing in his mind.

In his mind's eye, he saw Mickey's Tap Room, darker than midnight with dirty-yellow lighting. Mrs. Lyst was standing by the bar in her black skirt and white blouse, holding a bag full of money. The patrons were all staring at her, bloodshot eyes bulging and drool slathering from their lips. Their beer bellies hung low, restrained by overly tight belts cinched snugly to keep the pants from falling. Their meaty arms were beginning to reach for her. Jimmy knew what was on their minds, and it wasn't wondering about the contents of the bag she carried.

Jimmy rubbed his eyes to clear the vision, stood up, and stepped away from Lyst's desk. "I need to get going."

"Sit down, Jimmy." Lyst hadn't raised his voice, but Jimmy heard the firmness within and noticed the publisher's stern expression.

Jimmy sat.

"I haven't told you where she was going after the bank. If you went to Mickey's expecting to find Mrs. Lyst there, you'd be sadly disappointed and possibly cause a breakdown in the expected transaction."

"Okay. I'm sitting. Where's Wendi—Mrs. Lyst—going?"

"To your house. She's meeting you there. *You* are going to Mickey's, not Wendi, and you will negotiate the manuscript's return. She will give you five thousand dollars, and I am prepared to spend it all to get the story back. Now you may leave."

Jimmy stood to go.

Mr. Lyst held up a hand to stop Jimmy from leaving. "One last thing: if by some chance you can get it back for less, I would be deeply indebted to you, as will Mrs. Lyst."

***

Jimmy nearly ran down the hallway and out to the parking lot to his SUV. He rushed through two yellow lights, hoping no cops were watching. He pushed the speed limit as much as possible on A1A up to Yulee, then floored it on the Highway 17 straightaway. He flew past the trailer park on the right just before the interstate on-ramp and only began to slow down a mile or two later when he approached Mickey's Tap Room. There were no cars in the parking lot. That meant the person he was supposed to meet had not arrived, but neither had Wendi.

His graphic vision had shaken him. What was he thinking? She was his client's wife. Yes, she flirted with him – *she started it!* – but a part of him enjoyed it. Wendi made him feel like he was something special, something more than what he saw when he looked in the mirror. She made him feel … The only word he could come up with was desirable, which wasn't the kind of word guys used to describe themselves. Girls and women were desirable and sensual. Guys were … something else. Whatever that word was, Wendi stirred that feeling up in him. And regardless of what the word was, there was no way he would allow her to accompany him into Mickey's.

As he rolled past Mickey's and saw the blue bridge ahead, he noticed a car parked at his house. It was a red Audi A3. Not new, not old, not big, not small, but fancy. Like Wendi. He turned into his driveway and bounced across the yard, hurrying to catch up with her.

Slow down! he told himself. *Besides, she's somebody else's missus.*

As he rocked to a stop, he saw Wendi sitting on his front steps. She stood up, a smile spreading over her face. It was the kind of thing he could stand to see every day for the next sixty or seventy years. *Maybe I'll find a girl like her. Someday.* He hoped Hillary Lyst appreciated what he had. Jimmy took a deep breath before getting out of his SUV.

"Have you been waiting long?" Jimmy asked her as he came around the front of his vehicle.

"No. I just got here two minutes ago. I barely got seated on your steps before you pulled in." She held up a small paper sack. "It doesn't look big enough for five thousand dollars, does it?" She handed the bag of money to Jimmy.

"My mother always said good things come in small packages," Jimmy responded. "Of course, she was trying to make me feel better about being the smallest kid on the hockey team, so you can take that with a grain of salt."

She smiled some more. "I'll bet you were an adorable kid."

"If you consider Dennis the Menace adorable."

She laughed softly. Jimmy would have loved to stand there and say stupid things all night to make her laugh, but he had a previous engagement.

"It's after five," he told her. "And I need to meet someone at Mickey's Tap Room at 5:30 to negotiate the return of a certain manuscript."

"Mm-hm. I saw the place when I was coming here. It looks like a *very* high-class saloon," she said, sarcasm dripping from her words.

"If you consider the bottom-of-the-barrel high class," Jimmy replied, "and I know some guys who would find Mickey's an improvement over their current digs."

Wendi was still standing on his front steps, and Jimmy was leaning against the hood of his vehicle. It felt like those times as a teenager when he escorted a girl home to her door and then had no idea what to do once they got there.

"I'd invite you in, but I seem to have misplaced my key," she said, and Jimmy noticed the purr coming back to her voice.

"Luckily for you, I have a key that I'm pretty sure will fit," he answered. Jimmy climbed the steps, and she stepped back a bit to let him pass. Her position still forced him much closer to her than he intended. *Intentional? No doubt.*

Jimmy unlocked the door, but before he turned the knob, he took out his cell phone and opened an app. Tapping in a short series of numbers, he disarmed the alarm system. "It's a tough neighborhood sometimes," he said, shrugging slightly as he opened the door. "Alligators and raccoons are always trying to break in."

He held the door open and stepped back so she could cross the threshold. He could smell her hair as she slipped past him, a clean scent laced with some kind of tropical flower and a hint of citrus.

"Don't be too critical," he said as she disappeared inside. "I'm a bachelor, and it's the maid's year off."

"I'm impressed," she said as she walked into his living room. "No beer cans, paper plates, corn chip bags, or pictures of naked girls on the walls. Not like my vision of a bachelor pad."

"You haven't seen my bedroom," Jimmy replied. Immediately he felt warmth coming up from around the neck of his shirt and knew his face was turning red. He was tasting shoe leather again, thanks to his smart-alecky mouth.

"I didn't know it was on the tour," Wendi replied.

Jimmy felt embarrassed and a little guilty for implying a potential tête-a-tête. Jimmy had boundaries, and those boundaries clearly declared married women off-limits. Despite Wendi's playful flirting with him, he needed to maintain at least a *semi*-professional attitude with her, especially when he was working.

He checked his watch. 5:15. This wouldn't be a long tour. He had to be at Mickey's in fifteen minutes, but it was only five minutes by foot and even less by car.

She had checked out the kitchen and his office, and then Wendi opened the door to the guest bedroom, where Daani had slept—*alone!*—for two nights. The bedclothes were unmade, a towel hung from the corner of the bed's headboard, and a pair of pink, lace-edged panties were halfway under the bed but still quite visible. Daani must have missed them when she packed the morning she left.

Wendi walked over, picked up the panties, pulled them back like a slingshot, and sent them flying over Jimmy's head. He was horrified.

"They don't look like they're your size," she said, snickering. "But they look like your color. At least your color right now."

Jimmy knew his face must be beet-red.

"A-uh, a-a friend stayed here for a couple of days, and it was early in the morning when she left." Jimmy stammered. "She must have missed them when she packed."

"Uh-huh. And does this 'friend' have a name, Jimmy?" Jimmy was starting to understand how a rabbit or mouse feels when a cat stalks it.

Jimmy swallowed hard. "It's my ... niece. (*Yeah! That's it! Thanks, Daani.*) My niece was down here for a vacation and stayed with me for a couple of days before she drove back to Wisconsin. Her name is Daani. I'm her Uncle Jimmy."

He thought, *Who could've known <u>that</u> would come in handy?*

"Oh. Okay, then." And just like that, Wendi slid past him and back out to the living room.

It was time to go. *Just in the nick of time*, Jimmy thought.

"I have to get over to Mickey's Tap Room. I don't want to be late," he told Wendi. He went into his office, found an envelope, and put half the money inside, counting out twenty-five hundred dollars. Then he pulled out three more envelopes, putting a thousand dollars each in two and five hundred in the last one.

"What's with the envelopes?" Wendi asked. She hadn't said anything while he divided up the cash.

"Mr. Lyst told me I could use all five thousand dollars to get the manuscript back, but if I could get it back for *less*, that would be better," Jimmy replied. "I may play truth or consequences with them, offering what's behind door number one for a different envelope. Or maybe we'll play Whack-a-mole to see if they can win a prize. It all depends on how seasoned they are at negotiating. If they're smart, they'll open all the envelopes and count the money. That way, they get all they asked for. If they're newbies or nervous, they'll take the first envelope with twenty-five hundred and hightail it out. Either way, it's my job to get that manuscript back."

"Mind if I tag along?" Wendi asked, putting a hand on Jimmy's shoulder.

Stepping away and out of her reach, Jimmy said, "Sorry. Strict instructions from your boss and *mine*. You are not to be involved in the payoff."

Wendi produced a pout any three-year-old would be proud to claim.

"Personally, I would have chosen another route rather than paying a ransom," Jimmy said. "But I'm not the one calling the shots here. I'm just a go-between."

"Do you mind if I wait here at your house until you're done?" she asked.

"I promised Mr. Lyst that I would not allow you to be a part of this meeting at Mickey's. I won't break that promise."

"I promise I'll stay right here. I'll sit on the steps and enjoy the outdoor night sounds. I haven't done that in a long time."

All right," Jimmy said, "but I'm out of time. I have to go. Swear to me you'll stay here and that you will *not* come over to Mickey's."

"I *already* said I promise," Wendi replied. Jimmy didn't move. She pouted again and said, "Fine. I swear I'll stay here until I see you come out." Just to punctuate her promise, she made a crisscross motion over her chest, crossing her heart. As a final promise, she added, "Stick a needle in my eye."

"Just so you know," Jimmy said, edging to the door, "I have a feeling Mr. Lyst would skin me alive and use my hide for a book cover if I let anything happen to you. And I've become quite partial to wearing my skin over my bones."

Jimmy made eye contact with Wendi one more time, then turned on his heel and was out the door.

It was twenty-five past, but he knew he'd be at Mickey's in under a minute. He checked his waist in the back to make sure he had three envelopes still stuck in firmly under his shirt and one envelope on the passenger seat of his SUV. He pushed the ignition button. It was time to earn his paycheck.

Chapter 11

JIMMY DIDN'T WAIT FOR HIS watch to trip over to 5:30. He walked into Mickey's and headed toward the back. It wasn't a large or deep room, and he could see a man sitting at a table for two, a glass of something on the table in front of him.

Jimmy stopped, stood across the table from the guy, and put one hand on the chair next to his hip. The man flicked his eyes at the chair as if to say, "That's your assigned seat." Jimmy sat down.

"You Favreaux?" he asked Jimmy.

Jimmy nodded. "Who are you?"

"Just call me Gabriel. I'm a messenger for the Man. I was sent to negotiate for the manuscript. I assume you were sent to do the same thing for the old man with the books?

For no reason, Jimmy bristled at the term 'old man.' He knew Lyst was in his mid-to-late sixties, an age when most other men retire, but Hillary Lyst seemed to love what he did and probably had no intention of ever fully retiring. Without his publishing company, he'd probably just lay down and die.

"His name is Mr. Lyst," Jimmy replied.

He waited for Gabriel to say more. The silence was beginning to roar in Jimmy's ears when the messenger suddenly shrugged his shoulders and said, "Whatever. I don't have a dog in this fight. My client sent me to collect payment for the safe return of a document. I'm just doing my job."

A waitress shuffled over to their table. She looked like she had been working non-stop for years. "Whattaya having?" she asked.

Gabriel answered, "Whatever you have on tap."

She shrugged and looked at Jimmy, waiting for his order. She was wearing a faded shirt that had once been a Hawaiian floral print but was now just some swirls of white on a grayish-blue background. It was threadbare and stained. The stains were the only patches of actual color left. Jimmy hoped none of the stains were blood. Her shorts were denim, short-shorts like Daani wore, but the waitress's legs were skinny and shapeless. There was nothing sexy or sensual about them. They were just bones with skin, a means to get from table to table and take drink orders.

Jimmy waved his hand and said, "I'm good."

"Not today, you're not," she replied. "You want to sit here, you buy a drink."

"Bring me a tap beer, then," he replied. He had no intention of drinking it. It was just the price of admission to the show.

Gabriel chuckled as the waitress shuffled back to the bar.

"How old do you think she is?" he asked Jimmy. "She looks like she's at least seventy-five."

"She's probably forty," Jimmy responded. "It's not an easy life; she probably has to do favors for men to make ends meet."

"I don't think I could ever be so hard up that I'd ask her to do anything for me, let alone *pay* her for it." Gabriel's face showed contempt for the woman.

"Don't say it too loud, or she'll spit in your beer. Or worse."

The man looked disgusted at the thought.

They let the conversation go on hiatus until the woman brought their two glasses of beer. She set them down on the table – no coasters – and said, "Ten bucks. Five each." Jimmy knew she had probably opened a couple of two-dollar cans of Bud Light and called it draft on tap. He threw a twenty on the table. "Keep the change," he said. Her skinny hand grabbed the bill and shoved it in her shorts pocket. She had probably already paid the four dollars for the beer, so she was pocketing sixteen dollars in profit. Jimmy didn't care. She looked like she could use it. Besides, as he had told Pepé, his contract included expenses.

She grunted at Jimmy and left him alone with Gabriel the messenger.

Gabriel lifted his beer and drank half of it in one swallow. Jimmy slid his glass to one side of the table, moving it out of the empty space between the two men.

Gabriel wiped the beer foam from his upper lip on his sleeve. Jimmy could see inked skin under the man's shirt cuff. *Sleeved out,* he thought. Some kind of a vine or snake was inked onto his neck and creeping up from inside his shirt. Jimmy didn't have any tattoos, but he didn't carry a bias against those who chose to go that route.

"How did you come to be here today?" Jimmy asked.

"If you're asking if I stole the manuscript, I can assure you that I did not. I received a phone call from a man I know. He asked me to do him a favor. He said the manuscript got took on accident, and when he realized the mistake, he decided to return it."

"How decent of him," Jimmy said, not bothering to acknowledge the blatant lie. "A regular philanthropist. Since he admits it was a mistake and wants to return it, simply hand it over to me, and I'll take it back to my employer, and you can finish your beer in peace. I'll even let you have my beer."

"There is a matter of time and trouble. We used to call it shipping and handling. Everything you saw advertised on tv said 'plus shipping and handling.' Sometimes they would give you a second item free; just pay 'separate shipping and handling,' the ads said. My friend needs to recoup his shipping and handling. He had to store the document for several days, and he had to research it, too, to determine its value. His time is worth something, don't you think?"

Jimmy pulled the first envelope from his pocket, where he had slipped it after arriving at Mickey's. It was the envelope with twenty-five hundred inside, and he laid it to one side on the table, next to the glass of beer he was ignoring. A growing puddle of condensation stretched out from the glass, and Jimmy kept one eye on the liquid to make sure it didn't get too close to the envelope.

"As a freelance investigator," Jimmy said, "I understand the need to cover your overhead. Mr. Lyst understands it, too. He realizes there is always a cost to doing business. It's the American way of capitalism, after all. My employer wanted me to give this to you for your associate."

Jimmy reached over and slid the envelope from its resting place, pushing it across the table until it was next to Gabriel's beer.

The man reached for the envelope, but Jimmy's hand was quicker, covering the envelope of money.

"Not so fast, my friend. Remember what I just said: I'm a freelancer myself. I understand supply and demand and the need to pay the middleman," Jimmy said. "That's you, by the way. You're the middleman for your side, and I'm the middleman for my side. My boss is paying me a flat fee plus expenses, so I'm not too concerned about getting anything from this transaction. My money will come after the manuscript is returned safe and sound. But I'm sure you would like to be compensated for your time and trouble – your ... *shipping and handling*, I believe you called it?"

Jimmy reached back and slid an envelope out from behind his back, the one containing five hundred dollars. He placed it on the table. The puddle from his beer was growing, but he was careful to avoid it.

"We independent small businessmen need to watch each other's backs, don't you agree?" He nodded at Gabriel, who stared at Jimmy briefly, then redirected his gaze to the second envelope of money for a bit before finally nodding. Jimmy wondered if it had taken that long for the thought to percolate through his brain before he figured out Jimmy was offering him a bonus.

Gabriel lifted his beer and drained it. If Jimmy had been paying his own expenses, he would have thought, *That's two-and-a-half dollars per swallow.* But he let it go. Jimmy was going to see if the man would count both envelopes and wait for the rest or grab what he could see and run.

Jimmy opened the second envelope. He showed Gabriel that it contained five crisp, new one-hundred-dollar bills. One-hundred-dollar bills always look impressive, and even more so when grouped together. Jimmy took them out of the envelope, fanned them out like presidential flashcards, then straightened them up and slid them back into the envelope. He placed the envelope on the table, then slid it over until it rested next to the first envelope. Gabriel continued to look at the envelopes, especially the one Jimmy had intimated was for him with the pretty pictures of Benjamin Franklin inside.

"Can you use five hundred dollars, Gabriel? I'm betting you can. That second envelope is for you. No strings attached. Your boss doesn't even have to know anything about it."

Gabriel wiped his mouth with his sleeve again. Jimmy was getting ready to set the hook.

"Go ahead. Pick up the envelope. Open it up and look at the money. Five hundred dollars, and you didn't have to do anything to earn it except come to this gross little dive bar and drink some overpriced canned beer. And you didn't even have to pay for the beer." Gabriel picked up the second envelope and opened it. He pulled the bills out partway, recounted them, and slid them back in.

"Go ahead and put that envelope in your pocket. It's yours. Like I said, no strings attached."

The other man slid the envelope inside his shirt. Jimmy had him. All he had to do was reel him in.

"My boss talked with your boss," Jimmy continued, his voice even, calm, and soothing. "They agreed on a price. Five thousand dollars. I just gave you a ten-percent commission. Not bad for a half-hour's work, is it?" Gabriel nodded in agreement.

"This other envelope has the money for your boss." Jimmy picked it up and opened the flap to reveal many more one-hundred-dollar bills. Jimmy was careful not to count them or leave them exposed too long.

"All you have to do now is give me the manuscript, and then you can take the envelope and give it to your boss, and I will take the manuscript and give it to my client."

Gabriel suddenly looked sick. "Um ..." he began. "That could be a bit of a problem. I didn't want to bring the manuscript in here and get jumped and lose it *and* the money. So, I stashed it on the way here. But it's close by, I promise."

Jimmy rolled his eyes and groaned. Shaking his head, Jimmy said, "Gabriel, Gabriel, Gabriel. We were getting along so well, and you were getting a bonus, and then you pull this on me?" Jimmy reached out and quickly slid the envelope back to his side of the table. He didn't pick it up, though, letting Gabriel see it, just out of reach.

"I can go get the manuscript and be back in ten minutes. Honest, it is really close by," the intermediary spouted.

"Tell me where it is," Jimmy said. "I'll go get it. That way, you can take your money and your boss's money and call it a day. It's already dark outside." There were no windows in Mickey's, but Jimmy knew that sundown was at 5:30, which meant it was nearing total darkness outside.

Gabriel thought it over. He picked up Jimmy's beer and took a long pull. Three-quarters of the amber liquid disappeared down his throat.

"How do I know you're not going to jump me and take back the money when you know where it is?" Gabriel asked.

"I gave you a bonus, and this is how you repay me? How long do you usually have to work for five hundred dollars? A day? A couple of days? I gave it to you for a half-hour's work. And I showed you the money in the other envelope, right?" Gabriel nodded. Jimmy gave him the clincher: "I promise on my mother's grave that there are five thousand dollars in envelopes at this table right now."

Gabriel finished the beer. He looked at Jimmy, then glanced around the room as if looking for someone eavesdropping. He leaned toward the table and said, "Do you know where the weigh station is on 17 coming from Yulee?"

Jimmy nodded.

Gabriel continued. "There's a trash can by the far back corner. It doesn't get much use because most truckers pull through and use the dumpster at the other end on their way out. I put the manuscript in the can by the back corner. I laid it on top. It's all wrapped up in brown butcher paper, so nothing can get on it and ruin it."

Gabriel sat up and pointed a finger at Jimmy. "Now you wait here until I'm out of here. I don't want you jumping me from behind." He stood up and faced Jimmy as though afraid to turn his back on him.

Jimmy smiled and held out his hand like they were regular business partners. Gabriel looked at the hand for a minute before realizing what was happening. A sheepish grin rolled over his face, and he shook Jimmy's hand. Jimmy thought Gabriel's hand looked about the size of a small ham as it engulfed his hand.

Gabriel walked across the room toward the door. As he opened it, Jimmy saw that he was right. It was full-on night outside. He hoped Wendi was enjoying the crickets and highway sounds.

As Gabriel stepped outside, Jimmy glanced at the empty beer glasses on the table and thought, *An absolute pleasure to do business with you, Gabriel. And I mean that.*

✳✳✳

As soon as Gabriel closed the door, Jimmy stood up and walked over to it. He counted to ten and then pushed the door open and stepped out. He saw tail lights pull out of the parking lot. They turned right, heading toward Jimmy's house and the blue bridge. Gabriel was driving away from the weigh station, not toward it.

Jimmy ran to his SUV and jumped in. As soon as it sprang to life, he slammed it into gear, the tires spitting a small rooster tail of gravel out the back, and took off in the opposite direction Gabriel had. Five minutes later, Jimmy was at the weigh station on Highway 17. He saw the trash can Gabriel had mentioned. He pulled up next to it, shoved the gearshift into Park, and jumped out. The package was right on top, just like Gabriel had promised. Brown butcher paper. It was even tied with a string.

Jimmy grabbed the bundle, got back in his vehicle, and opened the package enough to see inside. It was letter-sized paper, and he could see a title page. He was able to read it under the overhead light. *Where the Ocean Swallows the Moon.* Jimmy had the manuscript back and still had two thousand dollars tucked into his waistband. *Some days are diamonds.*

***

Jimmy drove more sedately back to his house. He was glad to see Wendi's red car still parked in front, and she was still sitting on the front steps. As he drove in the driveway and up to the house, she stood and shielded her eyes against the Nissan's headlights. Seeing it was Jimmy, she sat down again.

He got out and handed her the package.

"You got it! Mr. Lyst is going to be so happy!"

"Well, if he's happy about that, he will be ecstatic over *this.*" Jimmy reached behind his back and pulled out the two envelopes. He opened the envelopes, took out the money, and counted twenty crisp one-hundred-dollar bills into Wendi's hands. Jimmy sat down on the steps next to Wendi.

"How did …?" she asked and looked at the investigator.

"I let the messenger's greed take over. I pulled out the envelope containing twenty-five hundred and laid it on the table. Then I gave him the envelope with five hundred inside and told him he could have it as a bonus. I opened it and showed him the five crisp hundreds, and then I just kept him thinking about that bonus. He never even counted the other envelope. The manuscript was exactly where he said it would be. Now you and I have to go back to your office, and you need to lock this up, but first, you need to make a copy of it. And if you can make a digital copy at the same time, that would be ideal."

Jimmy could barely make out Wendi's dark shape sitting on the steps next to him, and he suddenly realized she was getting closer. Her head was moving to intercept his. He quickly turned his head away, and she planted a warm kiss on his cheek.

He could tell she was staring at him in the dark, trying to figure out what was happening, so he stood up and said, "Come on. We need to go make copies of this book. We'll take two cars, so you don't have to come back out here again to pick up yours." He reached out a hand to keep her steady as she stood in the darkness. They got into their separate cars and headed back to Fernandina Beach and Lyst Publishing.

Following Wendi's tail lights, Jimmy thought about the aborted kiss on his front steps. He gently rubbed his cheek where her lips had connected. He wondered why he felt so lousy about doing the right thing.

Chapter 12

ILLARY LYST WAS PACING OUTSIDE by the office door when Wendi and Jimmy returned to the publishing company. They parked next to each other, Jimmy on the right, just like their seat assignments in Hillary Lyst's office.

Jimmy had kept the manuscript in his possession since Lyst had charged him with its recovery. He had also been charged with keeping Wendi out of it, and Jimmy knew if she returned carrying the manuscript, Lyst might get the wrong idea.

The publisher practically did a little jig as they walked down the narrow hallway leading to the offices. Wendi walked behind him, and Jimmy brought up the tail end of their little parade.

Arriving at the office door, Lyst opened it and went in, heading straight for his office. Wendi entered the reception area next, stopping just inside her office.

Hillary Lyst was over the moon with the manuscript's return, and the older man clapped his hands with joy when Jimmy handed him the leftover two thousand dollars. "Well done, Jimmy!" he crowed. "Well done, indeed! You have exceeded my expectations by leaps and bounds." Jimmy soaked up the compliment. He hadn't been praised so loudly and deliberately in quite some time. It felt good, and Jimmy decided it was okay to enjoy it since it was just the three of them in the office.

"Do you have a good copier that can handle this many pages?" Jimmy asked.

"Absolutely," Mr. Lyst answered. "We'll have this document saved as a printed hard copy, a digital copy on a thumb drive, and in the cloud for extra insurance against loss. It's not getting away from me again."

Wendi took the manuscript and left Mr. Lyst's office. Jimmy didn't see where she went, but he knew Wendi was overseeing the copy machine's production. Mr. Lyst had already invested sixty-five thousand dollars in this single manuscript, necessitating her personal attention. Fifty thousand were for Mcintosh, ten for Jimmy, and five more to trigger the manuscript's return. Luckily, Jimmy had brought Lyst a two-thousand-dollar rebate from that foray.

He had done precisely as Lyst had asked, simultaneously returning the manuscript for less than the five thousand the thieves had asked while keeping Wendi out of harm's way. Jimmy had to admit it had been a stroke of genius to convince Gabriel to take a personal bonus to distract him from checking the amount in the other envelope. Jimmy just hoped that wouldn't cause any problems in the future. It wasn't as though the thief could go to the police and charge Jimmy with breach of contract for failure to pay the total amount requested for stolen goods.

Back in Lyst's office, the older man with the goatee and round, gold-colored glasses was behind his desk again, still wearing the same clothes from when Jimmy met up with him seven hours earlier. Jimmy wondered if the man had eaten. His own stomach reminded him that he hadn't had anything since his mid-afternoon Blizzard on Jekyll Island with Pepé. As though reading Jimmy's mind – or hearing his stomach growl, perhaps – Lyst asked Jimmy if he would be amenable to sharing a pizza with them.

Jimmy replied, "All I ask is that there be no anchovies. Other than that, any pizza you order is fine with me."

"Splendid," Lyst said. "And would you be good enough to pick the pizza up?"

Jimmy laughed inside and thought, *Of course, there's a catch.* But he kept that thought to himself and said, "Sure, I'd be happy to run out for a few minutes and pick up a pizza, as long as I get to eat some, too. Just tell me where I'm going."

"I called the Loop and asked them to have two pies ready for an eight o'clock pickup. It's nearly eight now, so if you could pop over and pick them up, I'd be ever so grateful. And if you could pay for them and put it on your expense report, that would help tremendously, seeing as how the petty cash seems to be a tad low."

"No problem," Jimmy said. "Slip me one of those Benjamins I brought back, and if the Loop doesn't have a problem breaking it, I'll bring back the change, and you can replenish your petty cash."

"Capital idea, Jimmy, and yes, pun intended!" Lyst was unquestionably in a sunny mood, and who could blame him? He had saved money and could move ahead with producing a book he hoped would bring in a hundred thousand dollars or more just from the book sales. Jimmy wondered how high the movie rights would go. He hoped Mr. Lyst was savvy enough to make a bargain that included a percentage of the movie's profits, thereby guaranteeing him some retirement income.

Outside, Jimmy was getting into his Nissan when he noticed a car about a hundred feet behind him. He had seen it in his side mirror, and he could tell it was idling with its headlights off, but the owner either didn't know how to disable the parking lights or didn't care. Jimmy backed up and pulled out, keeping an eye on the vehicle. Sure enough, it pulled out as soon as he had departed, its lights still turned off. It followed Jimmy through the parking lot, past the Publix, and out the exit onto South 14th Street. The Loop was just across the street on the other side of 14th, but Jimmy turned right instead. The car tailing him finally turned its headlights on. They probably hoped Jimmy wouldn't notice, and it was less likely to draw attention to itself that way than by driving around in the dark with its lights off.

Jimmy led his tail on a circuitous route around the neighborhood. His newfound shadow stayed with him. As he drove, Jimmy called the Fernandina Police Department and told them who he was, reciting his PI license number. He explained that he was being followed after a meeting with an unsavory character earlier in the evening. While explaining the situation to the dispatcher, Jimmy took a lazy route between Sadler Road, 14th, and 8th Streets.

As Jimmy watched to make sure the tail stayed with him, he kept one eye peeled for a Fernandina police car. He asked the dispatcher to have the cops roll without lights or sirens. He didn't want to spook his shadow into running. When the dispatcher said they were a couple of minutes out, Jimmy asked to have the officers meet him at the Loop.

Jimmy turned into the Loop's parking lot, which was still reasonably full, considering it was past the usual supper hour. He parked, and as Jimmy exited his vehicle, his tail pulled up behind him and stopped. The driver's door opened, and – *surprise!* – Gabriel the Messenger got out and began walking toward Jimmy, who was standing next to the driver's door of his Nissan.

"Hey, Gabriel! Long time no see!" Jimmy called out. "It was a pleasure doing business with you this afternoon. I hope we can do it again sometime."

"You sonuva— you tricked me. And you lied to me. You said there was $5K in that envelope, and it was only twenty-five hundred."

"I never lied to you, Gabriel. I just never asked your boss if it was okay with him to give you a bonus out of his money. And there honestly were five thousand dollars in envelopes at the table, just not in the two envelopes *on* the table. The other twenty Benjamins were in envelopes tucked in my pocket. You were so busy thinking about how to spend your five C-notes that you didn't even count the money you could see. Haven't you ever heard the expression, 'There's no honor among thieves?' That means if you're a thief and lowlife, don't expect anything else in return. You got greedy, Gabriel, and so you got sloppy."

As Jimmy talked, Gabriel slowly tried to edge closer. Jimmy had been careful to maintain a safe distance from his new admirer, who was now about ten to twelve feet away from Jimmy.

"My boss wants the other twenty-five hundred, so pony up, smart mouth."

"I'm afraid that's not going to happen. I don't have the money anymore, and I only had two thousand anyway. *You* had the other five hundred. I guess I overstepped my bounds since it wasn't really mine to give to you. Any way you look at it, though, you're not going to give your boss that kind of cash tonight."

As if on cue, two police cruisers rolled up, one in front of Gabriel's car and one behind, hedging him in. Four officers streamed out of the two vehicles and grabbed Gabriel. Despite being cuffed, Gabriel was still hollering at Jimmy when they put him in the backseat of one of the cruisers and closed the door, mercifully muffling his ravings.

After explaining the situation to the officers and promising to come down to the station to press charges and fill out a report after making a quick pizza delivery, Jimmy walked toward the pizza parlor. He waved and smiled at Gabriel as he walked past the police cruiser and into the Loop.

Lyst had ordered an artichoke and bacon pizza and a Farmer's Market pizza – a vegetarian pie with mushrooms, Greek olives, green peppers, red onions, artichokes, and tomato sauce. Each pizza was eighteen dollars, so Jimmy gave the clerk a hundred-dollar bill for the pies. She got her manager, who initialed the bill after checking it. The clerk handed Jimmy his change back. Jimmy thanked her, stuffed a ten in the tip jar, and took the pizzas to his car.

A few minutes later, he was back in Wendi's office, which apparently served as the dining room in addition to the reception area and Wendi's office. It had more space than Lyst's office for eating, and there was considerably less chance of getting pizza sauce on the books lining the shelves. While Jimmy was out picking up the pizza and dealing with Gabriel, Wendi had finished copying the manuscript. Jimmy told her he was impressed with the speed of the printer.

"I made a thumb drive copy, too," Wendi said, holding up the USB device.

"Can you make me a copy of that for me?" Jimmy asked.

"Sure," she said. "Planning on doing a little light reading tonight?"

"Actually, yes," he replied, taking another bite of the artichoke and bacon pizza. "I want to see what Mcintosh wrote. He seems like the last person I'd expect to write one book, let alone two."

Chapter 13

IT WAS LATE WHEN JIMMY left Fernandina for home. After finishing up at Lyst Publishing, he had swung by the police station to file a statement about his friend, Gabriel. Jimmy had not told the Lysts about Gabriel's attempt at mugging him at the Loop. That was just between him and Gabriel. He didn't feel his employers needed to know.

Jimmy was aware some police officers – detectives, mainly – looked down their noses at private investigators, but not all of them. The wise cops understood where PIs stood in the pecking order. They accepted that an investigator could get information from a suspect that a police detective couldn't. It was partly usually because a PI couldn't arrest anyone but also because a PI didn't need a warrant to ask questions or search places. Private investigators were another tool in an intelligent police detective's tool belt.

Jimmy did his best to maintain good relations with all the local police departments he interacted with regularly, especially the dispatchers. They were not required to do anything Jimmy asked of them, and he knew it. So, he made it a point to discover all he could about the dispatchers and take care of them – birthdays, anniversaries, and other notable dates. In return, they helped Jimmy when he encountered occasional friction with persons of dubious character. Like Gabriel.

The Fernandina police were delighted to hold Gabriel indefinitely while pulling various threads together to see what pattern might emerge. They wanted to talk with him about his potential role in several local break-ins. Jimmy had told the police to check out any unsolved small extortion cases or holdups with no leads and examine Gabriel's alibis for those cases.

Jimmy didn't have specifics to share, but he was confident it wasn't the first time Gabriel had been involved in a shakedown. Jimmy was confident that Gabriel's familiarity with the process contributed to his sloppiness. Most people would pay the fee just to get their stuff back. It probably never occurred to anyone to give less than the asking price. Jimmy would give even odds that Gabriel's employer would insist all his associates count their collections each time in the future.

Jimmy left half an artichoke and bacon pizza with the dispatcher at the Police Department and headed home. It had been a long day but a fulfilling one. Challenging at times, yes, but fulfilling.

It was an easy half-hour drive from the Fernandina Police Department to his house. Jimmy had only gone a few blocks before his phone buzzed. Part of him hoped it was Wendi, but that thought was quickly doused with cold water when he saw the message from his security system. It said his front door had been breached, and the Nassau County Sheriff's

Department had been contacted. Jimmy dropped the phone into the cupholder between the seats, pulled his seatbelt a little tighter, and stood on the gas. This was one of those times he wished he had a lightbar on top of his SUV to make him look legit when he was flying to a scene.

Luckily, there were barely any cars on the road at that time of night, and Jimmy arrived at his place just twenty minutes later. Two Nassau County Sheriff's cruisers were in his front yard, their lights still flashing. His yard looked like someone was throwing a wild party with the rotating red and blue lights.

Jimmy rolled in and pulled up under the carport on the right side. When Jimmy stepped out of his Nissan, he saw a deputy exit the front door of his house, hand on his sidearm. When Jimmy ID'd himself as the homeowner and a private investigator, the deputy relaxed, removing his hand from his weapon.

The deputy told him there was no one inside when they arrived about fifteen minutes after the alarm had gone off. That meant they only arrived about five minutes ahead of Jimmy.

"It looks like someone wanted to find something," the deputy told Jimmy.

"Tossed?" Jimmy asked.

The deputy nodded. "But not too bad. They didn't have time to look very hard. We got here pretty quick," he said.

Jimmy said, "I appreciate that. I've never had anything like this happen before, so I wasn't sure how long it would take you guys to get here. That's a bonus to living this close to the

Sherriff's Office, though. It's good to know you can be here so fast."

"We were getting ready for a shift change, so we weren't all cruising around in various parts of the county. Let me give my partner a heads up, and I'll let you go in." Jimmy shook the deputy's hand before watching him step back inside the house. He returned about thirty seconds later.

"You can go inside, Mr. Favreaux. I hope you have a quiet rest of the night." The deputy put his hat on his head and strode over to his cruiser. He got in, backed up and around, and pulled out, headed back toward Yulee and Fernandina. The Nassau County Sheriff's Office was midway between the two towns.

Jimmy stepped inside his home. He didn't see the other deputy immediately, so he looked around the room from where he stood, checking for things out of place. The living room looked reasonably normal, just a few things from a side table knocked onto the floor. Whoever had been here had probably stood where Jimmy was; spooked by the alarm system, they knew their time to search was limited.

Crossing to his bedroom, Jimmy turned on the overhead light and looked around. His dresser drawers had been pulled out and dumped on the floor. The drawer to his nightstand had been dumped out, too. His closet door was open, but nothing was amiss. Jimmy couldn't remember if he had left it open that morning. *Probably.*

Until he cleared his presence with the other officer, Jimmy was careful about where he walked and what he touched. He walked carefully down the hallway to the office. Like the scene from his bedroom, anything in his office with a drawer had been targeted. No real damage, just inconvenience. The drawers had been crying out for his attention for some time, begging for reorganization. He'd take care of it in the morning.

Jimmy left the office and walked toward the kitchen, pausing to glance around the spare guestroom. Daani's pink panties were still on the floor where Wendi had tossed them. He couldn't tell if whoever rifled through his house had paused to pick them up or stepped over them without a glance. Turning around, Jimmy looked into the guest bathroom. The lid from the back of the toilet was lying on the floor. *What?* He went in and looked around. Nothing else was out of place. Why the toilet lid? Whoever had come poking around must have thought Jimmy would have hidden the … what? Hidden the what? In the where?

Jimmy sat on the toilet seat and began reviewing what he had seen. Nothing terribly out of place in the living room except the things from the side table brushed onto the floor. The dresser and nightstand drawers were all dumped out in his bedroom. The desk drawers in the office had been pulled out and emptied. The lid from the back of the toilet in the guest bath. Nothing had been touched in the guest bedroom. *Wait.*

He went back into the guest room. The dresser drawers were pulled partway out but not dumped on the floor. They were all empty, so there had been nothing to toss. The closet door was open, just like in his bedroom. But just like the drawers in the guest room, the closet was empty, so Jimmy's unexpected visitors hadn't bothered with it.

Jimmy went back to his bedroom and then into the master bath. The toilet lid was on the floor next to the toilet. Jimmy was still staring at the toilet lid when the other deputy spoke from behind him, causing Jimmy to jump straight up like a startled armadillo.

"What did you say?" Jimmy asked. "You surprised me."

"Sorry about that," the deputy replied. "I said, whoever was here was looking for something specific and thought you might have hidden it in the toilet tank. I saw the other tank lid on the floor, too. They knew they didn't have time to do an extended search, so they went to the obvious places. Drawers, closets, toilet tanks, refrigerator, freezer, and the other kitchen appliances. My guess is there were three people. Had to be three to cover that much ground in here and get back out of the house and away before we got here. One person took the master bedroom, one had the kitchen, and the last took the rest. Any idea what they were looking for?"

Where the Ocean Swallows the Moon," Jimmy said distantly. Gabriel's boss was either trying to take the manuscript back until he got the rest of his money, or he was looking for his money.

"What did you say?" asked the deputy.

"I'm sorry. It's nothing. It's a book title. But it's not here. It never was."

"Well, okay. If you don't need any help in the kitchen, I'm going to head back to the Sheriff's Office. That's a nice kitchen, by the way," the deputy told Jimmy.

"Thanks," Jimmy replied absently. He was wondering if the break-in crew would return to Lyst Publishing. They had gotten in there before, somehow. Jimmy was concerned for the safety of Hillary and Wendi. *They'll be fine,* he told himself. They should both be home, snug and safe in their beds. Or bed … singular? He just couldn't imagine them married. But she had repeatedly said she was Mrs. Lyst, and Hillary had confirmed it. Hadn't he?

Jimmy heard a thump as the deputy closed the door of his cruiser outside. A dispatcher's voice came over the radio, muffled by the sealed vehicle. Jimmy listened to the vehicle back up and leave.

He wondered if he should call Wendi or Hillary. He didn't have a cell number for Mr. Lyst, just Wendi's number. He started to scroll through his recent calls to let her know, then decided against it and hit cancel. Instead, Jimmy called the Fernandina Police Department again. The same dispatcher answered from earlier in the evening.

"Hey, Joe. It's Jimmy Favreaux."

"Hey, Jimmy. What are you doing still up?"

"Research," Jimmy answered, looking around his kitchen at the mess the break-in crew had left him. "Say, I had a visit tonight while I was out. Somebody broke into my place while I was down at the Police Department—"

"—Is everything okay?" Joe interrupted.

"Yeah, nothing was broken or damaged. Whoever it was, they were looking for something specific, but they didn't have much time to look for it. Besides, if they were after what I think they were looking for, it wasn't here."

"What were they after?" Joe asked, then said, "Hang on." Jimmy heard him talking in the background over the radio with one of the patrol cars. "Okay. I'm back. What did you say they were looking for?"

"I didn't. I think they were looking for a book manuscript, but I didn't have it. That's what Gabriel was all bent out of shape about tonight. He tried to shakedown Lyst Publishing for the return of the manuscript. I pulled kind of a fast one on Gabriel, and his boss apparently didn't appreciate it. So, it was probably Gabriel's boss or another of his crews that hit my place. They either wanted the book back or the money Gabriel neglected to bring home to Papa."

"Sounds like you could write a mystery novel, Jimmy, or a crime thriller," Joe replied.

"Maybe I will. Someday, but not tonight," Jimmy answered. "For now, though, can you ask the overnight guys to keep a close watch on Lyst Publishing? It's over by Staples. It would be good to put a car over by Starbucks. From there, they could see if anybody tries to enter the building."

"You got it, Jimmy. And thanks again for the pizza."

"No problem, Joe. Give my regards to Maria."

"Will do, Jimmy. Gotta go. Got another call coming in."

Jimmy hung up the call, feeling like he had done what he needed for the night. He doubted anyone would try to break into the Lyst residence. If anywhere, they'd go after the office again like before.

Jimmy used his cell phone to check the status of his alarm system. Everything was functioning correctly. He closed the door tightly, clicked the deadbolt, then tugged on the door a few times. It seemed secure enough for the night.

Jimmy dropped wearily into his recliner. He didn't feel like cleaning up the kitchen. It could wait until morning. He wasn't going to pick up the contents of his dresser drawers tonight, either.

"Alexa," Jimmy said. "Dim the lights to fifteen percent."

The lights did as he instructed, leaving just enough light for him to avoid obstacles if he had to get up during the night. He closed his eyes. He sat in the darkness, thinking. How could Wendi be married to a guy twenty or thirty years older than her? Jimmy had heard about May-December romances, but he never saw the attraction. Not for the May girl, anyway. He categorically understood the lure for the December man.

The other thing he couldn't get his head around was how strongly he was attracted to Wendi. It had been less than forty-eight hours since he had met her. How did *that* work? And why someone *unavailable*?

Jimmy pulled a small knitted afghan around himself and switched to full recline. Maybe, as his dad had always told him, things would look better in the morning, although he didn't know how Wendi could look any better.

Chapter 14

JIMMY TOSSED AND TURNED IN his recliner for a few hours before giving up on getting a whole night's sleep. He got up and went to both bathrooms, not to use them but to put the tank lids back in place. The office was next, a relatively simple job of scooping things back into their drawers. Most of the drawers in there were glorified junk drawers. He usually just tossed stuff in them, which made reloading them easy. His client records were on the computer instead of in old-fashioned hanging folders in a file cabinet.

He relocated to the kitchen next, picking up the cutlery and utensils dumped on the floor. After that, Jimmy picked up the food tossed out of the refrigerator during the burglars' search and left to warm on the floor for several hours. Then he bagged it all and dumped it outside in the trash bin. Finally, Jimmy returned to his bedroom and pushed the clothes together into a couple of piles.

I'll put them back in the drawers tomorrow, Jimmy told himself. He felt better about getting a jump on tomorrow's reorganization project.

He walked down the hall to his office again. He reached into his pocket and pulled out the flash drive from Wendi with the pdf copy of Trevor Mcintosh's book. Plugging it into his computer, he waited a moment while it checked the device for viruses. Once it was declared clean, he opened a window to show its files. The only file on the drive was the book manuscript pdf. Jimmy double-clicked it, and after a couple of seconds of thinking about it, the file popped open on the screen.

Just like Mr. Lyst had said, the manuscript read like an autobiography.

> *"I couldn't continue doing what I had done for years or continue being what I had been my whole adult life. So one day, I just walked away. I didn't tell anyone what I was doing, not even Mary, my wife. I walked a ways and then hitched a ride to the port authority. It was no trouble finding the ship I was about to join; it towered over everything at the dock. It was as though a skyscraper had laid down on its side to take a bath in the brackish water. Even on its side, it still towered stories into the air above.*
>
> *I was about to ship out on a container ship, not as a passenger but as a crewman. It was like a dream. But it became real once aboard and staring at the quarters I had been assigned. I wasn't sure when I would see Mary again or if I ever would."*

Jimmy sat at his desk, reading for the next several hours. When the sun began to illuminate the room, he stopped reading, stood up and stretched, then ambled down the hall to his bedroom to clean up the mess left from the night before.

He picked up the items that had been tossed by someone looking for either the manuscript or the rest of the money—not knowing Jimmy had given it all back to Mr. Lyst. After getting his bedroom semi-respectable, it was time to clean up Jimmy. He needed a shower and shave, and then he'd see if he had enough things left in the refrigerator to create some sort of breakfast.

As he stood in the shower and let the warm water cascade over him, he thought about the parts of the manuscript he had read. Something about the narrative nagged him. Several things, actually. He didn't know if it was his innocence in this arena or something else. It could simply be his lack of experience with this type of case and the whole book-publishing world. But the manuscript didn't feel like it lined up with the man who allegedly authored it.

Jimmy had spent a little time interviewing Trevor Mcintosh, and the man did not seem like a master of English. He had primarily spoken in Southern slang and mono-syllables, entirely different from the fluid story poured out on the pages of *Where the Ocean Swallows the Moon*.

The man was soft with callous-free hands and a belly that exposed the lie of his ever living any life other than idleness or entitled leisure. A shorter description would be that the man was lazy, and Jimmy could tell. Trevor wasn't independent or self-sufficient. He was used to people providing for him like he was entitled, and if he didn't get what he felt he was entitled to, he became fussy. It was clear to Jimmy that Mcintosh was still living off his fifteen minutes of fame from thirty-five years before. He seemed to think one home run put him in the same league as Babe Ruth and Hank Aaron.

Perhaps Jimmy should read Mcintosh's previous book, *Growing Up Southern*. Maybe it would clear up the confusion.

Drying off from his shower, Jimmy decided he needed to take a trip to the Camden County Public Library to see if they had a copy of *Growing Up Southern* available. He didn't have much faith in the three-decade-old book illuminating anything, but he was starting to feel like he was grasping at straws. Jimmy wanted to *earn* his fee.

Yes, he had secured the manuscript's return, which was his primary objective. But ten thousand for a day of driving around, talking to a once-upon-a-time famous author, and capping it off by outwitting a thug and extortion artist? Jimmy didn't feel right about taking the money for his role in that little comedy. *I'm sure I can get over that feeling, though!* he thought. He had ten thousand reasons to try.

And don't forget, there was the insult of having someone break into his house, but that could happen with any of Jimmy's jobs.

With his house and himself cleaned up, Jimmy stepped into the kitchen and took stock. He didn't have enough for breakfast, so he would stop somewhere in town. He made a short list of things from the grocery he could stop and pick up on his way home from the library.

Jimmy walked down the short hall to his office to grab the flash drive. No sense in tempting anyone to snatch it. He involuntarily yawned as he sat at his desk, waiting for the program to quit that he had been using to read the manuscript. Meanwhile, his body reminded him how tired he was. Staying up all night was definitely for younger people. Jimmy hoped he'd be able to sleep that night. Thinking about his to-do list for the day, he anticipated a less adrenaline-infused day would help him get a solid seven or eight hours of sleep that evening.

There was a message in Jimmy's Ancestry account, making an icon blink in the upper-right corner of the computer screen. He clicked it.

The app had uncovered a hint he had been looking for. It was a continuation of his search for more information about Dr. John Epps, murdered in 1881. The message said Ancestry had located the information about the trial of F.W. George, the man who shot Epps in cold blood. The newspaper accounts said the altercation was over a young woman. *Of course! What else?*

With nothing else pressing to do right that moment, Jimmy opened the file and began reading.

✳✳✳

"The quiet of yesterday and the Sabbath worship of our peaceful city was broken by a shooting affray that culminated in the tragic death of John Epps, sometimes known as "Doctor" Epps, who had been pursuing the vocation of a barber for some months

*under the Iowa National bank at the corner of
Fourth and Walnut streets."*

They didn't waste any time, Jimmy thought as he read. The shooting happened on Sunday, and the perpetrator was being tried by Monday. Either this was an arraignment—not the actual trial—or the newspaper was conducting its own public trial, much like it often happened today.

*"The affair is enveloped in considerable mystery
about the cause of the shooting. All the motives
ascribed as inducing the dark deed have been gained
from the perpetrator and are very unsatisfactory."*

Any court case where all the details come from the perpetrator would be "very unsatisfactory." 1881 sounded a lot like the twenty-first century.

*"The shooting was witnessed by only two or three
persons, and all agreed that very little passed
between the men at the time of the affair."*

To Jimmy, it sounded like a lot of the modern contests between men: a lot of aggression and minimal discussion. *We haven't evolved much since we were cave-dwellers,* he thought to himself before reading on.

*"The particulars as gathered from the eyewitnesses
are as follows: The shooting occurred at 11:30
o'clock, on the corner of East 5th and Allan streets,
just one block north of the house where the Swede
woman, Mrs. Helen Johnson, hung herself a few
days ago. The trouble between the men seems to
have grown out of a difficulty they had over a*

young lady who is boarding at the residence of Mrs. Bunce, in front of which Epps was killed.

It seems George was watching for his victim, for he was waiting near the house of Mrs. Bunce at the time of the affray. He had asked Mr. Manbeck, who lives nearby, if Dr. Epps was there. He was told that Dr. Epps had been there earlier.

Just then, Dr. Epps came down Fifth street, and George saw him coming, saying, 'There he is now.' When asked his destination, Dr. Epps replied that he was going to Mrs. Bunce's, whereupon George said, 'No, you are not; I am going in there myself. If you go in, I will shoot you.' George then drew his revolver, which is a large one, carrying a .32 caliber ball."

There was more—much more, so Jimmy skimmed the pages of information and testimony. It turned out F.W. George was pleading innocent by reason of insanity, a "side-effect" of epilepsy. The doctor treating his epilepsy? John Epps.

Jimmy closed the documents and stood up. He still didn't have a first name for George, just the initials "F.W." It was a very enticing rabbit trail, but Jimmy had other details to attend to.

He needed to get together with Pepé and compare notes and see if Pepé had made any progress on the *real* John Epps case, the one involving a missing person.

***

After a short conversation via text, Jimmy met Pepé at Panera Bread in Kingsland. The restaurant met the requirements of both men: food and beverages, tables, and Wi-Fi. Since Jimmy hadn't had any breakfast, he ordered an egg, bacon, and cheese on ciabatta bread with coffee. Pepé had already had breakfast, but it didn't stop him from ordering a bagel with a smear of cream cheese, a cinnamon roll, and a coffee. They took their cups, pumped their coffees from the air pots marked with the times they were brewed, and settled in at a corner table.

Pepé went first while Jimmy was doctoring his coffee with creamers and sweeteners. "What have you found on the interwebs about John Epps?"

"Which one?" Jimmy replied, his answer causing Pepé to stare at him as if he were speaking a foreign language. Jimmy smiled, waved a hand at his partner, and continued with his report.

"There's two John Epps from Des Moines – our guy from Jekyll and possibly an ancestor by the same name. Guess which one was murdered in July of 1881. Cold blood, broad daylight, right on the street in front of several witnesses. Can you believe it? Guess why."

Pepé sipped his coffee before answering. "A girl."

"Yeah," Jimmy said. "How'd you guess?"

"It's always a girl. In most fights, it's a girl the two guys fight over, and one guy kills the other. Kind of like the movie *10 Million BC* with Raquel Welch. It's either a girl who makes them steal, a girl who makes them leave their wives, or they accidentally kill the girl while fighting over her. And then one or both go to prison for her murder. But it's *always* a girl. Unless ..." Pepé held up a finger and paused, then rushed to the dramatic ending. "... it's the wife, who is also a girl, and so it also holds true. Boom!"

Jimmy laughed a little at Pepé's philosophy. "It was a girl, and – just like you said – two guys were interested in her. One had a gun, the other only his feet. The gun won. Hard to outrun a bullet from a pistol fired at close range."

"We all make choices," Pepé replied. "Like you choosing to look up stuff about a crime from nearly 140 years ago."

"Don't judge me. I had a rough day, coupled with no sleep. Literally no sleep," Jimmy answered his partner. "If you have a year or two, I'll tell you about it."

The location tile they had placed on their table started to buzz and dance, and a server brought their food. The conversation went on hiatus for a few minutes as they tore into their breakfasts.

When each man was about half-finished eating, they slowed down and settled back to discuss cases while they put away the rest of their food more sedately.

Taking a sip of coffee, Jimmy told Pepé, "I haven't had a lot of time to do a deep dive into the good doctor Epps from the twenty-first century. That was my plan for today. After yesterday's hijinks, stress, and travel, I decided to spend most of today at home focusing on *our* John Epps and doing some grunt work looking for any inadvertent trails he may have left. People think they can just disappear off the grid, but it actually requires a lot of pre-planning. It's not as easy as people think. You can't just go out into the woods and build a log cabin or live out of a tent or cave."

Jimmy paused briefly to take a bite of his sandwich but continued talking around the bread, chewing and talking simultaneously. "Most people no longer possess the wherewithal to fend for themselves without modern conveniences. They can't live off the land unless they've done it before. People today don't know where their food comes from. All they know is that it comes from grocery stores. There's a level of skill and expertise required that living in the modern world doesn't provide. Not only does our modern civilization not provide the training or the tools, it often *erases* any skillset you may have had previously."

Pepé was licking cream cheese frosting off his fingers from the cinnamon roll he had just devoured. He was smiling. "I could live off the land as long as it's right behind Panera. And a Taco Bell."

Jimmy chuckled at the remark and then asked the former cop what he had turned up about Dr. Epps from talking with the doctor's wife.

"Not much. Like you, I haven't had a lot of time to search. My wife had me drag the Christmas decorations out of the attic. I can't believe how close Christmas is. But first, we have to get through Thanksgiving. That's just a couple of weeks away."

"Think of the Christmas present we'll give Mrs. E. if we can find out whether her husband is alive or dead," Jimmy added.

"That's true," Pepé said, rising to his feet, coffee cup in hand. "But I'm still wondering if she wants him dead or alive. If we find out he's alive and hiding out on a desert island with Elvis and Marilyn Monroe, does she want him alive again? Or dead again? We could put out wanted posters with his picture that says, Wanted: Dead or Alive (Again)."

Pepé walked the few steps to the coffee refill station and pumped fresh coffee into his cup.

Jimmy laughed about the wanted poster idea and took a drink of his coffee. He only had a bite or two of his breakfast sandwich left. He popped the remains of the ciabatta bread into his mouth, chewed it up, and swallowed. Pepé was returning to the table with his fresh coffee.

"If nobody killed John Epps, where could he go that he could drop off the map so completely?" Pepé asked as he sat down again.

"We'll have to ask the airport in Brunswick to help us out to see if he left by plane. There's no train service, so no Amtrack. The nearest Amtrack station is over in Jessup, about forty miles from Brunswick. Instead of staying near the coast, the train tracks swing inland, then back north and east out to Savannah. Let's count the train out for now. Planes, trains, and automobiles. Did they ever find his car?" Jimmy asked.

"In the hospital parking lot. Locked. That means he drove to the hospital and got a ride to wherever he went. Unless he accidentally fell into the incinerator at the hospital. You know they have one of those, right?"

Jimmy looked across the table at him. Visions of the Dachau concentration camp from WWII flitted through his mind. "The hospital has an incinerator? What for?"

"They generate a huge amount of hazardous waste. Not hazardous after you burn it up, though. But you know, all the swabs, wipes, and stuff that get soaked with blood. Bio-hazards, they call it. They burn it at very high heat, so it doesn't produce a lot of smoke or ash. But it would do the same thing to a body, I'd bet." While Jimmy mulled that over, Pepé drank his coffee.

"Like a crematorium, isn't it?" Jimmy asked. Pepé nodded.

Jimmy continued, "But we don't know if that happened. Was he well-liked, or did someone have it in for him? Like a janitor or someone who would have access or knowledge of how to use the incinerator?"

"I'll ask around, but I think it's probably a dead end, pardon the pun."

Jimmy rolled his eyes. "So, if he wasn't burned in the hospital's incinerator and didn't leave by plane, train, or automobile, what's left? By foot or … what? Kayak?"

Pepé sat up a little straighter. "We're forgetting something. Brunswick is a port city. There are shrimp boats and commercial fishermen in and out of Brunswick all the time. There's a casino cruise ship that serves Brunswick, too. And Jekyll Island empties out on the mainland right by the river, at the base of the Sidney Lanier bridge."

"Okay. That's good," Jimmy responded, sitting a little straighter himself. Brainstorming was a good thing. He and

Pepé had often stumbled onto clues this way: carbs, coffee, and throwing ideas against a wall to see which ones stuck – like checking spaghetti to see if it was done.

Pepé snapped his fingers. He pointed at Jimmy excitedly, "Hey! One other place we need to check out is the Port Authority. All those cars and goods come in and out on those giant container ships. Those giant cargo ships go all over the world and *come in* from all over, too. Check out the names of the ships sometime when you drive by. Some of them aren't even written in English. But I'll bet they're always looking for crew replacements."

Jimmy swirled the last swallow of coffee in his cup before drinking it. "I wonder if they ever need doctors who want to go sailing? From there, they could end up anywhere in the world. Our job just got harder, Pepé. It's no longer a local scope; it's global."

"But I think we can forget about the other options for now," Pepé said. "I think you're onto something with the container ships. They probably do like to have doctors on board. They're out at sea for weeks at a time, and all kinds of mishaps, bumps, and boo-boos happen on a ship. A doctor is very valuable. He could even get a ride for free by working his way to wherever the ship was headed. You know, he pays for his transportation by taking care of the crew. I heard about cargo ships that used to let people ride along like on a regular cruise liner. They didn't have all the amenities, but they had nice cabins, three meals a day, and the passengers got to see the world. The captain charged a minimal fee, and they got a leisurely cruise – some would say boring – and saw how a cargo ship operated. I doubt Gwynn would go for that, though. I might suggest it the next time she asks me about going on a cruise for our anniversary."

"Good luck. There's not a lot of cargo ships offering to take passengers along anymore. And here's another thing," Jimmy said. "If Epps signed on to work as a crewmember, he could have worked out a deal to be paid in cash. Or, more likely, our doctor friend could have waited until he docked in another country where he opened a new bank account under a new, phony name. Then the shipping line could deposit his pay in that account, which has no connection to the U.S. After that, Epps was a regular crewmember. He had no need for his old credit cards. All his basic needs were met onboard. Three hots and a cot, as they used to say about prison. It was also true of the military and cargo ships."

Jimmy picked his phone up off the table and started thumbing the keyboard. After a few seconds, he said, "Listen to this, Pepé. 'Commonly, cargo ship cabins have a sink, a small refrigerator, a small cabinet, a bed, and a desk inside the cabin. Public showers and bathrooms are usually located outside the cabin if the ship is small to medium-sized. If the ship is an ultra-large, there might be ensuite showers, toilets, a gym, a cinema, and sometimes even a swimming pool.' Sounds like a cruise ship to me."

Jimmy looked at his search results for a moment longer, then added another tidbit: "The general store—the commissary—is called a 'slop chest.' And get this: the Coast Guard determines what an American ship has to carry. It says they must have clothing for the crew members, foul-weather clothes, and a complete supply of blankets and tobacco. And here's the best part: 'Merchandise in the slop chest shall be sold to a seaman at a profit of not more than ten percent.' I wish the stores I frequent were limited to ten percent."

"Right. As if ..." Pepé snorted.

Jimmy continued, "Merchant ships and smaller freighters – even most container ships – don't usually have a doctor on board as part of the crew. But if a crewman were proficient as, say, a cook *and* a doctor, he could be quite the prize to snag."

In response to the information Jimmy had found and the ideas they had tossed around, Pepé asked, "So, our medical friend may have hitched a ride on a cargo ship six years ago. But why?"

"That sounds like a question for the good Mrs. E, and that's *your* case, my friend."

Chapter 15

THE TWO INVESTIGATORS SPLIT UP in Panera's parking lot. They knew their assignments. Jimmy was going to search the internet for more clues about Dr. and Mrs. Epps – separately and together.

Pepé was going to poke around the Brunswick Hospital to see what he could find out about the doctor – mainly to check on his interactions with the other staff. Then he'd head back out to Jekyll and ask Mrs. Epps if she had remembered anything else that might help them figure out where her husband had gone six years before.

Regarding the other case, Jimmy had already recovered the manuscript for the Lysts, but the case didn't feel finished yet. What bothered him most was not that someone had stolen the manuscript or even that someone had held it for ransom. What rankled him most was the idea that Trevor Mcintosh supposedly wrote it. A man who couldn't string five words into a coherent sentence didn't seem like the best candidate to pen a prize-winning manuscript. Trevor had supposedly written a best-seller thirty or thirty-five years earlier, but Jimmy had his doubts about that, too. He could have stumbled across the original somewhere or hired someone to write it for him. Jimmy was pretty sure there were ghostwriters even back then who would write whatever you requested for a fee. Most of today's ghostwriters seemed to live in Africa and India and would write whatever you asked in less than a week for $25.

Jimmy was sure there were less honest and less respectable ways to acquire a manuscript, too. *Where the Ocean Swallows the Moon* was stolen from the Lysts. Who could say if it had been stolen from someone else before that? Was it possible *Growing Up Southern* found its way to daylight the same way, written by one set of fingers but claimed by another?

The library was closed, so there was no *Growing Up Southern* for Jimmy. As he drove toward home, he mentally reviewed the manuscript he had rescued and partially read. So far, *Where the Ocean Swallows the Moon* was like an autobiography, but it caused an itch in Jimmy's brain. He was simply unwilling to believe Trevor Mcintosh had ever crewed on a freighter, merchant ship, or cargo ship. The man was as soft as any 9-to-5 desk jockey. Working on a commercial vessel, Mcintosh's entitled attitude would have earned him a trip overboard within the first week, if not the first day.

Jimmy drove over the blue bridge, turned in his driveway, and up to his house. He parked, walked to the mailbox, and retrieved his daily portion of junk mail. As Jimmy walked across the lawn to his house, he surveyed the numerous tire tracks the previous night's traffic had left. There had been county deputies, Wendi's car, his car, and, at some point, at least one other car potentially carrying three second-rate burglars.

That caused him to wonder how his new best friend, Gabriel, was doing. Either the police were still holding him, or someone had bailed him out. If the latter, whoever paid his bail might send Gabriel to pay another visit to Jimmy to retrieve the twenty-five hundred dollars they felt was rightfully theirs. Or worse, somebody competent.

Jimmy wasn't overly concerned about encountering the dull-witted bully. If anyone should be concerned about his release from the pokey, it was Gabriel. Jimmy was reasonably sure whoever had Gabriel on their payroll might require a pound or two of flesh in exchange for losing the two-thousand dollars. It was like trickle-down economics.

Since Gabriel had twice failed to secure the total ransom from Jimmy, odds were that Gabriel could get a virtual trip to the woodshed. Jimmy hoped that it would end there. In these times of economic recession, even the bad guys had to watch their profit and loss statements. Jimmy hoped everyone chalked up the money as a loss or a failed business venture and let it go.

Jimmy sighed. He knew it didn't always work that way.

He went inside and checked his security system. It said no threats were detected. No messages from Alexa, his digital secretary. Jimmy felt the flash drive in his pocket. He had several options. He could stay at home and read some more in Mcintosh's alleged novel, do some internet sleuthing about Dr. John Epps from Jekyll Island, or go to Lyst Publishing in Fernandina and see how everything was in the light of day.

In the end, Jimmy opted to go to Lyst Publishing. Reading and internet searches could come later after checking in on his living, breathing clients.

Jimmy armed his security system and stepped out on the front steps. He noticed a bicycle by his mailbox, half hidden in the tall grass of the ditch, and tried to remember if he had seen it when collecting the mail. He shaded his eyes from the sun and checked the grass around the bike but saw no one. Hearing a slight creak on the little deck by his front steps, Jimmy turned his head to look, just in time to see a fist the size of a Boston Butt coming right at his face.

✱✱✱

Jimmy had no idea how long he had been lying on his steps and wasn't even entirely sure *why* he was lying on the steps. Suddenly, he felt rough, strong hands grab him by his shirt and turn him over. The meaty hands tore his back pocket off, picked up his wallet from where it fell on the steps, opened it, and took whatever cash was inside. Jimmy turned his head to see who was manhandling him.

Gabriel.

Just as Jimmy had figured, Gabriel had already taken a hit—literally, it appeared—for his part in the loss of revenue. His bottom lip was fat and split, his left eye a purple-brown and green, and his right eye similarly colored but swollen half-shut. Jimmy hoped he wouldn't sport a similar look after the thug was finished with him.

Seeing Jimmy looking at him, Gabriel growled at the PI, "You're eighteen hundred dollars short, Favreaux. Where's the rest of the two thousand?"

Jimmy tried to push himself up into a sitting position, but the bruised bruiser stomped a foot on Jimmy's back and held him down. *Okay. So be it. I can talk lying down.*

"I don't have it, Gabriel," Jimmy grunted, the heavy foot on his back making breathing difficult. "It wasn't mine to keep. I gave it back to my client. Tell your boss to send my client an itemized, notarized bill if he wants the money. And don't forget to include a self-addressed, stamped envelope with it. Courtesy never goes out of style."

"Har-dee har-har, Favreaux. This isn't about my boss. It's about you and me. The Man isn't after the money anymore."

Because he already took it out of your hide, pretty boy. Jimmy thought. "Well, I don't have the money, so I guess you're just out of luck. Write it off as a bad investment."

The foot holding Jimmy down on the steps began pressing harder, rocking back and forth and grinding Jimmy's chest into the wooden steps beneath him. "Wrong answer, Favreaux. I'm already out the two grand, and I need it for my mother's hip replacement. You better come up with it in a hurry because if she doesn't get her new hip, she'll get cranky and come over and kick your butt into next week."

"Nice to know the family that preys together stays together," Jimmy groaned at the oversized man. *Typical David and Goliath scenario,* he thought. *I wish I had five smooth stones and a slingshot!*

"What?" Gabriel asked, obviously confused by the word preys, thinking Jimmy was talking about prayer.

"Never mind, you big ape." Having had a few minutes to recover from the sucker punch, Jimmy started to push up against the foot again. When Gabriel raised it slightly to stomp him back down, Jimmy rolled sideways and off the steps, leaving the bully with his foot suspended in mid-air.

"Before you make another threatening move, Gabriel, I want you to take a look around."

"At what, Favreaux?"

"At the camera in *that* corner, the camera in the *opposite* corner, and the Ring doorbell straight in *front* of you. And you know what the beauty of a Ring doorbell is? It caught your entire attack on high-def video and recorded every word you said. You see, it records *audio*, too. And all of it is permanently uploaded to the cloud so it can be downloaded when I go to the police in a few minutes, right after you leave my property. I imagine you'll be spending another night as a guest of the county, but my guess is it'll be a much longer stretch this time."

The goon looked at the cameras and the doorbell, trying to figure out how Jimmy had snookered him again.

Jimmy pulled out his phone and said, "Siri, call the Nassau County Sheriff's Office."

In response, Siri replied, "Calling the Nassau County Ess-Oh."

Before she completed her reply, Gabriel was nearly halfway to his bike. Jimmy guessed Gabriel's boss now owned his employee's car in lieu of the money he had failed to collect from Jimmy for the manuscript.

"Nassau County Sheriff's Office. How can I direct your call?"

"Never mind. I'll be in after a while to fill out a complaint for an arrest warrant. This is Jimmy Favreaux, private investigator. I live over by the blue bridge."

"Hi, Jimmy. Everything all right? Did you get things cleaned up from last night? The night deputies told me about it."

"Yeah. It wasn't too bad. They got there in a hurry, so the mess was kept to a minimum. But I have footage of a guy trying to take my head off and then mugging me and taking my money from my wallet. He won't be hard to find. He was a guest of yours last night."

"That Gabriel guy? What a pain. Fernandina Police dropped him off with us."

"Well, he made the mistake of attacking me just now where my cameras could record him, video and audio."

"Sweet. I'll see you in a little while. Gotta run. Unless you have something else ..?"

"No. The call was primarily to get Gabriel properly motivated to leave. I'll see you in a bit. Thanks again."

"Ten-four."

As Jimmy hung up, he remembered that he hadn't checked the video from last night to see if he could make out who had broken into his house. Sliding around the steps and sitting down where he had been lying just minutes before, he called up the cloud where his camera videos were stored. Scrolling through several clips marked by date and time, he quickly found the timestamp he wanted.

From the doorbell's perspective, he watched as a car pulled off the highway and drove up close to the front door. Three men got out of the vehicle, a dark sedan, two from the front and one from the backseat. They wore COVID masks, making it impossible to tell who they were. The guy from the front passenger seat was the largest, even bigger than Gabriel.

Jimmy knew it wasn't Gabriel, though, because Gabriel had been chilling out at the Fernandina Police Department for harassing him outside the Loop when they broke into Jimmy's house. Back to the video.

The big guy stood on the top step, put one massive foot against the door, and leaned into it, pitting his considerable bulk against the door's integrity. After a moment, he stepped back, placed his shoulder against the door, and gave a hard push. The door popped open. The shrill system alarm immediately covered up any conversation the men made. The trio hurried inside, apparently following a pre-arranged plan as they scattered. Jimmy recalled that one of the deputies had been reasonably sure of the number of men involved based on the places in his house they had tossed before they fled. He was right.

Jimmy couldn't see what was happening inside, just shadows going from side to side as they hurried to find the manuscript or the money. He would be adding a few indoor cameras soon, he told himself.

After just a few minutes, the men hurried back out, took their places in the car again, backed out, and took off. A few minutes later, the first deputy arrived in a cruiser. It was another minute before he emerged from his vehicle, gun drawn. Jimmy knew he wasn't finishing a drink or a last bite of supper before getting out. He had checked with his partner to find out how soon he would arrive.

The deputy had barely stepped out of his vehicle when the lights of the second cruiser became visible in the video frame. It was only about thirty seconds before he pulled in next to the first squad car. The second officer stepped out of his vehicle, weapon in hand. Jimmy stopped the playback. He knew what had happened after that. There was nothing to find inside because the bad guys had already left the scene.

Jimmy would also give the Nassau County Sheriff's Office this video in case they could recognize any of the trio who had waltzed into his home the night before. If they could ID them, that would be icing on the cake, but Gabriel was the cake. His arrogance would cost him his freedom.

Jimmy wished there had been security cameras on the playground in elementary school when he was growing up. Some grown-up bullies might not be around to harass people today if there had been. *Or probably not.* Jimmy knew that prison did not rehabilitate the vast majority of criminals. It merely kept them off the streets while they learned a new trade inside the prison. Prisons were like colleges for developing criminal instincts and techniques. All the time in the world to learn, and "classes" conducted by the best in the business. "Best," except that each of them had been caught. Still, techniques were traded like currency in prison, and people often came out with new skills not learned in the prison kitchen, laundry, or woodshop.

Jimmy stopped at the Nassau County Sheriff's Office on his way to Fernandina and downloaded his videos. He filed a complaint against Gabriel, and after watching the video, the commander in charge said they would go pick the man up. Gabriel had been a guest of the county numerous times, but this time, the bully would be going away to serve time in a larger playground. He wouldn't be the top dog this time. He would be a small fish in a large pond full of much more deliberate, nastier predators with significantly larger teeth.

✳✳✳

After taking care of his business at the Sheriff's Office, Jimmy continued to Fernandina and Lyst Publishing. He looked in the vanity mirror on the back of the sun visor. Gabriel had missed Jimmy's eye and nose, delivering a glancing blow to his cheekbone because Jimmy had instinctively tried to turn away from the motion coming at him. It still hurt like a bugger, though, and it was already starting to discolor. Still, not too bad, and who knows – some women might like the rugged look. *Maybe Wendi's one of them.*

Jimmy wondered if Wendi would be at her desk and what she would say about his new facial decoration. He touched it and winced. He knew the bone wasn't broken, but it hurt like a son of a gun when he touched it. He carefully prodded it with a fingertip again, winced, and told himself to leave it alone. Part of him wanted to be able to withstand being touched because he was pretty sure Wendi would try to feel it and ask if it hurt. He didn't want to be wincing or, worse, yelping when she touched it. And, Lord knows, he didn't want any *tears* to leak out if she felt it. The embarrassment would end the contract for him.

Jimmy parked in the same space in front of Staples, just like every time he had been at Lyst Publishing. He walked down the long, narrow hall to the inner door, knocked lightly, and tried to turn the handle. It was locked. He rapped on the door again and waited. He was unable to hear anyone moving around inside. He knocked one more time, knowing that Hillary Lyst was relatively insulated back in his office. But no one came and unlocked the door.

Jimmy walked back down the hallway and stepped outside. He stood there momentarily, thinking, then turned to his right and started walking. Jimmy strolled past Staples and followed the sidewalk a short distance before arriving at his destination: Peterbrook Chocolatiers. He ordered a small cup of gelato and went outside to sit at the little bistro table in front of the confectionery.

Taking out his cell phone, he sent Wendi a text.

> I'm eating gelato at Peterbrook. Thought you might like some, too.

He took a couple more bites before her reply made his phone buzz on the table.

> Is something wrong? Why are you at the office?

Jimmy read her response, took another bite of gelato, and sent a reply.

> Nothing is wrong. I just thought I'd stop and check on you guys. There was trouble at my place last night after I left.

He finished up the gelato as her text came in.

> What kind of trouble? Are you okay?

> I'm fine. Had some unexpected visitors while I was in Fernandina. They were looking for the manuscript or the rest of the money. Or both.

> omg!

> Relax. They didn't have time to trash my place before the cops arrived. Besides, I didn't have the manuscript or the money. At least not when they were there.

> Are you still at Peterbrook's?

> Yes.

> Stay there. I'll be there in five minutes.

Jimmy got up, threw his cup and tiny spoon in a nearby trashcan, and went back inside the store, where the aroma of chocolate hung enticingly in the air. He gave in to the shop's seductive sales tactics. He bought some chocolate-covered popcorn before going back outside to wait for Wendi.

True to her word, about five minutes after her text, Wendi pulled up and parked next to Jimmy's Nissan. She got out of her car and walked briskly toward him. Wendi was one of those women who always looked like she should be on a fashion show runway. She was wearing tight jeans, white, open-toed sandals, and a jade blouse that made her hair look even blonder than it was. Her sunglasses were perched on top of her head like she was looking at the leaves on the trees. She gave him a small smile, but her concern was evident.

As she came closer and Jimmy's facial injury became more apparent, he could see her look of concern deepen.

"What happened to your face?" she asked, reaching out to touch his bruise. He leaned back to avoid letting her touch it. She pulled her hand back quickly.

"Does it hurt? What happened?"

"It does, thanks for asking. I got sucker-punched at my house just as I was leaving to come here."

"You what?"

"That big ape I met at Mickey's Tap Room to exchange the manuscript for the cash? It was him. When he didn't show up with the full five grand, his boss apparently took it out of his hide. Gabriel had two black eyes, a fat lip, and probably had some sore spots on his torso. I'd guess he probably has some bruised ribs to go along with those pretty eyes. Oh, and get this – he rode a bicycle to my house! I'm betting his boss took his car to cover his losses. He'll probably scrap it or sell it for whatever he can get. Either way, Gabriel let it slip that the boss isn't looking at *me* to produce the rest of the ransom. That means he took his pound of flesh from Gabriel while teaching him a lesson on following directions."

Wendi put a hand on Jimmy's arm. "The two thousand you brought back with you? That was supposed to be for the manuscript?"

"It was. But I got Gabriel so enamored with the feel of five hundred dollars in his pocket that he didn't count the money in the envelope I gave him. There were only twenty-five hundred-dollar bills in there, but it sure looked like a lot of C-notes. I told him the five hundred I gave him was a tip. Can you believe that? Gabriel believed it! He probably took the envelope I gave him and hurried back to the boss. I'd have loved to have seen his face when the boss told him he was twenty-five hundred short."

"So, he came to your house to get the money back that his boss took from him?"

Jimmy nodded. "Unfortunately for Gabriel, his sneak attack was captured in glorious color and hi-def on my security cameras and Ring doorbell, complete with crystal clear sound as he confessed to being the bagman for the manuscript ransom. When I pointed out the cameras, he just stood there staring, trying to figure out how I had outsmarted him again. When I called the Nassau County Sheriff's Office, and he heard them answer, he took off running for his bike. At that moment, I actually felt a teeny twinge of pity for him. But it went away as soon as I felt my cheek."

"I'm so glad you weren't hurt worse," Wendi said. They were sitting at the bistro table outside Peterbrook's, eating the chocolate-covered popcorn. Wendi's hand had shifted from Jimmy's arm to the irresistible bag of popcorn.

Jimmy waved her off when she tried to give him the popcorn back. He said, "I just stopped by to make sure everything was fine here with you and Mr. Lyst ... and the manuscript."

"Everything is right as rain," she said.

"Then I'll be on my way. I'm going to check in with Mr. Metz."

"What for?" Wendi asked, one hand paused mid-reach into the bag of milk chocolate-covered popcorn.

"I just want to meet him and get a reading on him. I'm not convinced yet that Trevor wrote the manuscript. And if he didn't, that could propel Metz in the standings from the silver medal to the gold. Mostly, though, I just want to get a feel for how Oscar's taking things, coming in second and all."

"I'm sure he's fine," Wendi responded. "Ten thousand is still nothing to squawk about. He can publish his book and do a lot of promotion and marketing for that kind of money. Or he can go the self-publish route and just enjoy having the extra money as a cushion for a change."

"But you know what they say," Jimmy replied. "Fifty thousand is the new ten."

Jimmy stood up and pantomimed tipping his hat to Wendi, then walked to his car and headed to the north end of the island to a trailer park where Metz still lived in his dead mother's mobile home.

Chapter 16

JIMMY HAD NO TROUBLE FINDING the home of Oscar Metz, freelance writer and prize-winning author, albeit second prize. Unfortunately for Jimmy—and even more unfortunate for Oscar Metz—the house was surrounded by police tape. It was a little after two p.m., and a solitary, bored cop in a squad car was parked in front of Metz's mobile home in what passed for a driveway in the trailer park.

Jimmy took his cred pack out of his pocket and walked over to the car. He held his ID against the driver's window for a second before the officer lowered it.

"Yeah?"

"I'm Jimmy Favreaux. I'm a private investigator. I work for Lyst Publishing. You might have heard that Oscar Metz was the runner-up in a writing contest. Got a ten-thousand-dollar prize for his manuscript."

"Yeah? I'm not that into reading. I prefer podcasts."

"Right," Jimmy answered. He stood mutely in the driveway momentarily, waiting for more. When nothing else was offered, he asked, "So, can you tell me what happened here?"

"Yeah. No big secret. Somebody busted in last night and beat that Metz guy nearly to death. Near as anyone can tell, it was one car with three guys. From what the neighbors say, one of the guys was pretty big."

"But Oscar's not dead?" Jimmy asked.

"No, but not for lack of trying. Whoever it was, they busted him up, but good. Then they tossed the place. There wasn't a drawer in the place that wasn't pulled out and emptied onto the floor. All the drawers in the kitchen and the fridge, too. Oh, and the toilet tank lid was taken off and dropped in the tub."

Jimmy recognized the description and style of the interior decorators but kept that sliver of information to himself. He'd let the local law enforcement agencies know if it festered into something more significant.

"Where's he at? Baptist Hospital out here?" Jimmy asked.

"Nope. The EMTs took him down to Jacksonville. Baptist Medical Center downtown. First, the ER, then into a room. Like I said, they busted him up. But good."

Jimmy jerked his head toward the mobile home and asked, "Is it okay if I take a quick look around inside?"

"Knock yourself out. It's all pretty well trashed. But watch your step. There's a lot of paper and other junk on the floor. I hope you're up to date on your tetanus shots."

***

Two hours later, nearly four-thirty, Jimmy found Metz's room at the Baptist Hospital. He asked a tired-looking brunette at the nurses' station how he was. She looked at Oscar's chart and said he was doing pretty well for a guy with four broken ribs, a couple of other cracked ones, three broken fingers that looked like they had been stomped on, a concussion, and a face covered in various other bruises, cuts, and bumps.

Jimmy went in and sat in a faux leather-covered chair next to the bed. Metz was napping, but not peacefully. *Reliving the beat down in his dreams,* Jimmy thought. The poor guy probably would for quite some time.

Eventually, Metz opened one eye and turned his head just enough to see Jimmy. He looked at Jimmy for what seemed like a long time. *Probably trying to get his eyes to cooperate and focus,* Jimmy thought.

"Who are *you?*" Metz asked.

Jimmy told him, showed him his credentials, and then pointed to his own bruised cheekbone. "I think we have something in common — the same decorators," he told the injured man in the hospital bed.

Metz turned his head away from Jimmy again and stared at the ceiling. "That's nothing. Did they tell you what those jackals did to me?"

"Yeah, they did," Jimmy said. "But I'm not talking about this love pat on my cheek. I was talking about the *interior decorating* they did at my place before they hit yours. The only reason my place didn't look like yours is because I'm a private investigator, and my house is wired up pretty well for security. As soon as they kicked in the front door, my system called the Nassau County Sheriff's Office. It doesn't even wait for me; it just does it automatically. Those guys didn't have enough time to do much at my place. I got lucky. Plus, I was lucky because I wasn't there. This kiss on my cheekbone? That was from today – someone on their B-squad. If I had been there last night when the varsity came knocking, I'd be lying in a bed in here, too. Or possibly on a slab at the funeral home."

Metz didn't say anything. He gazed at the ceiling above his bed.

Jimmy asked, "Did the guys who did this say anything to you? Explain what it was they were looking for? Did they explain why they were giving you a beat down, or who sent them?"

Even with the bandages and bruises, the frustration was evident on Metz's face. A tear escaped from the corner of his eye. He tried to bring up one hand to brush it away, but the IV in his arm made it too difficult, and his other arm was in a sling and unavailable. The tears began to flow more freely, and Jimmy knew it wasn't simply from the painful ribs. After a minute or so, Oscar started to sigh but inhaling cut it short with a painful gasp and whimper, courtesy of his four broken ribs. The tears continued.

"What's the use? It's all going to come out anyway," Metz said. "I didn't tell those guys, and this is what I got for my trouble. The only good thing is that I haven't received my prize from Lyst yet, or they'd have taken that, too."

"Too?" Jimmy replied. "What else did they take?"

"A-a manuscript. I-it's for a book," Metz stammered, "but I don't think they found it."

"A book you wrote?" Jimmy asked.

Oscar automatically started to shake his head but immediately winced and stopped. The wrecking crew had busted him up, "but good," just like the cop said.

"A book I *rewrote*. But they didn't find what they were looking for because I hid it."

"I'm a little confused, Mr. Metz. You are a writer and won second place in a publisher's contest with your submitted manuscript. What manuscript were those goons after?"

"*Where the Ocean Swallows the Moon*. The original copy. The one I used to rewrite the book for Trevor."

"The book Trevor Mcintosh supposedly wrote? The manuscript he submitted that won the contest?" Jimmy asked incredulously.

"Trevor didn't write it, but neither did I. He got it from some guy who died from COVID in 2021. He hired me to rewrite it so he could enter it in the contest. Neither one of us had any idea it might win. Or maybe he did ..."

"Why did he want it rewritten?" Jimmy asked, pulling his chair closer to Metz's bed.

"He wanted me to remove some of the things that personalized it. Change a few characters' names, a few locales, and some minor details. He just wanted it changed enough that it wasn't the same book. You know, in case someone came along and claimed they had written it. But I couldn't simply rewrite it; I had to *retype* the whole thing, from the cover page to the end. And I almost got it done in time for the contest deadline."

"*Almost?* Why didn't you finish it, Oscar?"

"I decided to enter a book of my own in the contest. I had a manuscript I had been working on for a long time, and I decided it was good enough to enter. But it needed a final edit before I entered it, and it simply took longer than I expected. So, I didn't get the other manuscript retyped in time."

Jimmy sat back in the pleather-covered chair and asked, "What manuscript did Trevor submit?"

"The original, which is to say, the manuscript he found that the other guy wrote. I was using this old manual typewriter that Trevor has. He told me I had to use a manual typewriter, and he provided me with one, so I did. Then he hired some goons to steal back the original, so I could finish the copy. They were supposed to put the retyped copy in Lyst's office, but someone got the bright idea to *sell* it back. I still had the original at my house when those ruffians came last night. I hadn't given it back to Mcintosh yet." Metz stopped, licked his lips, and said, "Can you give me my water glass with the straw, please?"

Jimmy picked up the water glass from the rolling table and made sure it was full. He snapped the lid back on the glass and gave it to Metz, who sat up gingerly and took several short sips from the straw. Apparently, sucking on a straw involves the ribs, too, because every time Oscar took a sip, he winced. After his drink, Metz laid back slowly in his bed. He closed his eyes briefly, and Jimmy was afraid he would go back to sleep. But then his eyes opened slowly, and he started his story again.

"Trevor insisted the rewrite look just like the original. That's why he had me retype it on that old Royal manual typewriter."

The one he wouldn't let me see the other day, Jimmy thought to himself. He couldn't let me take a picture of him with it because it wasn't at his house. Not pawned, either!

"Using the old typewriter was the primary reason I couldn't finish. It was so much slower than using my computer—the keys required much more force to get them to work. Have you ever used a manual typewriter, Mr. Favreaux?"

"It's Jimmy, and yes, I have, but not since junior high. Miss Heery's typing class."

"Hmm. Yes. I think it was almost that long ago for me. Trevor said a computer-produced manuscript wouldn't have the same look. When you use a computer and laser printer, the letters result from a laser fusing the dry ink powder – the toner – onto the page. Even if you use the same font and typestyle to look like an old typewriter, it won't show the impact of the keys transferring the ink from the ribbon to the page. You can actually feel the difference, almost like braille. And if you hold a typewritten page up to the light, you can often see stars – little holes in the paper – from hitting the period key at the end of a sentence."

"And you still have the original, Oscar?"

Metz nodded his head slightly before the pain reminded him again to avoid nodding or shaking his head to answer questions. "I think I do. Those hooligans stole the original *back* from the publisher after Trevor was announced as the winner, and then I finished the rewrite. I gave the reworked copy to some guy a couple of days ago, but I still had the original."

"Can you describe the guy you gave the rewrite to?" Jimmy asked.

"Big guy, didn't seem very bright. I think he said his name was Gabe or something like that. He seems to have anger issues."

"Gabriel," Jimmy replied. "He's the one who provided my pretty cheekbone decoration. You're right: he's not very bright, which is why he's currently chilling out in the Nassau County jail. When he sucker-punched me today, he did it on my front porch, in full view of three security cameras, complete with sound."

"Good," was Metz's one-word response.

"So, you gave Gabriel the rewritten copy you had finished *after* the contest was decided?"

"Yes. I gave him the rewritten copy, and he said he was going to meet some guy at a bar and swap the copy for some money. Not only would the Lysts be paying Trevor, but they'd be paying some thug for a fake copy – not the original. Gabriel told me the Lysts would be so happy to get the manuscript back that they'd never notice it wasn't the same one Trevor submitted."

Jimmy chuckled. "That's ironic! I used a similar tactic with Gabriel when I met him in a bar to make the exchange. I distracted him with an envelope of cash, saying it was a tip for him. He was so excited about the tip that he never counted the rest of the money. I shorted his boss two grand, twenty-five hundred if you count Gabriel's 'tip' money. Unfortunately for Gabriel, his boss counts the money he collects. He took it out on Gabriel and apparently took his car to make things even. That's why Gabriel attacked me on my porch – looking to get repaid for what the boss took from him. But like I said, his performance was caught in hi-def for the police."

A painful expression crossed Oscar's face, and he said, "Please don't make me laugh; it hurts. But I'm glad about Gabriel. For what it's worth, I don't think he was one of the guys who attacked me last night. From what you said, he was probably nursing his own wounds, and yes, he's a B-squad player."

Jimmy smiled at Oscar before he said, "I made a quick stop at your place earlier, and I didn't see anything that looked like it could be the manuscript. You don't think your interior decorators found the original last night, do you? Were you unconscious at all while they were there looking for it?"

"I think I went in and out a couple of times, but only for a second or two each time. The manuscript was always in my sight. It's in two halves, and both parts were always there when I opened my eyes. The pieces are moveable, but neither one moved. It was in plain sight to them, too, but they didn't know what to look for."

Jimmy waited, hoping Oscar Metz would tell him without being prompted. Instead, he closed his eyes again. Jimmy was starting to get nervous that a nurse would throw him out soon, so he cleared his throat. Once, then again, but he got no reaction either time. So, Jimmy took a deep breath and nearly coughed up a lung. That time, Oscar's eyes fluttered open.

"I'm sorry. Did I doze off? This morphine is *wonderful.*" His hand came out from beneath his blanket, revealing a button connected to a wire. His thumb was poised over the button, and he had a big grin on his face. Jimmy grinned back.

"Yeah, it's great stuff. Can you tell me where you hid the original manuscript so I can make sure it wasn't taken and retrieve it?" Jimmy asked, a little jealous of Metz's painkilling button. After his sleepless night and his run-in with Gabriel's fist, he could use a little snooze and something to ease his pains.

Oscar answered slowly, his speech a little slurred from the morphine. "It was right in the living room with us the whole time. It was too big for a lot of the places I thought about using, but then I saw the perfect place for the first half. Did you happen to notice the condition of my carpets, Mr. Favreaux?"

"It's Jimmy, remember? And no, I really didn't take a close look because they were covered with papers, pens, clothes, pots and pans, and everything else that had been kept in a drawer at your house. Why?"

"You didn't notice the antique Electrolux vacuum cleaner in the corner by the sofa? It was my mother's, bless her soul. It's one of the models from the 1950s with chrome skis to glide on while you pull it around the room. It has a big, tube-like body just the right size to hold half the manuscript. It's inside the canister in a manilla envelope."

Jimmy smiled at Metz. "It's good that the goon squad didn't try to clean up after themselves. What about the other half, Oscar?"

"It was in plain sight, too. Did you notice the shelves by my desk?"

"Sure. A few pictures and knick-knacks. I guess there were some supplies, too. I think I saw some reams of paper and packs of pencils and notepads."

Metz smiled, and not from the morphine. "I put the second half in a ream of paper and taped it back up, so it looks like a new ream. There are a few sheets of plain paper on top, and then the manuscript starts. It was under their noses the whole time. I tried to watch them, but I didn't know if they tossed the stuff from the shelves while I went in and out of consciousness." Metz had a big tear running down his cheek again. "I don't suppose …" He stopped.

"You don't suppose what?" Jimmy responded, standing up next to the bed.

"I don't suppose I'll be able to keep the ten-thousand-dollar prize for second place."

Jimmy sat down again in the pleather-covered chair to think. Whether or not Oscar Metz received the prize for his novel wasn't Jimmy's decision, but he felt he could convince Lyst to allow the writer to keep his award. After all, Metz was a freelance writer working for a client. Rewriting the manuscript for Trevor didn't affect the manuscript Oscar had submitted.

Besides, if Mcintosh hadn't hired Metz to rewrite it, he would have chosen someone else. He probably picked Metz for his proximity to Lyst Publishing and Mcintosh's house.

"I don't know, Oscar. I'll put in a good word for you with Lyst. In the end, Mcintosh turned in the original manuscript, but it's not his work. *You*, on the other hand, turned in your own work. When I was at school, the teacher always said to show your work. You showed yours. I don't know if they'll disqualify the other manuscript or just Mcintosh. That's not up to me. It's all a work in progress."

Jimmy rose and stepped toward the door. "Rest. That's what you need, Oscar. Lots of rest."

Oscar smiled a sloppy grin and held up his morphine button. "And a little of this."

Jimmy waved and stepped out into the hall. He was going to go back to Metz's trailer and retrieve the manuscript.

✳✳✳

The Fernandina Police squad car was gone when Jimmy arrived back at Metz's trailer. The police tape was still partially up, but since the officer was gone and the tape was beginning to blow around, Jimmy assumed the scene had been released. It was after six p.m., the sun and the cop were gone, and night was taking over.

Jimmy walked up the metal steps to the locked front door. PIs in the movies were always experts at picking locks. Jimmy had never picked up the habit. Luckily, the door frame was bent so severely that it took only a slight nudge to persuade the door to open. Jimmy slipped in, closing the door behind him.

He walked over to a nearby window and looked out. Nothing was happening outside, and nobody was out wandering around. Jimmy noticed a movement in a window at one of the trailers across the street, like a curtain had been allowed to return to its normal position. He knew a close-knit neighborhood like this would be up on all the goings on. He figured he needed to be quick, or he'd have company from the "neighborhood watch," official or not.

This won't take long, he thought to himself. He walked directly to the Electrolux vacuum circa 1955. He flipped a catch, and the tube opened up. He reached in and pulled out a manilla envelope, taped shut with the word "WOSM" scrawled across it in marker. He figured it was an abbreviation for *Where the Ocean Swallows the Moon.* A few steps to the right was Metz's desk. On the wall over the desk were some shelves, one holding several reams of paper.

Jimmy looked at the packages. Each appeared pristine and unaltered from a front view. He took them from the shelf one by one and turned them around. The middle one in the stack had nearly invisible tape on the backside holding the corners down. He took out his pocket knife, slit the tape, and opened the package. It was just like Metz had said: a few sheets of blank paper and then typewritten sheets. He taped the end shut again, grabbed the manilla envelope, and quickly glanced around the room. He opened the door and stepped out, nearly knocking down a woman coming up the steps to Metz's trailer.

"Excuse me! I'm so sorry! I didn't see you there," he apologized, holding out a hand for her to grasp for stability. She took it briefly while she collected herself.

She let his hand drop and smoothed her hair back into place. "It's quite all right," she said. "I was just about to knock. I saw you go inside and figured you were a plainclothes detective. I saw the uniformed officer leave about an hour ago. You *are* with the police, aren't you?"

She put one hand up near her neck and leaned back against the railing, slightly increasing the space separating them. The black metal railing was between her and the house, and Jimmy was in front of her. Where she would go if Jimmy intended to do her harm, he didn't know.

"I'm a private investigator," Jimmy said. "I'm helping out with the case." *Not really a lie,* he told himself. "I was just down in Jacksonville visiting Oscar – Mr. Metz – at Baptist Medical Center. He asked me to get him a couple of things. That's why I'm here."

"Is he all right?" the neighbor asked.

"He's pretty banged up and bruised, but I think he'll be home in a day or two. It would be very helpful if you would keep an eye on his trailer until he gets back. If you see anyone other than the police going in there, I'd appreciate it if you would call the local police to alert them. Oscar would appreciate it, too, Mrs. ...?"

"Mrs. Campbell. June Campbell. Like the soup people but without the money." June Campbell laughed at her joke, one Jimmy was sure she had told a few thousand times before.

June Campbell looked about seventy, wearing pink and white striped capri pants, white sneakers, and a pink sleeveless blouse. For Jimmy's taste, she was a bit on the high side of years, but she still had a figure that had probably opened more than a few doors for her when she was younger. Her hair was a stone-gray color, the kind most women want to avoid in their senior years. Everyone desires beautiful, soft white hair, but you can't always get what you want.

"It's nice to meet you," Jimmy said, intentionally omitting his name from the conversation. "As I said, Oscar should be home in a few days, and it would be helpful if you kept an eye out for people going in and out of his trailer. I'm afraid I have to leave to take some things back down to Oscar before it gets too late today."

Jimmy walked quickly down the steps and over to his SUV. *Ten-to-one says she goes in as soon as I drive away*, Jimmy told himself. Climbing into his vehicle, he started it up, put it in gear, and began to drive away. He slowed slightly and adjusted his rearview mirror in time to see June Campbell reach into her pocket, pull out a key, unlock the door, and slip inside. *Probably got it from Metz's mom once.*

Jimmy smiled and drove on. *There's a fine line between a neighborhood watch and nosy,* he thought to himself. At least *someone's* watching over things.

Chapter 17

JIMMY WANTED TO READ THE original manuscript or, at least, a portion of it. He had gotten a copy of the rewrite on a flash drive from Wendi the night before, so he could easily compare the two documents for changes.

Driving back through Fernandina, Jimmy considered swinging past Lyst Publishing to see if Wendi was at the office, but in the end, he chose to go straight home. Enough bad things had been happening there the last few days, and he felt he needed to be there.

He was relieved to find everything at home exactly as he had left it. A quick check of his security system and its videos in the cloud revealed no new break-ins or visits. Jimmy carried the manuscript with him – a large manilla envelope and what appeared to be a ream of paper – while he locked his front door, got some sweet tea from the fridge, and went to his office. Once in his office, Jimmy consolidated the two packages into one, then gazed at the four-inch-tall stack of pages they produced.

Jimmy didn't need to read it to recognize it was different from the fake copy he had bargained for with Gabriel. Clearly, the original manuscript had come from multiple reams of paper of varying whiteness and weights. It was like analyzing layers of stone in a canyon wall. Slight variations in paper caused distinct "eras" in the stack. Stock from different reams introduced different color elements and contributed to the stratified effect. There were dark brown smudges on the side of the stack, like someone with dirty hands had repeatedly riffled the pages. Some corners were slightly bent, and a small, light brown mark on the cover sheet looked like a cigarette ash had landed there, toasting the paper slightly.

Jimmy thought back to his conversation on Jekyll Island with Trevor Mcintosh. The eccentric author had asked Jimmy for a cigarette, and when Jimmy said he didn't have any, Mcintosh replied that he didn't really smoke. Jimmy had encountered Trevor's kind before: people who *say* they don't smoke, but what they mean is they don't *pay* for cigarettes.

The discoloration from dirty fingers and different batches of paper didn't prove anything by itself. Trevor had told Lyst he had written the book over several years, so the variations in paper quality were entirely plausible; expected, actually.

Jimmy settled into his desk chair to read and compare the two manuscripts. He had a stack of papers from the original manuscript and the pages from the flash drive on his computer monitor in front of him. He took a big drink of his tea and started reading.

✳✳✳

Two hours later, Jimmy had not digested a significant percentage of Mcintosh's manuscript, but he had read enough to uncover several distinctions between the two documents. Chief among those differences was the *near-absence* of a prominent character in the original: Lottie Evans. Her character was still featured in the new, mangled storyline, but her name was now Mary Fiske. A number of her physical attributes had also been altered. The original Lottie was described as a raven-haired, brown-eyed beauty. The rewrite listed Mary as flaxen-haired with dark-blue eyes the color of a clear sky at dusk.

Most of the other changes Jimmy found were cosmetic, little things that would only catch your eye if you had read either of the stories before. Or, like Jimmy was doing now, reading the two stories side-by-side for comparison.

The original story was about a man called Chris, who, tired of his chosen life, walked away from it to see the world aboard a cargo ship. The rewrite was the same premise, but the main character and storyteller had been renamed Samuel. Ports of call were changed along with crew members' names and descriptions but placed side-by-side, the story was obviously the same.

Jimmy felt a little disappointed. He was hoping for more glaring inconsistencies between the two copies. He had hoped Metz had written in new adventures and interactions with new characters, but it was mostly just replacing names with new ones. Jimmy knew he wasn't an expert in the law in general and definitely no authority on copyright and trademark cases or where intellectual property was on trial. Still, he felt it was a clearcut case of unauthorized duplication. Jimmy doubted anyone could fail to see they were the same story if it ever went to court for plagiarism.

It seemed like only a few years since a movie release in which Tom Hanks portrayed a captain on a container ship that encountered modern-day pirates. Jimmy could understand Lyst's belief that the new manuscript could translate to the big screen.

Jimmy paused his reading, pulled up a search window, and looked for "tom hanks cargo ship captain." He quickly found it on IMDb.com – the Internet Movie Database website owned by Amazon (who else?): 2013's *Captain Phillips*. The description blurb read, "The true story of Captain Richard Phillips and the 2009 hijacking by Somali pirates of the U.S.-flagged MV Maersk Alabama, the first American cargo ship to be hijacked in two hundred years." [1]

One distinct advantage to having the manuscript on his computer was the ability to search for terms electronically. He searched Metz's rewrite for pirates and got a hit.

Similar to the Tom Hanks movie, both versions of the book detailed an attack by pirates in the Indian Ocean off the Somalia coast. Unlike the film, though, the container ship's captain in the book chose to *run over* the pirates' boat, crushing it and sending it to the ocean floor. There was no mention of survivors. The ship's wake had tossed the pirate crew into the Indian Ocean, leaving the high-seas thugs to take their chances with sharks.

---

[1] (Sony Pictures Entertainment, 2013)

In real life, distinguishing heroes from bad guys isn't as easy as in fiction. Unlike the old movies, where bad guys wore black hats and good guys wore white, determining whether someone was a hero or an anti-hero these days depended on your point of view. Jimmy had long ascribed to the belief that history was determined by the winners, not the facts. Even facts were not necessarily facts – since history was written by the winners. Those winners, therefore, delineated truth and fiction, crafting the enduring version of the facts.

Trevor Mcintosh had paid Oscar Metz to alter the manuscript he supposedly "got" from a guy who died of COVID in 2021. Did paying Metz for a product and the original author's absence—and subsequent inability to protest—make Mcintosh the *de facto* owner? As the old saying went, possession was nine-tenths of the law. Trevor *possessed* the original manuscript and had paid for the rewrite Jimmy had rescued for the Lysts.

Jimmy was glad he didn't have to be the judge in that case. There were too many grey areas and arbitrary decisions. Jimmy was satisfied with his role as an investigator, a finder of people, places, and things – like a missing manuscript – and not assuming the mantle of universal referee for all things existential.

Not someone who ordinarily reads a book's last chapter before reading the rest, Jimmy zoomed ahead with his digital copy, located the same place in the original manuscript, and began reading for differences. He wanted to see if both versions ended the same.

Twenty minutes later, he was shaking his head. *Not the same, not even remotely.*

In the new, rewritten version, Samuel – the main character – looks back at all his adventures while serving aboard the container ship and all the people he has met during his time at sea. He lists the captain and crew he's worked with and then begins to enumerate the women he's wined, dined, and slept with. *Cue the music: To All the Girls I've Loved Before,* Jimmy thought.

Samuel, the rewrite's hero, plans to get a good night's sleep because the ship departs in the morning, setting sail for other exotic ports with new food, people, and experiences. *Pull the covers up to his chin and fade out on his smile.*

In the original, however, Chris – the main character, looks back at his life at sea and compares it to his previous life. There's no mention of women or amorous adventures, just an honest reflection on the opportunities with Lottie Evans he missed by traveling the world. Chris discovered his heart wasn't truly in seeking adventure and new places; he longed to be at home with Lottie. His heart was always yearning to go home and resume where he had left off with Lottie.

In the original version's ending, Chris was packing his seabag and preparing to *quit* the sea and find Lottie to discover if she would take him back. If she had moved on with her life and no longer desired him, Chris would return to his cabin and job on the container ship and go wherever the big ship carried him. But his heart would always remain behind with Lottie.

Jimmy realized that all this reading – coupled with a punch in the face – had given him a headache, so he got up from his desk and went to the kitchen. He never used the crushed ice feature on his fridge and skipped it this time, too, pulling a bag of frozen peas from the freezer and placing it against his cheek. Stopping in the bathroom on his way back to the office, he tapped out three ibuprofen, then another for luck, and washed them down with a glass of water.

Back at his desk, Jimmy straightened the typewritten manuscript and put it into a single box, tossing the manilla envelope and paper wrapping Metz had disguised it with. Jimmy put his computer to sleep and walked down the hall to the living room, where the wall clock showed ten p.m. He wasn't ready to go to bed for the night but needed a break from the computer screen. Stretching out in his recliner, Jimmy pulled a small afghan over his legs and closed his eyes, the bag of frozen peas against his bruised cheek. Within two minutes, he was snoring softly.

***

As Jimmy slept, he dreamed he was on a container ship, hundreds of feet above the water, standing on the prow like in the movie *Titanic*. Instead of Rose, he was with Wendi. Together they shouted "King of the World!" as the ship knifed through the sea, dolphins keeping pace alongside, soaring up out of the water and gracefully diving back under the surface. Since it was a dream, Wendi still wore the black skirt and white blouse from the first time Jimmy had seen her.

Suddenly, Jimmy felt someone tugging on his arm, pulling him away from Wendi. Turning to see who it was, he found a crew member repeating a phrase to Jimmy over and over: "You must come and help; you're the doctor. You must come and help; you're the doctor."

Dream-Jimmy looked from the crewman back to Wendi, who was holding out one arm and trying to draw Jimmy back to her the way people always do in dream sequences. Jimmy looked at the crewman again and saw that the man's hands were covered in blood. The man kept repeating the same phrase: "You must come and help; you're the doctor."

The crewman stretched out a bloody hand, grabbed Jimmy's arm, and started pulling him back toward the crew's quarters. Jimmy stretched his other arm toward Wendi, but she turned away, saying, "I never wanted you to go, but you're the doctor." High above the waves with the wind in her hair, she stretched her arms wide as Jimmy was dragged into the darkness of the crew's quarters.

Jimmy jolted awake, his eyes wide and his breathing ragged. He looked around his living room; it was still dark outside. He was unsure if he had slept all night and through the next day or had just taken a cat nap, but he definitely felt better. He pulled out his phone to check the day and time and discovered he had only slept a little over an hour. The bag of peas, no longer frozen, had fallen between the seat cushion and the chair's arm. The peas felt like puréed baby food or mashed potatoes. Feeling the thawed vegetables, he realized he must have moved around in his recliner while he napped.

He got up from the recliner and stretched, trying to limber up, twisting right and then left, feeling the little audible pops in his back. He shuffled to the kitchen and dropped the bag of peas into the trash. If this case was a harbinger of things to come, he would have to consider purchasing some reusable ice packs. Although, at eighty-nine cents each, the frozen peas were an effective and economical alternative.

He stood by the sink and looked out the window at the darkened backyard. He could see moonlight off the St. Marys River as it flowed under the blue bridge, almost within rock-throwing distance. The shimmering light on the water reminded him of his weird dream.

Why had the crewman thought Jimmy was the doctor? Research about container ships said they didn't carry a doctor as regular crew. The small crew size made a full-time doctor economically unrealistic. The captain and other officers were trained in basic first aid in case of emergencies. They would contact the Coast Guard—or its equivalent in foreign waters—if there was a severe accident. But having a crewman who happened to be a trained EMT or other licensed medical personnel could be a definite plus for any ship spending long stretches far from land.

"You must come and help; you're the doctor."

"I never wanted you to go, but you're the doctor."

"You're the doctor."

"I never wanted you to go."

Who was the doctor? Why was he on the ship? Container ships didn't bring doctors.

Jimmy had barely slept the last couple of nights. Maybe it was just a weird dream brought on by a lack of sleep. Plus, he had been punched in the face, his house had been broken into, he had been threatened multiple times, and he knew the threats were not idle – Metz was a testament to that, as was Jimmy's bruised cheek.

Jimmy stretched out in his recliner again and picked up the remote to turn on the tv but stopped. He sat frozen, rewinding the dream in his mind, hearing the phrase, *You're the doctor* repeated over and over. He put down the remote, laid his head back on the chair, and closed his eyes. He was just about asleep again when one more scene from the dream suddenly became sharp in his mind.

The crewman was pulling him into the darkened quarters, Wendi was pretending to fly over the ocean ahead, and both were saying, *"You're the doctor."* In this other scene from the dream, Jimmy said, "I'm not the doctor. I'm Jimmy."

The crewman had tugged him closer to the looming darkness and said, *"No, you're Chris! You're the doctor!"*

Jimmy sat up straight in his chair. He pulled out his cell phone and called Pepé. It went to voicemail. *Of course, it did.* It was eleven p.m., and Pepé had a wife and a life. Frustrated and not wanting to lose the forward progress he felt he was making, Jimmy canceled the call without leaving a voicemail. He sent his partner a text instead.

> Idea. Check with Bwick Port Authority. See if anyone died on a ship in 2021 while docked at Bwick. Plz check. Important!

Chapter 18

WHEN MORNING CAME, JIMMY DROVE back to Lyst Publishing, the original manuscript on the seat next to him. He wasn't sure if he was refreshed from getting more than a couple of hours of sleep or jazzed from the weird dream. Giving in to his hunger, Jimmy pulled in at Chick-fil-A on A1A to refuel with breakfast. He used their app on his phone to order his food and, while waiting for it, sent a quick text to Wendi.

> I need to speak with Mr. Lyst. Important. Meet me at the office in a half-hour.

It didn't take long for her to reply.

> K. We'll be there. Is everything all right?

He thumbed a reply that everything was fine, but he had uncovered some new information and needed them both to be there to see what he was bringing. Shortly after hitting the send button for the text, his food was brought out, and he was on his way again, the smell of food filling his vehicle.

He pulled into the lot and parked in what he had begun to think of as *his* spot in front of Staples. He opened the window to let the Chick-fil-A aroma escape while he snarfed down his sausage-egg-and-cheese biscuit and hash browns. He washed it down with a coffee – three sugars and three creamers. After checking his teeth for stray surprises, he closed his window and exited the car with the box containing the manuscript clutched under one arm. He didn't pace in front of the door, just went in and walked down the narrow hall. It was mid-morning, but the sun didn't travel straight overhead this late in the year, so the enclosed hallway would have been quite dim if not for the overhead fluorescent lights. Situated between the two buildings, the only natural light came from the front door.

The door to Lyst Publishing was unlocked at the end of the hallway. Jimmy tapped lightly on the door as he opened it. Stepping inside, he saw that Wendi was not at her desk, but he heard voices from Hillary's office. He walked toward the voices, knocking on the open door as he walked in and announced his presence with a hearty "Halloo!"

Wendi was sitting in the same chair she had occupied three days before when they first gathered here. She was wearing jeans and a dark blue blouse. Everything he had seen her wear looked better because she wore it. Mr. Lyst sat behind his desk in a white shirt with a button-down collar, the sleeves rolled halfway, and no tie. His uniform. Mr. Lyst smiled at Jimmy.

"Wendi said you had something to show us, Jimmy. I would postulate it's encased in the box you carry, yes?"

"You have hypothesized correctly, Professor." Hillary Lyst raised his eyebrows in response. Jimmy continued, "I'm going to show you something, and I want you to tell me what it is. Ready?"

"Indeed," Lyst answered.

Jimmy placed the box on the desk in front of Mr. Lyst and removed the lid. His original broad smile faded quickly, and a look of utter confusion passed over Hillary Lyst's face as he looked at the cover sheet of the manuscript the box contained. His mouth opened slightly, but he refrained from speaking.

The publisher reached into the box, picked up the top sheet, and examined the next several pages. Holding the sheets of paper in his left hand, he opened a desk drawer with his right hand. He pulled out the manuscript Jimmy had brought him two days ago after his tête-à-tête with Gabriel at Mickey's Tap Room. He scrutinized the pages one at a time, then placed the individual manuscripts side by side on his desk. He compared each sheet, turning them over to the right and left—away from each other—keeping them safe from becoming mixed.

Wendi had risen and stepped behind Hillary's desk, looking around his forearms at the pages on his desk. Mr. Lyst surveyed a dozen or so pages, then stopped. He looked at Jimmy, his mouth slightly open, his lips pursed like he was about to say "what," but had stopped as confusion paralyzed him. He finally found his voice but was still baffled.

"What am I looking at, Jimmy?" Lyst asked, still examining pages on his desk. He was doing manually what Jimmy had done the night before with a paper original and a digital copy.

"What do you *think* you're looking at, Mr. Lyst? You have two copies of a book, of which there should be only one copy."

Lyst flipped through a few more pages. He looked over his glasses at Jimmy. "Do you remember when I quoted Sir Winston Churchill the day before yesterday? 'It is a riddle, wrapped in a mystery, inside an enigma?'" Waving his hands over the two manuscripts on his desk, Lyst pronounced, "This is a riddle, wrapped in a mystery, tucked inside an enigma, and *covered thoroughly in a conundrum!*"

Jimmy continued to smile at the publisher. "What we have here is not a failure to communicate, but *too much communication*. According to the alleged author, Trevor Mcintosh, there should only be one copy. But somehow, we have two copies, and I know how."

"Do tell," Lyst said, sitting back in his chair.

"Yes, do tell, Jimmy," Wendi echoed, coming around the desk to sit in her assigned seat.

"I paid a visit to Oscar Metz. His trailer was festooned in police tape—"

"—my word!" Lyst interrupted. "Is he—?"

"No, he's alive, but not for lack of trying by the three strong-armed brigands who accosted him in his home two nights ago," Jimmy explained. He was secretly proud of himself for using the term brigands. "Those guys beat him within an inch of his life. He's in Baptist Hospital in Jacksonville. I went down to see him yesterday. From what he told me, it sounds like the same three delinquents who hit my place two nights ago.

They must have had a busy night. When they didn't find the manuscript at my place, they moved on to Oscar's. Thankfully for me, I was not home when they came calling. Unfortunately for Oscar, he *was*."

Lyst sat up and nearly hollered, "*Your* place?" He eyed Wendi sternly, and she seemed to shrink slightly in her chair. Her cheeks flushed at his indignation.

Wendi turned to Jimmy and said, "I hadn't told him about that *yet*, Jimmy. I didn't want to upset him, and since you were okay ..." She trailed off.

Lyst scrutinized Jimmy more carefully and said, "What's that *mark* on your cheek, Jimmy?"

Not wanting to get Wendi in more hot water, Jimmy said, "It's nothing. Really. It comes with my job sometimes. You'll be glad to know the guy who did it performed his pugilistic act in front of a command audience on my three security cameras. He's now a guest of Nassau County for the foreseeable future. Incidentally, it's the same guy I met at Mickey's who neglected to count the cash in the envelope I gave him. He's the same guy who tried to jump me at the Loop the other night when I was here with you and Mrs. Lyst, and I left for a bit to go get the pizza—"

"—jumped, w-what?!" Lyst's features displayed his understandable irritation at not being in the know. His brow was so furrowed Jimmy thought the older man could grip a quarter in the wrinkles between his eyes. Lyst looked at Wendi, who pointed her index finger at Jimmy. Hillary shifted his stern, schoolmaster-like gaze to Jimmy.

"What?" Jimmy replied with mock ignorance. "You got your pizza, and the local cops took Gabriel in for the night for trying to rough me up *and* to question him about holding your manuscript hostage. Full disclosure, this Gabriel-guy dropped the envelope off with his boss, thinking he had completed his assignment while scoring an extra five hundred dollars for himself. Unfortunately for Gabriel, his boss is much more fiscally-minded and took the time to count the money I gave Gabriel. He decided it was Gabriel's fault and took it out on him physically, then confiscated Gabriel's car to make up the difference. So, when Gabriel came to my place to try and shake me down, he had to ride a bicycle there. He looked pretty comical. Let me assure you, it's tough to outrun the cops on a bike."

"Is there more the two of you have withheld?" Lyst asked, sitting back in his chair, interlacing his fingers over his chest.

"Um … I really can't remember, so if we hit something, stop me, and I'll explain," Jimmy responded.

Lyst looked at Wendi, who shrugged her shoulders and raised her hands as if to say, "What can you do?"

Jimmy was trying to get his train of thought back on track, mumbling under his breath to himself, "Okay, I explained about Gabriel, the break-in at my house, and the break-in at Metz's—"

"—Okay, Jimmy," Mr. Lyst interrupted. "The story behind these two copies of *Where the Ocean Swallows the Moon* if you would please," he said tiredly.

"Gotcha, Professor." It was the second time Jimmy had referred to the publisher as 'Professor,' and Jimmy realized from the subsequent frown on Lyst's face that he was pushing his luck.

"So, *Mr. Lyst,* I went down to Baptist Hospital yesterday afternoon to see Metz, and I barely said anything to him before he started crying and confessing everything. Mcintosh hired him to rewrite *Where the Ocean Swallows the Moon,* taking out names and changing details, so it's not quite so obvious that it's the same book. Then Oscar popped the ten-thousand-dollar question: if he'll be able to keep his prize money."

"Absolutely not!" Lyst barked and snorted with derision through his nose. He adjusted his glasses and looked away from Jimmy at the many volumes of books lining the shelves of his office, fuming silently.

Wendi cleared her throat and softly asked, "What did you tell Oscar, Jimmy?"

"Well, I told him it wasn't my call, of course; it was up to *you,* Mr. Lyst. I *did* say that, from my point of view, what he did for a client should have no impact on writing his entry for the contest." Jimmy looked at Lyst, who was still looking at the hundreds of books lining the room, his fingers still interlaced.

"But I made it very clear that it would be up to *you,* Mr. Lyst," Jimmy reiterated, then stopped, waiting for a response.

Lyst finally tore his eyes away from the books on the wall and fixed his gaze on Jimmy. "We'll return to that issue after I hear more about Mcintosh's manuscript. Proceed, *Mr. Favreaux.*"

Lyst's use of Jimmy's proper name did not go unnoticed, and Jimmy figured it might take a little time to get back into Lyst's good graces. As he continued his report for his client, Jimmy tried to present all the relevant details.

"Metz told me he rewrote the story for Trevor, but he was very clear that Mcintosh didn't write the original. Oscar told me Trevor got it from a guy who died last year from COVID. Apparently, it was written on an old manual typewriter, so Mcintosh required Oscar to retype the story on a similar typewriter. When I went up to Jekyll and saw Trevor, I tried to convince him to let me inside his house to take a picture of him with the typewriter he wrote the story on, but he staunchly refused. He finally came up with a story about needing to pawn it for some quick cash. I chose not to push it, but from what Oscar told me, that's the typewriter he used to rewrite the story. That's the real reason Trevor couldn't let me see it."

Wendi spoke up. "I don't understand what Mcintosh expected to do or say if what is happening right now happened, where there are suddenly *two* copies."

Mr. Lyst answered the question. "He would say one is a rough draft and one the final. He could just say he thought he had gotten rid of the draft copy or that he typed it at his mother's, for example, and she kept the draft, unbeknownst to him. But that story is replete with gaping holes. As I see it, the problem is that he already told me he wrote it *without* a carbon: one copy and *no drafts*. The existence of another copy proves his dishonesty."

"What about the issue of authenticity?" Jimmy asked. "According to Metz, Mcintosh got it from a dead guy. I wonder if the author would have given it to Trevor if he had lived. I sincerely doubt it."

"Are you suggesting Mr. Mcintosh acquired the manuscript illegally?" Lyst asked, looking at the twin manuscripts before him.

"I'm suggesting that Trevor – or someone who knew him – was an acquaintance of the unfortunate COVID victim. Upon his demise, somebody discovered the manuscript. Whether Trevor or someone who knew Trevor, I'm willing to bet they claimed finders' keepers on the manuscript, citing the proverbial possession is nine-tenths of the law axiom."

"Indeed," Lyst answered. "Do we have any idea who the deceased might have been?"

"*We* don't," Jimmy replied, "but *I* might. I put a bug in my partner's ear to have him do some checking with the port authority to see if they had any onboard COVID deaths last year while ships were docked in Brunswick. I'm waiting on him to get back to me. It may take some time."

"Why the Brunswick Port Authority?" Wendi asked.

"A couple of reasons," Jimmy replied, crossing the room to sit in the vacant chair. "First, Trevor lives on Jekyll Island. Brunswick Port Authority is the nearest international port to where he lives. Quite handy, actually. It's not far on Highway 17 after coming off the Jekyll Causeway. You don't even have to go into Brunswick to get there. Secondly, the main character in the book – both books, I might add – spends five years working on a container ship. He recounts the various exotic ports he visits during his travels. If the story is about Trevor, it makes complete sense that he would have crewed out of the Brunswick Port Authority."

"He couldn't have written it about someone else?" Wendi questioned.

"He could have, I suppose," Jimmy answered, "but if you read it, it's an autobiography. It's written in the first-person – I did this, I did that, and I went there. I suppose it's *possible* he wrote it about someone else or a fictional character, but just barely within the realm of possibility. Whoever wrote it *did* those things and *went* to those places. There's almost no reasonable chance Trevor wrote it. He may have told Metz it came from a dead man just to lend an air of mystique to the story. You know, trying to effect an air of eccentricity. Why not go bigger? But if Mcintosh has ever been on a watercraft larger than a bass boat, I'll eat my non-existent hat."

Jimmy continued his explanation, "While I was talking with him the other day, I noticed his hands. They're soft and white. He not only doesn't get much sun exposure, he doesn't use his hands for any work more strenuous than bumming cigarettes and drinks from strangers. Those hands have probably never seen a solid hour of manual labor. No callouses anywhere and no grease or oil under his nails or embedded in the skin of his hands. A man who crews on a container ship uses his hands. Container ships aren't pleasure boats; they're work ships. It's like the difference between a real farm in the country and a postage stamp garden in the middle of a city. I can smell fraud all over him. I'd be willing to bet he didn't write *Growing Up Southern*, either."

"I've often wondered the same thing since meeting the man, Jimmy," Lyst responded. Jimmy was glad to hear Mr. Lyst use his first name again. He genuinely liked the publisher and hadn't meant to keep him out of the loop. Life comes at you fast sometimes, though, and you need to roll with the punches and write a *mea culpa* report afterward.

"So, we're agreed that Trevor didn't write the book and tried to cover it up by hiring a freelancer – Oscar Metz – to rewrite the book and change it slightly in case the original should ever be found?" Jimmy asked, taking an informal poll. All three nodded.

"But what was the point of stealing the manuscript?" Wendi asked.

"Metz hadn't quite finished his rewrite when the contest deadline came," Jimmy explained. "He gave the original back to Mcintosh, and *that's* what Trevor submitted. After you contacted him and told him he had won the big prize, Trevor got some local goons to break in here and steal back the original so Oscar could finish. Metz gave the rewritten copy to another thug – Gabriel – later. That's the one I got with the ransom money. I think the original plan was to break in here again and simply swap copies, but someone decided they could make a little money off the transaction, so the plan morphed a bit. Fifty grand for Trevor didn't include a spiff for the guys who broke in and stole the original back. So, they decided to sell the copy back to you for an extra five grand. Does that make sense?"

Wendi answered, "They stole the original and sold us a copy?" Jimmy nodded.

"What tipped you off?" Wendi wanted to know.

"Other than Oscar spilling his guts about it? Look at the two copies on the desk," Jimmy instructed. "Is the one from your desk drawer today the same copy you were given during the contest?"

Mr. Lyst looked at the two copies. He put his hand out toward the original Jimmy had just delivered. "This one has the earmarks of time. Bent corners, dirty smudges where the pages have been riffled multiple times over a long period by hands that were not always clean."

Jimmy nodded. He said, "Look at the cover sheet. See the light brown dot? Like an errant cigarette ash landed there?"

"Yes. What of it?" Lyst replied.

"I think that's Trevor's sole contribution to the manuscript."

Hillary Lyst's eyebrows rose, but he waited for Jimmy to explain. Wendi looked at him, too, questions in her eyes.

"When I visited Trevor this week, he asked me for a cigarette, but when I told him I didn't have any, he said it was okay because he didn't really smoke."

"So?" Wendi asked, waiting for more to connect the dots.

"He also asked if I had any beer or alcohol. He said he was thirsty. I recognized him as one of those people who mooch off others all the time. He didn't mean he doesn't smoke; Trevor meant he doesn't *buy* cigarettes. And when he had the manuscript, he bummed a cigarette from someone, and a tiny ember fell on the manuscript, toasting the paper lightly. Take a look at the copy of the manuscript Wendi ran on the copier the other night, making sure you would have an extra copy. The cover page is enough."

Wendi went and retrieved the cover page. "No burn mark," she said.

"Because you copied a copy," Jimmy replied. "If the goon squad had left Metz alone, you'd have published the rewritten version, and no one would have been the wiser."

"I disagree. I believe I would have noticed," Mr. Lyst responded to Jimmy's assertion. "But with only the 'rescued' copy to compare with my memory, I would have eventually been forced to capitulate. I would have ultimately blamed it on a failing memory. I'm afraid you are correct."

"So, assuming Mr. Mcintosh is no longer the grand prize winner," Jimmy asked, "what do we do about Mr. Metz?"

Lyst leaned back in his chair, made a steeple with his fingers under his chin, and told Jimmy, "Mrs. Lyst and I will take it under consideration. Nothing needs to be done this morning, correct?"

"Nothing," Jimmy answered, then added with a sly grin, "unless you think it would be prudent to stop payment on a certain fifty-thousand dollar check."

"Indeed," Hillary Lyst replied. "Yes, indeed."

Chapter 19

JIMMY WAS FRUSTRATED. HE WANTED to discuss his suspicions about the manuscript's origin with Pepé. However, his partner wasn't answering calls or texts. That left Jimmy in a pickle: he could go back to Metz's house again and talk with his neighbors and poke around inside Oscar's mobile home, or he could drive to Baptist Hospital and see Metz again, or he could burn more gas and run back up the interstate and out to Jekyll for another visit with Mcintosh. Unfortunately, he didn't have enough solid information to necessitate any of those things, so he decided to go home.

While driving, Jimmy's phone rang. A quick touch of a button on the steering wheel connected him before he even looked to see who was calling. He answered, "This is Jimmy."

"Jimmy! This is Pepé. You done good, partner. We got a hit at the Port Authority."

At last! Things are falling my way! Jimmy thought. "I'm driving, Pepé, so tell me what you uncovered. I'll be home in about five minutes, and then I can get in my office and use my computer."

"Okay, dude. No sweat. So, I asked whether there were any ships that lost crewmen to COVID last year while in port. There were five," Pepé said, his voice filling the confines of Jimmy's mobile office courtesy of his iPhone's Bluetooth connection.

"Five? Wow! That's more than I expected," Jimmy replied.

"Yeah, that's what I said, too. Then I had them break the results down by country of origin. Only one was American. The other four were Panamanian."

"Really? Panamanian? That sounds odd to me. I mean, we have a huge Navy and a zillion shipping companies here in the U.S., plus we import so much stuff that I figured we'd have a huge fleet of container ships. But Panama?" Jimmy questioned.

"Panama is actually the world's largest flag state for container ships," Pepé answered. "That's what they're called: flag states. According to this handy-dandy brochure I got, 'International law requires that every merchant ship be registered in a country, called its flag state. A ship's flag state exercises regulatory control over the vessel and is required to inspect it regularly, certify the ship's equipment and crew, and issue safety and pollution prevention documents.' Almost sounds like I know what I'm talkin' about, doesn't it?"

"Almost," Jimmy replied with a light laugh. He knew that Pepé liked to hide behind a façade of ignorance, but the retired policeman was far more intelligent than he let on. He had been a Charleston cop and Navy Watch Commander for over thirty years.

"The U.S. only has like seventy-five container ships under its flag. Pretty wild, huh?" Pepé continued.

"Yeah," Jimmy replied. "That's crazy. So, tell me about the dead American person. We'll let Panama worry about the rest of the bodies."

"You got it, dude. White male. About fifty. Had been part of the ship's crew for five years. He ran the galley. He was the main cook, but he was also a dietician, they said. And get this: he was a medical guy."

Here we go! Jimmy thought. *Now it's getting interesting!*

Jimmy said excitedly, "Hold on, Pepé! I'm almost home. I'm practically pulling into the driveway. Did they have a name on this white male, about fifty, who was a medical person?"

"They did," Pepé said, "but it's not John Epps. They said his name was Christopher Evans."

Jimmy slammed on the brakes and pulled the SUV onto the shoulder, skidding to a stop on the loose gravel. He took a big breath and said, "Say that again, Pepé. What was his name?"

"I said it's not John Epps, Jimmy. They told me this guy's name was Christopher Evans. Why? What's going on?"

"Give me a minute, Pepé," Jimmy said.

It was like he was in the middle of his dream again. He heard the words in his head, repeated over again, *"You must come and help; you're the doctor. You're the doctor."* And then the final admonition: *"You're <u>Chris</u>; you're the doctor."*

Could Chris, the unofficial, *ad hoc* ship's doctor, be an alias for John Epps? Could Dr. Epps have called a time-out on his career and life as a doctor and husband to run off to sea? Had he gone searching to find if he had missed something vital by choosing one fork in the road over another? Could he have gotten up one morning and decided to backtrack and take the road less traveled? The timeframe was a good fit with his disappearance, and the Brunswick hospital was only a few miles from the Port Authority. It would have been simple for him to catch a ride with someone or take a taxi from the hospital to the docks.

"Pepé?" Jimmy got back on the phone. "I'm going to stop at home and do some quick research. We may have an answer for your client, which may also be part of the answer for mine." Without waiting for a response from Pepé, Jimmy clicked off the phone and put the car in gear. He let his reflexes navigate the last mile home while his brain cruised along at a mile a minute, turning over and examining puzzle pieces to see how they fit.

✳✳✳

A few minutes later, in his home office, Jimmy did something he should have done a few days ago—and *would* have—but the discovery of two John Epps a hundred and forty years apart had distracted him. He typed in the name Charlotte Epps and let the computer do the heavy lifting.

In less than half a second, he had over a million results ranging from obituaries to Facebook profiles to Twitter accounts, LinkedIn accounts, images, and even TikTok videos. He scrolled down the list and finally found the information he hoped to find. Ancestry.com had recently updated its databases. Coupled with Charlotte's name and some guesswork about their wedding, the genealogy website provided what he was looking for and more.

Charlotte Epps was born Charlotte Evans in West Virginia in 1973. Robert and Cynthia Evans, her parents, had moved to Iowa when she was a toddler. She had grown up in the middle of the state in Marshalltown, Iowa, where she graduated from high school before going to Coe College in Cedar Rapids.

While in Cedar Rapids, her path crossed with that of John Epps, a pre-med student at the University of Iowa in Iowa City, just a half-hour south of Cedar Rapids. Epps graduated a year before Charlotte, and they were married in the summer of 1994.

In the fall of 94, John moved into the next phase of his education, continuing his studies at the University of Iowa to become a doctor. Charlotte graduated in the spring of 1995, and that fall, she took a teaching position in West Branch, just a few miles east of Iowa City on I80.

Three years later, John Epps was *Dr.* John Epps. He had often said that after twelve years of elementary and high school, doctors have to start over in kindergarten, facing twelve more years of school and laborious study. John was lucky enough to stay in Iowa City for his four years of residency, finally becoming a full-fledged doctor when he was thirty.

Midwest winters had rubbed the shine off the young couple, and they began looking for a warmer place for the next chapter of their lives. One of John's former classmates contacted him about the Southeast Georgia Health System in Brunswick, GA, an hour south of Savannah on the coast. It had opened a new program at the Brunswick Port, the International Seafarer's Center's medical program. Designed to take care of merchant mariners – most from other countries – who otherwise have little or no access to medical care, the program would be an extension of the medical center and a much-needed service for the crews of container ships berthing in Brunswick. John applied to the hospital, highlighting his interest in the new program and his desire to use his skills to aid those traveling on the enormous ships.

In his cover letter, Dr. Epps quoted John Masefield's poem, Sea-Fever, a poem Epps had studied once in high school and had never forgotten. It stirred something deep within the Iowa boy, something he had never had the opportunity to experience in his landlocked home state. Eschewing the typical quote, "all I ask is a tall ship and a star to steer her by," Dr. Epps chose the final verse of the 1916 poem.

I must go down to the seas again,
to the vagrant gypsy life,

To the gull's way and the whale's way
where the wind's like a whetted knife;

And all I ask is a merry yarn
from a laughing fellow-rover,

And quiet sleep and a sweet dream
when the long trick's over.

(John Masefield, 1916)

Dr. Epps and his wife, Charlotte, moved to Brunswick in 2003, where he served on staff at the hospital and in private practice with several associates. Seven years after relocating, the couple purchased a home on Jekyll Island, loving its proximity to the beach and the endless expanse of the ocean.

Six years later, Dr. John Epps disappeared.

Six years after that, Jimmy Favreaux found him.

***

Jimmy called Pepé back. "Hey, dude, Sorry for hanging up so abruptly. It's just that I realized I missed something, and I needed to get it done. It's important to the case. Both cases, actually."

"Both cases? You mean mine and yours? How's that?"

"I'm not a hundred percent sure yet, but I think Dr. Epps gave in to his wanderlust and then wrote it in a journal or log, and it grew into a book as he kept writing through the years."

"I think you lost me," Pepé said.

"Okay," Jimmy replied. "Let me try again. Dr. Epps came to southeast Georgia back in 2003, in part to work at the hospital but also to work with an International Seafarer's Center medical program that the Southeast Georgia Medical Center started in 2002. The International Seafarer's Center – the ISC – was established in 1982, and they're still there, in old downtown Brunswick on Newcastle Street. One of the many things they try to provide to the crews of these container ships is access to health care."

"So?" Pepé asked. "How does that tie in?"

"I think – and this is just me talking here – but I think Dr. Epps spent a lot of time helping out the crews from the ships. I think that he became so enamored with their stories of the sea, tales of the exotic ports, and the slower pace that he abandoned ship, so to speak, and joined the people he was helping. I think Epps got tired of the day-to-day medical grind at the hospital and his private practice. I think he went to the dock and somehow talked his way onto a ship. Dr. Epps knew enough about cooking, and coupled with his medical skills, he convinced them to take him on. Maybe he offered to make that first trip for free, earning his passage. You know, 'I'll work the first trip for free, and we'll both see if we like it.' I don't know. Whatever way he did it, he got on a ship as the main cook, but his medical skills are the real reason they kept him on, I would guess."

"And then he caught COVID in 2021 and died," Pepé added. "He walked out on his wife six years ago, but when he died last year, there was no returning anymore."

"He wanted to," Jimmy said quietly.

"What? Why do you say that?" Pepé asked. "He walked out without saying anything, and she never heard a peep out of him during those six years. What makes you think he wanted to come back?"

"In the original manuscript – not the rewrite Mcintosh commissioned from Metz – the main character packs his ditty bag at the end. He's going to see if his wife will take him back. If she does, he's done with the sea. If she doesn't take him back, he'll return to his cabin on the ship and never leave again."

"He says that in the book?" Pepé asked.

"He does, man. He was going to try and make a go of it with his wife again, but I think he got sick and never made it home."

"Well, that really sucks."

"Tell me about it, Pepé. But I haven't told you the main reason I think the book's author is our missing doctor," Jimmy said to his partner.

Pepé was silent. He knew Jimmy was secretly dying to tell him, so he just waited until Jimmy couldn't stand it anymore.

"You ready?" Jimmy asked.

"Still," Pepé replied.

"What was the name of the guy the Port Authority said died in 2021 while in port?"

"Christopher Evans. So?"

"In the book, the main character's name is Chris. And I know you don't believe in coincidences, so let me tell you another one. I looked up the information on Dr. Epps and his wife, going back to Iowa and their wedding and college days, and everything I could find. Any guesses what her maiden name was? Go ahead and guess."

"Jimmy, just tell me," Pepé answered, sounding a little tired of playing question-and-answer games.

"Charlotte *Evans*. In the book, the main character's name is Chris, and he's in love with a woman named Lottie Evans, short for Charlotte. Lottie – Charlotte – is the woman he left behind when he went down to the sea to ride the gigantic ships. And the name of the man who died of COVID in port last year? Christopher Evans. He chose her last name. I think he wanted someone to figure it out if anything serious ever happened to him."

Jimmy let the silence linger on the phone. He knew his partner – the ex-cop – was weighing everything Jimmy had told him. He was assembling his own version of the puzzle the case had dropped in his lap.

Pepé took a big breath on the other end of the phone. Jimmy knew he was going to summarize things to make sure he had it straight.

"Christopher Evans, white male, about fifty, died of COVID last year on board a container ship while in port at Brunswick. Evans was actually Dr. John Epps, last seen in 2016 when he left home for work and never showed up or left a goodbye note or any other communication with anyone. But while at sea, he wrote a book about his experiences. After Epps died from COVID in 2021, Trevor Mcintosh somehow came into possession of that same manuscript. Then Mcintosh paid a freelancer – Oscar Metz – to change it. And that's the manuscript you were chasing at the beginning of all this, isn't it? Did I miss anything?"

"The only question I haven't answered yet is how Mcintosh came to possess the manuscript for *Where the Ocean Swallows the Moon*."

"Good work, Jimmy. Let me know when you figure it out."

Jimmy said goodbye, then tipped backward in his La-Z-Boy until fully reclined. He was apparently not as refreshed as he thought by his sleep the night before because, in a few minutes, the room was filled with the loud snores of a man deep in sleep.

The rest of the afternoon was taken up by a well-deserved visit with the Sandman.

After his long nap, Jimmy spent part of the evening reading *Where the Ocean Swallows the Moon* by Dr. John Epps (with modifications by Oscar Metz). After a quick supper, he decided to pursue the backstory of John Epps, the one they were being paid to investigate.

Jimmy had already collected enough information on Epps from his school days up until he disappeared six years ago. Now Jimmy wanted to put his curiosity to rest about a connection with the John Epps from 1881.

Using what he knew about Charlotte Epps, he carefully sifted the marriage records and digital newspaper clippings. Jimmy found John Epps's parents: Daniel Epps and Annie Martin. Daniel was born in 1950 and died in 2014. Daniel's father had been Harold Epps, and his grandfather was Clarence

Epps. Another click brought up Clarence's father, and Jimmy stopped and stared at the screen. The name he read was Christopher Columbus Epps – the oldest son of Dr. John Epps, the part-time barber and part-time doctor who was killed in broad daylight in Des Moines in 1881.

The John Epps who was murdered in 1881 was the great-great-great-grandfather of the John Epps from Jekyll Island. One was killed by a .32-caliber bullet sent airborne at close range, while the other was killed by an airborne germ. Jimmy sat back in his chair. He had connected the dots and the Epps, so to speak.

Jimmy sat and let his mind idle for a bit. He pushed the mouse around aimlessly, then accidentally clicked on the ancestry link for Clarence Epps. It opened his profile, and on the side of the page was a suggestion for findagrave.com. Jimmy clicked it without really thinking.

It showed the gravestone of Clarence C. Epps and a picture of his obituary. Under survivors, the obit included five grandchildren, seventeen great-grandchildren, and one great-great-grandchild. That was John Epps, born in 1972 and died in 2021 after going missing for five years.

Although Epps was no longer missing, Jimmy wasn't sure if his passing was mourned. He would check into that tomorrow.

He put his computer to sleep and then went to do the same with himself.

Chapter 20

THE FOLLOWING MORNING, JIMMY THOUGHT of another question he didn't have the answer to yet, but he knew who might: Hillary and Wendi Lyst. Jimmy already knew Mcintosh wasn't going to get the prize money; that was certain. But whether Oscar Metz would get it was another matter.

The hitch was that *Where the Ocean Swallows the Moon*—the original, not the rewrite—was still a better book than Metz's entry, *Three Devils and an Angel.* The question in everyone's minds at Lyst Publishing was not whether Oscar should get the first-place prize but whether he should get a prize at all, based on his complicity in manufacturing a plagiarized book.

Jimmy could make a case for letting Oscar keep his award since his own book was original and better than the other entries, save for the winner. His illicit editing of Epps's book did not impact the production of his own manuscript. If the Lysts decided to rescind his runner-up prize *and* the grand prize, they would either need to choose two new winners or declare the whole thing a crapshoot, which Jimmy was pretty sure wouldn't fly with anyone.

The good thing is, he thought, *I don't have to make those decisions.*

A half-hour later, Jimmy was parking in his *private* spot in front of Staples in Fernandina. Two minutes later, he was tapping on the door to Lyst Publishing as he opened it. The door was open; good sign number one. As he stepped in, the woman with her back to him turned around and smiled broadly at him: Wendi. Good sign number two.

"Hey, good lookin'. What's cookin'?" Jimmy adlibbed as he entered the office. A corny line, but he had heard his dad say it to his mother for so many years that it was the first thing that came to his mind when talking with an attractive woman.

His upbeat mood dipped slightly as he remembered: an *unavailable* attractive woman. But then he decided that particular issue would not ruin his day.

He realized Wendi was blushing. "Hey, what's up?" Jimmy asked.

"What do you mean?" she replied, answering a question with a question.

"I mean, you're either blushing, or you were out in the sun yesterday."

"Neither," she answered, but Jimmy thought she looked flustered. "I … was just … running an errand and just got back before you came in. That's probably what it is."

"If you say so," Jimmy responded. Inside he was a little confused. Wendi's face hadn't reddened until he dropped the corny line on her desk. Usually, *she* was the one doing the overt flirting.

"Did you need to see Mr. Lyst?" Wendi asked. She wasn't making solid eye contact. And, yes, Jimmy was sure she was blushing, maybe even more now than before. *This is new!*

"Um, yeah. I do. Is he in?" Jimmy answered.

"He is. Go on in. Just give a little knock first."

Jimmy walked past Wendi's desk to Mr. Lyst's door, the portal to the boss's inner sanctum. He rapped once with a knuckle, but not a cop knock.

"Come."

Jimmy opened the door. Hillary Lyst was in his usual white shirt, sleeves rolled to the elbows. He stood up as Jimmy came in, reaching a hand toward him to shake hands with the private investigator. Jimmy didn't know if Lyst was wearing the same black slacks as the day before or just another pair from a closet filled with black slacks. The two men shook hands, and Jimmy sat in the right-hand chair. Even though Wendi was not joining them, this was Jimmy's assigned seat.

"What delightful update do you bring today, Mr. Favreaux? I'm sorry. I meant *Jimmy.*" The older man smiled at Jimmy, his eyes peering over his glasses to meet Jimmy's.

"I have some good news, and I have some questions. Let me spread the good cheer around first. We figured out who the actual author of *Where the Ocean Swallows the Moon* is."

"Do tell!" Lyst said gleefully, and Jimmy thought the publisher might applaud audibly at the news.

"His name was Dr. John Epps."

"Was? He's expired?" Lyst's eyebrows furrowed, and his mouth frowned.

"Unfortunately," Jimmy replied. "He passed away from COVID last year. As I'm sure you've gathered from reading the book, he spent the five years prior to his death as a crew member on a container ship, traveling around the world. The book was autobiographical, like we thought, recounting his experiences at sea. I think he finished it shortly before succumbing to COVID. Had Dr. Epps lived, the story might have had a completely different ending."

"How terrible," Lyst said, shaking his head. "Such a horrid disease, so completely arbitrary in who it attacks and who it takes from us."

Jimmy nodded in agreement, then continued. "I have more information about Dr. Epps, but I thought I'd see if you could answer a few questions first if that's alright with you."

"Perfectly fine, Jimmy," Lyst replied.

"You recall that Metz asked me if he would be allowed to keep his runner-up status and award."

"I do."

"And, have you come to a decision?" Jimmy asked.

"I have. I have decided to let Oscar keep his runner-up status, but I have decided to withhold the cash premium. We'll handle publishing his book, but there'll be no additional monetary award. If his book sells well, he'll receive the compensation he deserves. Does that seem fair to you?"

Jimmy nodded. "Fair? Yes. Adequate? That's another question. It's not my money, but I think Metz did you a favor by rewriting the book."

Hillary Lyst sat forward, took his glasses from his eyes, placed one elbow upon his desk, and balanced his chin on top of his fist as though holding his head up to keep Jimmy squarely in his line of sight. A completely random notion entered Jimmy's brain: Lyst looked like he was posing for a high school yearbook picture. Jimmy shoved away the thought.

Mr. Lyst stared at Jimmy for a long moment, then uttered one word: "Explain."

In for a penny … Jimmy thought.

"If Oscar had not rewritten the book for Mcintosh," Jimmy began, "none of this excitement or confusion would have occurred. Trevor would still have entered the original manuscript as his own, you would have declared him the winner, paid his prize money, published his book, sold the movie rights, made some money for your company, and all without knowing Mcintosh was a complete fraud. Thanks to Oscar's hand in the matter, you now know the truth, inadvertent though it may be. My question is: what's the truth worth to you?"

Jimmy sat back in his chair, steepled his fingers, and tried to keep his external appearance calm. He wasn't a good poker player, and going up against a client was not his strong suit.

"So, Jimmy, are you suggesting we give him the *entire* runner-up prize or a portion as a *reward*?"

"His work on a project for a 'client' didn't impact his writing in his own story, *Three Devils and an Angel*, did it? He said it was something he had been working on for a while but had never published, so all he did was finish it, polish it up, and enter it in your contest. Whatever freelance work he did at the same time has no bearing on the quality of *his* story. Does it?"

Lyst put his glasses back on and sat back in his chair, sighing as he did. "No, I suppose not."

"And no one knew Mcintosh's story was not really his until after he had been declared the winner, correct? And then only because of the kerfuffle with the Three Mouseketeers and their greed."

"Point conceded," Lyst grumbled.

Feeling like he was on a roll, Jimmy continued to press his case for Metz. "You had already declared Trevor the winner. The fraud wasn't discovered until after the book was stolen and the fake copy recovered. If Mcintosh had just left well enough alone, no one would have been the wiser. You awarded Trevor the prize based on the original copy you had seen, *not* on the copy Metz produced for him. So, you really can't penalize Oscar without taking on some of the blame yourself."

"How do they say it in the movies? You're 'pushing it,' Jimmy," Mr. Lyst responded to Jimmy's continued pressing.

Jimmy was trying to read the man seated across the desk. He had known Lyst less than a week, but he felt like he understood the publisher's desire to do the right thing. The older man was a stickler for propriety and correctness.

"So …?" Jimmy tossed the word out like a fly-fisherman casting into a pool of still water, waiting to see if he would catch a big, speckled trout lying just beneath the surface.

"Fine," Lyst declared, picking up a manilla envelope and setting it on the right corner of his desk. "Metz gets his prize as originally established." Jimmy could see the name METZ written across the front of the envelope in big, black letters.

Lyst leaned forward and pointed one finger at Jimmy. "But we are not giving Mcintosh a single penny. I'm researching ways to deal with him legally. He foisted a fraud upon me – us! – and I will not allow him to escape retribution." He lowered his arm and holstered his finger. Jimmy relaxed a few notches, but Lyst wasn't done yet.

"The legal repercussions from committing plagiarism can be considerable," he continued. "Copyright laws are absolute. One cannot use another person's material without citation and reference. What Mcintosh did goes significantly beyond that. Some plagiarism may also be deemed a criminal offense with prison time as a consequence. The defamed author of a work so besmirched has the right to sue the plagiarist."

Jimmy sat up and asked, "Or their estate if the author has passed away?"

"Absolutely! Beneficiaries have the right to sue for loss of royalties and income from the theft of intellectual property."

"Um, I have a hypothetical question for you, Profes— um, Mr. Lyst. If I were able to produce the widowed spouse of the true author of *Where the Ocean Swallows the Moon*, would they be able to claim the prize for the book? I mean, if they were interested in pursuing that?" Jimmy was working on the idea as he spoke, winging it.

"Hypothetically speaking," Lyst answered, "the estate of the rightful and true author of the manuscript could make a case for the receipt of the premium despite not personally or even knowingly entering the manuscript into the competition. Or, in layman's terms: yes."

Jimmy sat back and stroked his chin, letting the publisher's words percolate through his mind.

Lyst spoke again. "Perhaps before I give away the store, as it were, I should inquire into the identity of the proper author of the book in question, this Dr. John Epps."

"You should," Jimmy said, "but I can't give you any details right this minute." He rose from the chair and opened the door to leave Lyst's office. "I promise I'll pull together all the loose ends very soon and reveal the finished product."

Jimmy walked through Lyst's ersatz lobby. Wendi was standing next to her desk and turned as Jimmy walked toward the exit. His path brought him face-to-face with her, usually one of her favorite ways of making *him* uncomfortable. This time, Jimmy took her right hand in his left, put his right arm around her waist, did a couple of quick steps, and twirled her as he passed her. Wendi leaned against her desk, one hand near her throat, her other hand resting on the desk for stability. Whistling to himself, Jimmy walked down the hall and out into the Florida sunshine.

***

The first thing Jimmy did after getting into his SUV was call Pepé. After giving his partner an update on their cases—which had now become a single case with multiple tentacles like a jellyfish, Jimmy asked, "What's Mrs. Epps's financial situation?"

Pepé replied, "She's not destitute if that's what you're asking, but she's not rich, either."

"Could she use fifty thousand dollars?"

"*I* could use fifty large, Jimmy. *You* could use that much money, too. What are you trying to do, *hermano*?" Pepé asked. Before Jimmy could respond, Pepé answered his own question. "You're trying to be the white knight who saves the maiden, aren't you? You still think every case and every story can have a happy ending."

Glad that his partner couldn't see his frown, Jimmy said, "I'm just trying to do what's right. Her husband wrote this book, and a cash prize goes with it."

"Have you forgotten why I was hired in the first place?" Pepé asked. "She wanted him *declared dead*. Most people who do that are trying to get on with their lives."

"Do you remember the question I asked when we started this case, Pepé?" Jimmy replied. "I asked you, 'If we find out he's alive, does his wife want him back? And if not, does she want him dead?' It turns out he *is* dead, but my question now is, would she have taken him back if he was still alive? Would she want the money or her husband? Did she want us to find him dead, or did she want him alive again?"

Pepé sighed. "What do you want me to do, Jimmy?"

"I think we have to go out to Charlotte Epps's place on Jekyll and let her know we found John. I'd like to go along because I want to see her reaction. I want to know if she still loves him like he still loved her during the six years he was gone. Like he still loved her right before he died. If she does, I say we *tell* her about the prize money. If she's only trying to get clear of her marriage to hook up with someone else ... well, I guess Hillary Lyst will have more in the pot for another contest next year. How does that sit with you, Pepé?"

Pepé answered, "So if she would rather have her husband back than money, we give her the *money*? And if she would rather have money than her husband, we *don't* tell her about his book or the prize money?" Jimmy could see Pepé in his mind as they talked, visualizing his face as he worked through Jimmy's suggestions. He would have enjoyed the look when Pepé gave in to Jimmy's persuasion.

Pepé sighed again. Jimmy smiled.

"Where are you, man?" Pepé asked.

"On my way to meet you. I was down in Fernandina. I'll meet you at Taco Bell's drive-thru in Kingsland for a quick lunch on the way?"

"And you're buying!" Pepé added.

"Yes, I am. I love gigs where expenses are included. They're few and far between. See you soon."

Chapter 21

JIMMY MADE GOOD TIME, BUT Pepé was already parked in the lot at Taco Bell, leaning against his pickup's front bumper. Jimmy pulled up next to him, and Pepé jumped in the passenger door. Jimmy drove up to the drive-thru's speaker, and they placed their order.

Within a few minutes, they were on their way up I95, cruising at 78 miles per hour, a little over the speed limit but still getting passed occasionally. In only twenty minutes, they took the off-ramp for Jekyll Island at exit 29.

"I need to ask you for a favor, Pepé," Jimmy said as they turned onto the six-and-a-half-mile-long Jekyll Island Causeway. They'd be on the island in under ten minutes, and then it would take another ten minutes at residential speeds to arrive at the Epps's home.

His tummy now filled with Mexican fare, Pepé was amenable to suggestions. "Wattchu need, mi amigo?" he asked, still in Mexican mode, even though he was half Puerto Rican, not Mexican.

"When we get done visiting the good Mrs. Epps, how about you accompany me to break the news to Trevor that he's fifty grand lighter today than yesterday?"

"Ouch! That's going to leave a mark. But … heck, yeah! You know I love to disappoint people who try to take shortcuts. I learned that years ago as a cop in Charleston!" Pepé filled the vehicle with his raucous laughter.

Jimmy joined in the laughter but was sincerely glad to have Pepé along for the confrontation he expected with Trevor. Pepé *and* his Smith and Wesson, that is. Jimmy had no idea if Trevor would try to kill the messenger, but Jimmy wasn't taking chances. Losing fifty thousand would definitely "leave a mark," as Pepé said. He reminded Jimmy that people had killed other people for far less money. Jimmy was right to be cautious with an unknown factor like Trevor.

A few minutes later, Jimmy pulled up to a nice but modest two-story house, its exterior made of tabby, a centuries-old building material made primarily with oyster shells. Composed of equal parts lime, water, sand, oyster shells, and wood ash – tabby is a simple concrete with oyster shells for strength and decoration. Structures from the 1500s made with tabby still stand along the Georgia and Florida coasts and barrier islands.

This was not Pepé's first visit to the house. He led the way up the driveway and rang the bell without waiting for Jimmy. Jimmy had nearly caught up with his partner when he heard Pepé greet their hostess. Jimmy couldn't see her yet, but he noticed she had the same Ring doorbell he had – the one that captured Gabriel's attack in living color for the police. Pepé waved to Jimmy to hurry up and held the door open for Jimmy to join them inside.

Mrs. Epps was about fifty, like her husband. Jimmy knew from his research on them that she was a year younger than John – she wouldn't cross the fifty benchmark until sometime in 2023. She wore jeans and a patterned tee shirt, and her feet were adorned with sandals. Like Lottie Evans in the book, Charlotte Epps had raven hair and dark brown eyes. However, the hair was lightened somewhat by the sun and salt or the natural aging process. Like the house's exterior, the living room inside was nice but not ostentatious. Jimmy assumed the furniture was all purchased while John lived there and worked at the hospital. He wondered how well she was getting along without his income.

Pepé and Mrs. Epps – Lottie, she said, when Pepé introduced her to Jimmy – chatted about the weather and the neighborhood she lived in, and Jimmy heard a quick mention of the Bulldogs. It sounded like Mrs. Epps had high hopes for the Dawg's chances for another national title this year.

"Go, Dawgs," Pepé agreed. Jimmy smiled and nodded.

Both men declined any beverages, and the trio settled into the couch and chairs in the living room. Once everyone had found a seat, there was silence for an uncomfortable period, no one anxious to deal with the news about to be revealed.

Pepé cleared his throat and started. "I wanted to come up today and speak with you in person, Mrs. Epps. My partner,

Jimmy, has uncovered information about your husband and his whereabouts for the past six years."

Jimmy heard Lottie inhale quickly, not quite a full-fledged gasp, but his partner's news had caught her off guard, even though that was the reason for hiring Pepé. It only took Charlotte a few seconds to get over her initial surprise.

"Where is he?" she asked. "Is he alive? Do I want to know? How did you find him? Is he nearby? I'm sorry," she paused. She took a deep breath in and tried to calm herself. "I'm sorry to ask so many questions at once. Tell me what you found. But please answer one question first: is my husband still alive?"

Jimmy was glad to have Pepé there. Although Jimmy had performed the distasteful chore of telling someone their loved one was dead, he had done so only twice. He felt he had done a poor job of it both times. No matter how often you see someone else deliver the news, whether in real life or on tv cop shows, it isn't the same as doing it yourself. Pepé made eye contact with Jimmy for the briefest of seconds and gave him a nearly imperceptible nod.

Pepé looked Mrs. Epps directly in the eye and said in an even voice, "I'm sorry to be the one to tell you that John has passed away."

This time, her intake of air was much closer to a gasp. Lottie reached for a tissue from the box on the side table.

"C-could you tell w-when or did someone know?" she asked, stumbling slightly over the question.

Jimmy answered, "It was last year. He died as a result of COVID-19. He was onboard a ship at the Brunswick Port

Authority. He had been a crew member since disappearing in 2016."

Charlotte Epps let out a sudden, short wail and buried her face in her hands, the tissue pressed tightly to her eyes. Her sobs seemed to be coming from the core of her being, Jimmy thought. Lottie cried for a minute or two before saying, "H-he was so close to home. If I had only known …."

Pepé tried to console her, saying, "It was his choice, Mrs. Epps. Leaving was his choice, and staying away was his choice. I'm very sorry for your loss, Charlotte."

She cried softly for a moment longer. Sitting on the couch but feeling useless, Jimmy screwed up his courage and asked, "Did your husband do much writing?"

Mrs. Epps sniffled, trying to get her emotions under control. "He used to keep a journal when he was younger. It helped him unpack the stress of school, his internship, and the unbelievable load that medical school and private practice put on a doctor. But a few years before he disappeared, he quit journaling. I tried encouraging him to take it up again, but he said he didn't have time."

Jimmy thought carefully about his next words, then asked, "Would it make you feel better to know he had started writing again?" Lottie stared at him as an array of emotions washed over her.

"No. Yes. I don't know. Maybe." She sniffed again and took a deeper breath. "Was he writing again?"

"The entire time he was working on the container ship. And your name is scattered throughout his journal. He repeatedly mentioned how much he wished you could have seen the things he had witnessed in far-off, foreign ports."

"Do you have it, his journal?" she asked hungrily. "Is it possible for me to have it? I would *dearly* love to read it, to feel close to him again. I know it can't bring him back, but I could see what he saw through the words he wrote."

Jimmy caught his partner's eye and saw Pepé lift his chin, a subtle nod of agreement. "Better," Jimmy told the grieving widow.

He explained about the manuscript's discovery and being entered in the contest, leaving out the part about Trevor trying to rewrite it so he could pass it off as his own.

"It's going to be published?" Charlotte asked, surprised at the revelation.

"Professionally edited, designed, printed, bound, and available for you and the rest of the world to read. And, if the publisher does his job well, it could even be made into a motion picture. You might have to think about who you want to play you on the big screen."

"Oh, my ..." she responded, taken aback by the sudden possibilities.

"There's, uh, one more thing that goes along with it," Jimmy finished. "There's a fifty-thousand dollar prize. As the wife of the deceased author, it belongs to you."

"Oh, my ..." she said again, her dark eyes filling with tears. "If only John were here to share it with me."

Pepé nodded at Jimmy and gave him a wink and a brief but sincere smile.

✳✳✳

It was another fifteen minutes before Jimmy and Pepé left. Jimmy had asked Mrs. Epps if she had any of John's journals from previous years, and it had taken her a few minutes to find one. Jimmy had brought it along to give to Hillary Lyst to compare with the autobiographical writing in Epps's novel about his years on a container ship.

The two investigators were headed to the island's north end to pay a visit to Trevor Mcintosh. Neither man expected it to be a very social call, and both imagined Mcintosh's reaction to their news would be less than sociable. That was half of the reason Jimmy had invited Pepé. The other portion was that Trevor Mcintosh was an unknown factor. No one could know for sure what his reaction to the message might be.

Despite Mcintosh's soft, doughy exterior, Jimmy knew that native Southerners often maintained ready access to firearms, especially in their homes, similar Jimmy thought, to the woods and forests of northern Minnesota and southern Canada. People who relied on the land to help provide food were keenly familiar with weapons and their use. Years of hunting with firearms could cause them to act quickly to fill their hands with protection.

Jimmy was taking no chances. Pepé carried his reliable .38 caliber Smith and Wesson revolver, identical to his service revolver from his years on the Charleston police force in the mid-70s, nearly fifty years ago.

Jimmy had asked Pepé once why he chose the revolver with its six shots over a newer Glock 9-millimeter with a standard fifteen-shot magazine. Pepé had responded, "If I can hit them with my .38, I don't need all those other bullets. And after all these years, I know I can hit what I'm aiming at. I'm too old to break in a new gun or a new wife. I like what I have." Pepé liked the familiar heft of his weapon and the extra punch the larger caliber gave him. His proclamation that he liked what he had for a weapon and a wife was about as close as he got to public declarations of love. Jimmy smiled at the unexpected glimpse at Pepé's soft side.

Jimmy turned off the paved road and onto the sandy dirt path that led to Trevor Mcintosh's ramshackle home. He couldn't see any changes around the "family manse" since he had been there last. The lawn chairs under the carport were in the same positions, and still rusty. Jimmy stopped just past the end of the house rather than directly in front.

The duo dismounted from the car and crept quietly toward Trevor's house. Pepé stayed to the left when they got close to the house, and Jimmy prepared to try the front door. Pepé was positioned in an advantageous place where he could simultaneously see the front and back of the house. He gave a sign to Jimmy, who stepped up to the door and gave a sharp, cop-like knock: authoritative and impossible to ignore if you were inside. Jimmy called out in his best law enforcement tone, "Trevor Mcintosh! Open the door! Do *not* make me ask twice!"

Jimmy stepped back from the door and slid over to his left. If the door opened and a shotgun or rifle barrel emerged, the gun owner would need to open the door all the way to aim at Jimmy, providing precious time to either run or drop to the ground.

Jimmy snuck a glance at his partner. For some reason, Buffalo Springfield's song, *For What It's Worth,* was running through Jimmy's head.

> *There's something happening here*
> *But what it is ain't exactly clear;*
> *There's a man with a gun over there*
> *Telling me I got to beware;*

Jimmy was aware that Mcintosh could be dangerous, but he hoped his initial assessment was correct: Trevor was too lazy to get into an altercation and too afraid of going to prison or dying to start a shootout. But there was always the potential for mischief.

Jimmy and Pepé were there to tell him he was no longer the winner of fifty thousand dollars, a message they were sure would not be greeted with smiles, hugs, and tea cakes. Jimmy hoped the afternoon visit would end peacefully, but he couldn't be sure.

The 60s song intruded on his thoughts again.

> *There's battle lines being drawn;*
> *Nobody's right if everybody's wrong.*

In his peripheral vision, Jimmy saw Pepé assume a crouch, Smith and Wesson in hand. He must have seen something or heard movement in the house, but Jimmy's brain was too focused on the earworm to have heard anything inside.

It's time we stop
Hey, what's that sound?
Everybody look, what's going down?

Jimmy forced himself to focus on the present situation, hearing the footsteps in the house and the movement of curtains. His body was prepping for fight or flight, and he felt the adrenaline release into his bloodstream. He wished he had used the restroom before coming out here. But he wasn't a Neanderthal; he was a thinker. He decided to use his mind.

"Trevor!" Jimmy shouted, not moving from his spot to the left of the front door that was hopefully out of harm's way. "This is Jimmy Favreaux. I was here a few days ago to talk to you about your new book—Where the Ocean Swallows the Moon."

No reply from inside.

"Trevor! I'd really like to have a conversation with you, but I don't like hollering through a door to do it. C'mon out, and we'll sit under the carport again, like the other day."

Nothing was coming from inside the house since the initial footsteps and curtain movement. For some unknown reason, Jimmy recalled how he once convinced a skunk accidentally jailed in a live trap to leave by kicking the trap.

The skunk had accidentally walked into the trap set for another critter, lured by the smell of apple slices and peanut butter attractively arranged on a bed of lettuce. The skunk was in no hurry to depart its cell because … well, peanut butter, apple slices, and lettuce were in the trap, and none were outside. Holding a blanket in front of his body, Jimmy had walked over to the miniature prison, pulled open the spring-activated door, and gave the trap a good wallop with his foot. The skunk came waddling out as fast as his little legs would go, seeking refuge in the trees rather than pausing to spray Jimmy.

> *What a field day for the heat;*
> *A thousand people in the street*
> *Singing songs and carrying signs;*
> *Mostly say, 'Hooray for our side.'*

Jimmy looked at Pepé briefly and held up a fist to indicate Pepé should hold his position.

At least, that's what Jimmy hoped the raised fist meant.

He had seen it done in multiple movies with soldiers on covert ops. The whole squad stops whenever someone raises a fist in movie situations. He hoped it didn't mean to take a deep breath and start shooting.

Luckily, Pepé nodded and gave Jimmy an OK symbol with his fingers. Jimmy was familiar with that one.

Jimmy stepped closer to the house, still to the left of the front door, and flattened himself against the wall. Raising one hand high above his head, he paused briefly before slamming the hand down against the siding, producing a loud BAM as his hand connected. He repeated the action two more times, then hollered, "Trevor! I mean it! Get your butt out here now! We need to talk to you!" He paused two seconds, then slammed his hand against the siding three times in quick succession.

"Okay, okay!" came a voice from within the house. Jimmy heard a few more muffled steps, like a person walking on carpet, and then the front door opened a crack. Jimmy held his breath and waited. He hoped his hunch was right about Mcintosh being too lazy and timid to attempt a shootout à la Butch Cassidy and the Sundance Kid. If Jimmy was wrong, he was the only party-goer out of costume. Bad.

As the door opened a little more, Jimmy also hoped he'd been right about the potential for a rifle or shotgun as Mcintosh's weapon of choice. A long barrel couldn't maneuver around the door and quickly catch Jimmy against the siding, but a pistol, on the other hand, could easily be poked out and turned in Jimmy's direction. But neither style of weapon appeared from within. Just the head of Trevor Mcintosh.

He stepped out on the front step and looked to his left toward the carport, then back to his right, fixing his sight on Jimmy for a brief second before reorienting on Pepé. A look of alarm passed over Trevor's features, and he ducked back behind the relative safety of the door.

"Who's that?" he yelled to Jimmy.

"That's my friend, Pepé. He and I work together sometimes. He used to be a cop up in Charleston. And he knows how to use that gun he's holding, Trevor, so I hope we won't have any trouble today."

"Okay, okay," Mcintosh said. He didn't immediately show his head outside again. Trevor's brief exodus outside had revealed beard stubble a few days longer, hair a little stringier, and the same clothes from their first encounter several days before.

"Come on, Trevor. Get out here," Jimmy reiterated. He gave the house a single thump with his hand to express his impatience.

"I'm coming!" Mcintosh whined. Jimmy wanted to get a look inside the house. He was reasonably sure Mcintosh had just put down a weapon of some variety inside the door.

Paranoia strikes deep,
Into your life it will creep
It starts when you're always afraid
Step out of line,
The men come and take you away.

Trevor stepped outside and closed the door behind him.

Jimmy walked toward him.

As Jimmy came up the steps, Mcintosh extended a hand like they were best buddies, and he wanted to shake. Jimmy grabbed Trevor's elbow and guided him down the short steps and over to the carport. Jimmy gave him a little push toward the lawn chairs. Trevor chose one where he could see Pepé, but Jimmy had no qualms about turning his back on his partner. He knew Pepé was vigilant. He heard Pepé sit on the front steps.

Jimmy focused his attention on the scruffy man sitting across from him. Trevor's white pants were as dirty as the last time Jimmy had been here, suspenders still hanging loose, and his wife-beater t-shirt had more food stains down the front. Jimmy hoped the breeze would blow in his favor and carry the man's odor away.

"Trevor, I'm going to lay it out neatly for you. I've already spent more time here at your house than I wanted to, so I'm going to skip the niceties and get right to the point."

Mcintosh's hands were in his lap, and his head hung down like he was examining his cuticles. He raised his head and started to speak but stopped almost as soon as he began.

"What?" Jimmy asked curtly.

"I was just going to ask if you had a cigarette, but I remembered you told me the other day that you don't smoke." Trevor paused, then tilted his head at Pepé. "Does he? Smoke, I mean?"

"No. He thinks it's a dirty, smelly habit, just like me."

Trevor's head lowered again.

Jimmy's usual nature was not to act the bully, the bad cop in the good-cop, bad-cop scenarios. He glanced around the alleged author's yard. He noticed the sunshine on the saw palmettos growing around the bases of some of the tall, straight long-leaf pines that stretched to the sky overhead. With all the pine straw and the sand, there was no chance for grass to ever take hold here.

He wished he was back at Mrs. Epps's house, sitting on the back patio, enjoying fresh coffee, and listening to her tell about her missing – now dead – husband. Instead, he pulled his focus back into the moment. Time to turn up the heat on Trevor Mcintosh.

"You lied to me, Trevor. You lied to Mr. Lyst, and you lied to Wendi—the pretty lady who drove here—and you lied to Metz. Did you know that Metz is in the hospital in

Jacksonville because three thugs tried to beat him into telling them where he had hidden the original manuscript?"

Mcintosh's head hung a little lower.

"And you lied to yourself, Trevor. You told yourself you were a writer, but you can't write anything now – if you ever could. You're living in the past, although if you ask me, you're probably recreating the past."

Trevor tilted his head slightly and gave Jimmy a mock-quizzical look.

"I think you did something similar with Growing Up Southern, Trevor. I think you either stole someone else's book or bought it from someone because you can't write a story, let alone a novel. That's true, isn't it, Trevor?"

Mcintosh squirmed in his lawn chair, the aluminum frame creaking.

"Here's what I want to know, Trevor. Are you listening to me?"

Trevor's head tilted slightly again in response. Good enough, Jimmy thought.

"Where did you get the manuscript you gave Lyst Publishing? We know you didn't write it. Metz told me that when I saw him in the hospital. I knew it as soon as I read the first page. There is no way that a man who wears the same clothes for a week or more at a time and bums cigarettes and alcohol from strangers could write about the adventures John Epps had on that container ship for those five years."

"Who?" Trevor stirred and looked at Jimmy. "What name did you say?"

"John Epps. Doctor John Epps."

"He told me his name was Chris."

"Excuse me. What?!"

"I kinda met him once last year in a bar downtown. He said his name was Chris. I was having a drink with a friend when this Chris came in. I guess he knew my friend, so he sat with us. He bought a pitcher of beer, which was good because I had a powerful thirst that night. I had been fighting a fever for a couple of days, and I thought maybe I could burn it out from the inside if I could get some alcohol. So that's what I was doing, trying to drown my fever."

"Trevor," Jimmy said, trying to remain calm, "did you get tested for COVID before you went to the bar?"

Trevor lowered his eyes and began to pick at a stain on his shirt. He shook his head.

"Have you had any vaccinations for COVID?"

Trevor shook his head again.

"How long did you sit with 'Chris' that night?"

"Um … until they threw us out at closing."

Jimmy rolled his eyes. He asked another question, one to which he was pretty sure he knew the answer. "How long after that night did you get the manuscript from your friend?"

"M-maybe two weeks?" Trevor answered with a questioning tone. He wanted to answer the right way so Jimmy wouldn't be mad.

"Two weeks? Maybe a little more or a little less?

"Y-yeah, I guess."

Trevor had likely given Chris Evans – John Epps – COVID, and it had taken his life. Not in broad daylight on a Des Moines street but in a dirty dive bar in Brunswick, GA, after midnight.

In Jimmy's mind, it was an admission that Trevor had essentially stolen the manuscript and tried to pass it off as his own. Mcintosh had never even read it. Someone else had and gave Trevor a synopsis. Mcintosh just turned it in as his own.

Jimmy glanced at Pepé, who smiled and nodded. Pepé holstered his revolver and was about to stand when Jimmy gave a quick head shake. Pepé eased back on the step and waited.

"Chris was the name he used on the ship, but his real name was Dr. John Epps. What I want to know, Trevor, is, why did you kill him for the manuscript?"

Chapter 22

TREVOR HAD RISEN SO QUICKLY from the rusty lawn chair it had tipped over behind him. "What? NO!"

"Sit down, Trevor. Tell me more about how you came into possession of that manuscript. Remember, Pepé used to be a police officer in Charleston, and he worked in Navy security after that. He doesn't take kindly to liars, thieves, killers, or people who make him do extra work."

Pepé had to stifle a laugh and quickly look away. Jimmy managed to stay in character, though, channeling a county sheriff.

"C'mon, Trevor. Pick up your chair, sit down, and tell me how you ended up with the story."

"Okay, okay. I'm telling you the truth, though. I just want to make sure you know that." Trevor was sniveling.

"Tell me the truth, Trevor, because I'll know if you lie. The truth has a way of ringing true when you hear it. Lies are dull, like hitting a lead pipe against a stump. Truth sounds clear and beautiful, like windchimes in a light breeze. Let me hear the windchimes, Trevor."

Mcintosh had picked up his chair and resettled himself in it. He had his hands on the knees of his dirty trousers.

"Okay," Trevor started. "This is the God's-honest truth. The guy I went out with that night – the one who works at the port – he told me that Chris had died. A-and he had to help take care of removing the body and talking with the police and everything, you know?"

"I know, Trevor. Keep going. I want to know how you got the manuscript," Jimmy replied gruffly, trying to keep Trevor on edge. Pepé was also interested in hearing the story since the dead man was the subject of his case, even though the main point had been discovering whether Epps was dead or alive.

"Okay, I know, I *know*! I'm getting there," Mcintosh whined at the two investigators. "My friend came out to see me and brought this box with him. I was hoping it had Cuban cigars inside, but it was just paper. It was the manuscript. He said he had kept it when they cleaned out the dead guy's cabin on the ship. Nobody else wanted it, and this guy thought I might want to look at it since I, you know, have a book."

Jimmy snorted. "If you don't tell me the complete truth, Trevor, I'm going to look into whether or not you actually wrote the first book."

Trevor ran a hand through his stringy, greasy hair, pushing it off his forehead. "I *am* telling you the truth. My friend gave me the manuscript. I read it a little, anyway, and decided I could try and get it published. People are always asking me when I'm going to write another book. And the dead guy – Epps, you said? – Dr. Epps didn't need the manuscript anymore. It wasn't going to do him any good, and it could do me a whole heap of good."

Mcintosh looked up at Jimmy, who circled his finger in the air, the sign for "keep going." Trevor kept talking.

"I heard from my old agent about this contest and the prize and everything. I hadn't heard from my literary agent in years. I didn't even know she was still alive, to be honest. I guess it was just the right place at the right time, you know?"

"No, Trevor. It was the wrong place at the wrong time. Did it ever occur to you that Dr. Epps might have a family somewhere?"

Trevor hung his head again, his whiskered chin nearly resting on his chest. Without raising his head, he asked, "Did he?"

"Yes, Trevor. He has a wife who lives right here on Jekyll Island. She hasn't seen him in six years."

"Well, I couldn't have known that! You can't blame me for what he did! I never met him or saw him or nothing!"

"I'm not blaming you for what Dr. Epps did, Trevor. I'm blaming you for trying to take credit for writing something you didn't. It's bad enough that you did it at all, but it's worse because you won and kept your mouth shut, lying to people so they would think you wrote the book. The truth came out, Trevor, but not because *you* told it."

"I told it now, though," Mcintosh said, sounding like he was on the verge of crying. "You believe me, don't you?"

"Oh, I believe you, Trevor. I don't think you're creative enough to come up with a believable lie on your own. When I came here the other day, and I wanted to see the typewriter, you told me it wasn't here. That was true because it was at Metz's house in Fernandina. But you said you pawned it, and that was a lie. That's when you started to get angry and wanted me to leave. Your little castles built on lies can't stand up to scrutiny, and you're not quick enough on your feet to talk your way out of it."

Trevor said nothing, glaring at Jimmy. His attitude had shifted from crying about being caught to anger over not getting any slack. *Too many years of feeling entitled.*

Jimmy was still scolding Mcintosh. "Now let me tell you what we came here to tell you: Lyst Publishing has disqualified you and rescinded the grand prize. There's no check with your name on it coming to you."

"I don't get the money?"

"No, you don't get the money. If you're lucky, Mr. Lyst won't sue you for fraud. He could still turn you over to the police since fraud is a crime."

Jimmy paused, debating whether to provoke Trevor even more, then chose the box marked 'YES; LET'S.'

"And, just so you know, the grand prize has been awarded to someone else," Jimmy added, not feeling sorry at all for taking delight in Trevor's misery.

"Not Metz, is it?" Mcintosh asked, a mixture of anger and disappointment in his voice to match the look on his face.

"No, it's not Oscar. He's luckier than you, though. Mr. Lyst agreed with me that Oscar did him a favor by changing the story. Mr. Lyst would have noticed when he began editing the manuscript, but you sped up the whole deal. No one would have noticed if you had simply turned in the original manuscript and left it at that. You'd have fifty thousand dollars in your bank account, a new book, renewed interest in *Growing Up Southern*, and a serious boost to your non-existent career. Instead, we're leaving."

Jimmy decided not to divulge Charlotte's name and connection to the prize. He turned away from Mcintosh and then turned back. "But before we go, I just want you to know that we're filing a report with the Glynn County Sheriff's Office about this, so they know what you did. We're not pressing charges *at this time*, but we can change that at any time if you make any trouble for Oscar, the Lysts, or *anyone* else connected to the book. Do you understand, Trevor?" Jimmy put his hands on his hips and waited to see if Mcintosh would answer.

Trevor glared at Jimmy, his normally pale face getting red and blotchy, but he said nothing.

"Glad to hear it, Trevor. That's the best thing you've ever come up with on your own: nothing." Jimmy took a step or two away and stretched his back. "Let's go, Pepé. We have to stop at the Sheriff's Office on the way back."

As Jimmy turned to leave, Mcintosh came out of his chair and tackled Jimmy, carrying them both to the sandy ground. Mcintosh landed on top of Jimmy, his heavier body keeping Jimmy pressed to the ground. The author reached into his back pocket and brought out a fillet knife, intending to gut Jimmy. But in the short span it had taken Trevor to tackle Jimmy and reach for the knife, Pepé had risen, drawn his .38, crossed the short span between them, and placed the gun barrel firmly in Mcintosh's ear.

"The choice is yours, maggot," was all that Pepé said, his voice colder and scarier than Jimmy had ever heard before.

Trevor went utterly still. It was like he was a string puppet, and the gun controlled the strings. Trevor rose, the gun barrel never breaking contact with his ear. Pepé relieved Mcintosh of the knife, and the author took a step back from the investigators.

Jimmy rose from the ground and brushed the sand and pine straw from his clothing. "Thanks, Pepé. I owe you," he said.

"Yes, you do," Pepé replied, keeping his eyes on Mcintosh.

The duo backed up to Jimmy's vehicle, Pepé watching Trevor while waiting for Jimmy to get in and start the SUV. Pepé holstered his weapon and got in. He rolled his window down.

Jimmy hollered out the open window at Mcintosh, "We'll let the Sheriff know you like to play with knives when we see him about the fraud, Trevor."

With that parting word, Jimmy pulled away from Trevor Mcintosh's dirty, ramshackle house. Looking in the rearview mirror, he saw Trevor sink to his knees in the sandy dirt under his carport, his shoulders rising and falling as he wailed over his loss.

✳✳✳

Jimmy called Wendi when they were on the causeway leaving Jekyll Island. He explained that he had met with Charlotte Epps and had decided to offer her the prize money. He asked her to tell Mr. Lyst that he had a previous journal to compare writing styles. He also mentioned briefly that he had explained the situation to Trevor Mcintosh.

"How did he take it?" Wendi asked.

"Like most anyone would," Jimmy replied. "He cried, cajoled, cussed, and tried to make a deal. When that failed, he tried to relieve me of my spleen."

"My God!" she answered. "Are you okay?"

"Fine as frog hair, like a friend of mine says. I made sure I brought protection with me." Jimmy winked at Pepé, who grinned and gave him a thumbs-up.

"I'm going to come down to the office after I drop my 'protection' off in Kingsland. Is that all right with you? I have to finalize some things with Hillary and report on my two meetings this afternoon on Jekyll."

"I'll be waiting to hear all about your adventures," she responded. Jimmy clicked off the call.

"She sounds nice," Pepé said after a moment.

"You don't know the half of it," Jimmy sighed. He turned on the radio to the oldies station. The sounds of Buffalo Springfield filled the cabin.

"You better stop
Children, what's that sound?
Everybody look, what's going down?"

As the two friends turned onto Highway 17 to get back on I95, Jimmy asked his friend, "You doing all right, Pepé?"

"Fine as frog hair," came the reply.

A few miles went by, the silence sharing space with classic oldies. Jimmy replayed the confrontation in his mind.

"Maggot?" Jimmy asked.

Pepé grinned. "That's what we used to call the disorderly guys in the 70s when I was a cop in Charleston."

"You didn't say, 'Go ahead, punk. Make my day?'"

Pepé shook his head. "Nah. That's only for movie cops. We were the real deal."

You still are, my friend; you still are, Jimmy said to himself.

Chapter 23

THERE WERE NO TRAFFIC JAMS on the way back to Kingsland, and Jimmy dropped Pepé off at Taco Bell. He noticed the former peace officer went inside the restaurant rather than to his car. Jimmy smiled knowingly.

It took Jimmy nearly an hour to arrive at his client's office in Fernandina. He made the mistake of opting for I95 and got tied up in a traffic snarl caused by an overturned semi. When he pulled into the lot in front of Staples, he was pleased to see his parking space was empty. He entered the building through the front door and walked down the hallway, which seemed to get shorter every time he visited.

He rapped on the door to the publishing company and opened the door. Wendi was away from her desk. He continued through her office, knocking lightly on Hillary Lyst's door.

"Come."

Lyst was alone in his office, which was fine, Jimmy thought to himself. He wouldn't be distracted by Wendi's presence as he and Mr. Lyst discussed the case and its likely conclusion. The two men exchanged the usual greetings, and Jimmy took his right-hand seat. Lyst asked him how things had gone with Charlotte Epps.

"It went as well as it possibly could have," Jimmy replied. "We were there to tell a woman her husband had died. In the end, she didn't want closure as much as she wanted her husband returned to her. I truly wished we could have provided that for her. She asked if she could get a copy of the manuscript before it was published, and I promised her that was doable. I hope I didn't overstep, Mr. Lyst."

Lyst waved away the potential slight as though he were shooing away a fly trying to get a snack from his desk.

"It will be advantageous for her to have a copy," Lyst responded. "She knows the author better than anyone and may have insights we might overlook. I thought I might prevail upon her to write a Foreword for the book and supply us with information for the About the Author page. Between you and I, Jimmy, I am quite pleased that Trevor Mcintosh didn't write the book. I would have absolutely *hated* putting a picture of him in the book as well as on advertising and marketing materials for the book."

Jimmy laughed at Lyst's comment. Jimmy had brought along the other journal sample Charlotte Epps had loaned him, and explained, "This is an example of Dr. Epps's previous writing. I thought it might be valuable to you for comparison's sake if nothing else. His widow said he used to journal regularly, especially in college and during his internship."

"Splendid! If she has enough, there may be a follow-up book based on his previous writings. As it is, I've already decided to split *Where the Ocean Swallows the Moon* into two volumes, possibly three."

Jimmy was pleased for Lyst Publishing and Mrs. Epps. The books would be a lasting legacy to her husband.

"There is one thing, though," Jimmy added. "Mrs. Epps intends to donate a portion of the royalties to the International Seafarers' Center in Brunswick. It was a primary reason they moved to Brunswick, and even though it may have been indirectly responsible for her husband abandoning her, it also held a special place in his heart."

"We'll work that out as we move forward, but I don't foresee any issue with that request," Mr. Lyst replied. "How did things turn out with Mr. Mcintosh?"

"Let's just say Trevor didn't take the news as graciously as Mrs. Epps did."

Lyst looked at Jimmy over his glasses and stroked his white goatee. "Hmm. No, I wouldn't suppose he did. Was there any trouble?"

"Nothing that I couldn't handle with the help of my business partner. It got a little dicey at the very end when Mcintosh realized it was all slipping away. His plan was held together with fragile threads, and we unraveled it, causing his whole scheme to fall apart. He wanted something for nothing, you know? Getting fortune and fame without doing the legwork."

"Indeed," Lyst replied.

Jimmy decided to skip over the part where Mcintosh tried to slice him into serving-sized portions, and Pepé was forced to convince him otherwise with his gun barrel.

Instead, Jimmy told Lyst, "We filed a report with the Sheriff's Office, but more as an FYI than a complaint. We told Trevor we would be doing so, and if he ever tried to cause trouble for you, Mrs. Epps, or anyone involved with the book, we'd change it from an FYI to a complaint."

"Excellent plan, Jimmy. I'm quite pleased you returned in only one piece, as well."

Jimmy's head snapped up at the phrase, and he knew that Wendi had shared the small portion of information about the altercation he had shared with her. Lyst smiled at him, gave him a conspiratorial wink, and slid his finger alongside his nose like Paul Newman in *The Sting*. Hillary Lyst leaned back in his chair, his hands clasped over his belly.

"Let's confirm I have all the details, shall we?" Lyst said, summarizing Jimmy's report. "Trevor is out, purely and simply. He tried to foist Dr. Epps's manuscript on us as his own. The manuscript wins on its own merits, with the prize money going to Dr. Epps's widow, Charlotte Epps, with the possibility for a benevolent royalty donation in the future. Oscar Metz remains the runner-up, and his book wins on its own merits since, without *your* convincing argument, he would have been disqualified along with Mcintosh. Metz retains the prize money at your behest since it was through him that we became aware of the attempt to pass off *Where the Ocean Swallows the Moon* as Mcintosh's work. Is that how you understand the results, Jimmy?"

Jimmy nodded and added, "Yes, Metz saved your company from significant embarrassment, don't you agree?"

"Indeed, we would have become the laughing stock of the publishing world when it became clear that Mcintosh could never have written the manuscript. And it would most certainly have been discovered; it's just a question of when," Lyst continued. "As to your fee, the quoted amount for your services was ten thousand, plus expenses, if I recall correctly."

"We can just call it ten thousand," Jimmy replied, trying to appear magnanimous. "There weren't that many expenses— a few trips up and down I95 to Jekyll, a few trips to your office, a few meals, a bag of frozen peas for a bruised cheekbone, and a trip to Jacksonville to see Metz in the hospital."

Lyst raised his eyebrows. "Didn't you keep your receipts, Jimmy?"

"I, um, did," Jimmy stammered, "but I don't have them with me or totaled up. If you insist, I'll put it all together with mileage and submit it tomorrow or the next day at the latest."

"Calm down, Jimmy. Just ballpark it for me."

Jimmy pulled out his phone, tapped the screen a few times, swiped it a few more, tapped again, and announced, "$350 should cover the mileage and meals."

"I'll have Wendi cut you a check tomorrow for ten thousand, three-hundred and fifty dollars if that's acceptable with you."

"Or the day after if you need."

"I'm sure tomorrow will be adequate." Lyst swiveled in his chair, turned his attention to his computer screen, and once again, Jimmy knew their meeting was concluded.

Stepping out into the front office where Wendi's desk was, Jimmy felt disappointed to discover it vacant. He strolled to the door, looked around briefly, then walked down the hallway and out to his car. He had enjoyed being a part of their world for the short time the door had swung open for him. However, the case's conclusion would resolve the issue of the appealing—*but unavailable*—Mrs. Lyst.

Tomorrow would be another day and possibly another case, Jimmy thought to himself as he began his drive home.

∗∗∗

Once at home, Jimmy turned his attention to the matter that had distracted him at the beginning of the case: the first Dr. John Epps – the one murdered in broad daylight in 1881 in Des Moines, Iowa.

A few days before, all Jimmy had for the killer were the initials F.W. However, while Jimmy was unearthing information about Dr. John Epps from Jekyll Island, ancestry.com had filled in the blanks about Dr. John Epps from Des Moines. Jimmy opened his Ancestry account and examined the clues Ancestry had uncovered about the antiquated murder case. He saw that "F.W." stood for Fountain Watkins. Fountain Watkins George killed Dr. John Epps.

George's personal testimony at his 1882 trial revealed that he killed Epps because they were both sweet on a young girl, then only eighteen years old. George said Dr. Epps was going to perform an abortion on the girl, and he – George – had promised the girl's father that he would protect her as she had only recently arrived in the big city of Des Moines.

George told Epps he would kill him if he tried to go into the boarding house and meet with the girl. George was good to his word, and as Epps attempted to enter the boarding house, George shot him in the back. Epps fell where he had been shot, and George ran over and shot him a second time, this one in the heart at point-blank range. Multiple witnesses on the street corroborated the testimony, and George was found guilty and sentenced to death.

At age 35, Fountain, a first-time offender, was committed to the Iowa State Penitentiary for murder in the first degree on May 16, 1882. His original sentence was to be hung, but the sentence was commuted to life on August 10, 1883. George died in the prison hospital on May 31, 1887, and was buried in the prison cemetery on June 2, 1887. His case had been appealed to the Iowa Supreme Court, but George died before the court could hear his case.

Fountain W. George had removed his competition for a young girl's affection using a .32-caliber pistol. He acted impulsively, not planning his actions or escape, and paid for his impulsivity with imprisonment and, eventually, death.

Nearly a century and a half later, Trevor Mcintosh opted to take the easy way to the top, claiming someone else's work as his own. He also acted impulsively, but at least his victim was already beyond caring. Mcintosh's unofficial sentence included imprisonment in a trashy little house and a continued decline into obscurity.

∗∗∗

As Jimmy finished indulging his penchant for chasing rabbits and wild geese on Ancestry, his phone rang. His iPhone screen displayed

no number

Jimmy hit the little green phone icon on the screen to accept the call.

"This is Jimmy Favreaux."

"Good evening, Mr. Favreaux. Or can I call you Jimmy? I feel like we're already acquainted."

The voice was electronically disguised, just like the one that Mr. Lyst had heard. Even though Jimmy knew anyone with a cellphone could download an app and do the same thing, it was still creepy. Normal, average people didn't disguise their voices.

"Sure. Call me Jimmy. But tell me how we're acquainted? I know you spoke to my client, but you and I have never crossed paths. At least, not that I'm aware of." Jimmy sat back in his desk chair in his home office, but he was anything but relaxed. Something about a disguised voice set his nerves on edge. Too much tv and movies, probably.

"It's true that you and I have never directly crossed paths, Jimmy, but you have encountered several of my associates. Therefore, I feel I know you to a degree."

The app the caller was using had an algorithm that made the s's extra sibilant, causing extra hisses. Crossssed pathssss. Sssseveral assssosssiatessss. Jimmy got a mental picture of a lizard man, a reptilian humanoid such as on Dr. Who and other sci-fi shows.

"Ah. You're talking about the goon squad who tossed my place and Oscar Metz's trailer, not to mention the star pupil in your class: Gabriel," Jimmy replied to the disguised voice. "How's Gabriel doing, by the way?"

"Yes. Mr. Gabriel. I'm afraid he's not doing well. Not well at all. It seems he so regretted being apprehended multiple times recently and disappointing me in his engagements with you that he chose to retire. Permanently."

Jimmy sat straight up in his chair. He felt the hairs on his arms rise with his motion.

"G-gabriel's dead? How? He's in the lockup."

"Something to do with wrapping a blanket around his neck and securing the other end to the top bars of his cell. My understanding is he stood on his bed and jumped off, like doing a cannonball. He had made the blanket length short enough that it was sufficient to snap his neck. I understand it happened on a shift change when deputies and jailers were coming and going and no one was paying close attention to the cells."

Jimmy had never meant for Gabriel to be subjected to anything like this when he tricked him at Mickey's and their other two encounters. He had a sick feeling in his stomach. *It's not your fault*, he told himself. *Gabriel didn't kill himself. He had help from someone.*

"Are you still there, Jimmy?"

Jimmy swallowed. "Yeah. I'm here."

"I thought you should also know that Mr. Mcintosh has been, how shall we say, *disciplined* for his failure to hold up his end of a bargain."

"What?! Did you kill him, too, you sadistic—"

"Calm yourself, Jimmy. He's still alive. He just received a visit from the Three Musketeers. The same associates who toured *your* house and visited Mr. Metz. I'm afraid those boys get a little carried away in their zeal for their work sometimes. But Mr. Mcintosh will continue to live his pathetic life, albeit with a considerable amount of arthritis in the future, I'd wager."

"How did you get my number?" Jimmy asked, at a loss for the right question at the moment.

"Oh, come now, Jimmy. Your webpage, Facebook, and business cards; do I need to go on? That's not the real question you wanted to ask, though, is it?"

Jimmy let the electronic silence between them swell. Even that was electronically disguised with hiss and background distortions.

"Who are you?" Jimmy finally asked, cracking the silent void.

"There you go. That's where a friendship starts, with the exchange of names, although friendship isn't quite the right word, is it? Either way, I'm sure you've heard my name before, a long time ago. My associates call me The Man, but you know me by another name. *Le Bonhomme Sept-Heures.*"

Jimmy took the phone away from his ear and stared at it. He knew the name, but it wasn't real. It was a term from his childhood. In French-Canadian, it means the Seven O'clock Man, a north-of-the-border version of the bogeyman. Kids who weren't home and inside before seven o'clock ran the risk of becoming Le Bonhomme Sept-Heures' next victim.

"And now that we've been properly introduced, Jimmy, I bid you adieu. I'm sure we'll cross paths again. I look forward to it. Bonsoir, Jimmy."

Jimmy continued to stare at his phone. The screen read,

CALL ENDED

Jimmy thought about what he remembered from his childhood about Le Bonhomme Sept-Heures. Legend said he was an old man with a big hat and big coat carrying a sack. When kids stayed out after dark – seven o'clock – the old man would catch them and put them in his sack. Some of Jimmy's friends said the man *ate* the kids he caught, while others said he kept them locked up underground forever.

Jimmy couldn't help himself. He typed the phrase "le bonhomme sept-heures" into Google, which returned a half million hits. Dozens and dozens of children's books carried the title. Kids were the exact audience you wouldn't want reading something like that. Wonderful scripts for nightmares.

Chapter 24

THE CREEPY ATMOSPHERE FROM THE phone call the night before had mostly dissipated, but Jimmy could still sense its lingering presence. It had rattled him. Jimmy told himself it was kids' stuff and to forget it. Someone must have come across his Canadian roots and was using that for kicks. A healthy dose of normalcy and routine should dispel the malevolence he still felt in the air, so Jimmy was drinking his morning coffee and looking at the headlines on his computer.

An incoming text stirred his phone to life. It was from Wendi.

> I have a check for you

Jimmy texted back,

> Can you mail it or hold it for a few days?

Her response arrived quickly.

> I would prefer you pick it up today. I have something to ask you. In person.

Jimmy had no idea what that could be about. She probably just wanted to make him uncomfortable one more time. In retrospect, he *had* felt disappointed that she wasn't at her desk when he left the day before. If nothing else, he wanted to thank her for all her help and wish her well. He texted back.

I'll be there in an hour, ok?

Wendi's reply came quickly.

Looking forward to seeing you. Thank you.

Jimmy jumped through the shower in near record time, shaved carefully, applied some cologne, dressed, and joined the traffic on 17 and A1A to Fernandina Beach.

✳✳✳

Jimmy parked in his place in front of Staples. To the left, he saw Peterbrook Chocolatiers but decided it was too early for gelato or chocolate popcorn. He hadn't had lunch yet, and his breakfast had consisted of coffee. Just coffee.

He checked his watch before walking down the hall to the Lyst's office. Nearly an hour had elapsed since Wendi's text. He was right on time.

He gave a light double-tap knock as he opened the door to the office and walked in. Wendi was at her desk and looked up when he knocked. She wore a charcoal grey skirt and a light blue button-up blouse with frills down the front. *She looks good in blue,* Jimmy thought. *She'd even look good with nothing on.* He immediately felt his face grow hot. *That's not what I meant!* He was just glad she wasn't a mind reader.

Wendi stood to greet him, extending a hand, saying, "Good morning, Jimmy. I want to congratulate you on a job well done. Speaking of well done, were you out in the sun yesterday? Your face seems a bit pink."

He felt his face deepen in its red hue.

"Yeah, um ..." he said. "We were outside most of the time we were up on Jekyll. I must have gotten some sun."

He realized he was still holding her hand. She cleared her throat, and he released her hand, wishing there was a chair to sit on or a hole to fall into and pull the dirt over himself.

"I, uh ..." he mumbled and stopped. He had no idea what he thought he was going to say. He looked down at Wendi's desk while he stood there. He opened his mouth, but nothing came out. It was like being thirteen again. He forced himself to look up at Wendi, only to find that she was also looking down at the desk. She looked up at last, and he saw that her face was also a light shade of pink. She looked almost as flustered as he felt. *What the ...?*

She moved away, stepping behind her desk and opening a drawer. "I have your check. Ten thousand, two hundred and fifty, correct?"

"*Three* hundred fifty," he replied. "But it's no big deal. I told your ... um, *Mr.* Lyst yesterday that I didn't really care about the expenses. It's not like I had to fly down to Miami, rent a car, and stay in a hotel for a week while I tracked somebody down."

Wendi was looking at a yellow post-it note. "No, I see that it's my fault. I misread his note. I'll write you a new check.

It'll only take a minute," she said, sitting back at her computer and bringing up her accounting software.

Jimmy stood in front of her desk, painfully aware of his awkwardness. He watched her type the numbers and his name into the check-writing program on her computer, watching her hands as she did. Her nails were smooth and shiny, a light silvery color, complementing the skirt and blouse. Suddenly, she stood up. Jimmy looked at her, confused.

"I'm just going to go to the back and get the check off the printer," she said and walked quickly away. It was less than a minute before she strode back, handing Jimmy the check. He glanced at it and handed it back.

"What?" she asked, looking at the check. "The date's right, the amount correct, and your name is spelled right, too, isn't it? F-A-V-R-E-A-U-X."

"But your name isn't," Jimmy answered.

"My name?"

"It's not signed," Jimmy said with a smile.

She sat at her desk, signed the check, and handed it to him again. "Better, Mr. Smarty-pants?" she asked.

"Yeah. The bank is funny that way. They prefer checks that are signed. Now, what did you want to ask me about? You said it had to be in person."

"Well, uh, … Jimmy. You know it's Thanksgiving in just a couple of weeks. You've never mentioned any family, and I was wondering if you might like to have Thanksgiving dinner with me—I mean *us*. Thanksgiving dinner with *us*—Hillary and me."

Jimmy realized he hadn't paid much attention to the calendar. He usually got a rotisserie chicken from Publix the day before or ordered a pizza. He could count on one hand the number of times he had shared a Thanksgiving meal with someone since moving to the First Coast. As a single, unattached guy, holidays didn't carry the importance they did for people with close family or family-like friends.

"Only if you let me bring something," he replied.

"That would be fine—" she started.

"—and only if it can be store-bought if I don't have time to make something homemade," he added, leaving himself an escape.

Wendi laughed. "That's fine, too, Jimmy."

"And let's see – Thanksgiving is on a Thursday, right? The 24th?"

"Yes," she replied. "Oh, that's right. You're from Canada originally, right? Do they do Thanksgiving in Canada?"

"We do, but it's the second Monday in October."

"So, we already missed it?"

"Yeah, but I did, too, so this will make up for it."

"Is it like American Thanksgiving?"

"It is, but without the Pilgrims and Native Americans," he laughed, and she did, too. "We have the same foods – turkey, corn, mashed potatoes, green beans, pumpkin pie. I think Canada appropriated it from America because they were jealous of the food." She laughed again. Jimmy loved hearing her laugh.

He finished his discourse on Thanksgiving, saying, "In Canada, it's the last chance some people get to go out and close up their lake cabin for winter, so that's part of it. It's a nice three-day weekend."

"But no Black Friday?" Wendi asked.

"We are always happy to take advantage of Black Friday and Cyber Monday savings. They're simply not a part of our Thanksgiving. *Our Thanksgiving?* Listen to me. I've been an American citizen for over a decade, but I still think of myself as Canadian sometimes. I suppose it's time to embrace the holidays, right?"

Wendi laughed again, then said, "It'll be at my house at 1 p.m."

It was as if the world suddenly stopped spinning. Jimmy looked at Wendi and said, "*Your* house?"

Wendi's face turned bright red this time. There was no mistaking her embarrassment. She quickly walked around her desk, took his arm, and led him to the door. "Yes, my house. I'll text you the address later. I have a lot of work to do today, Jimmy. Thank you again for your help with our situation." She opened the door to the hallway and practically shoved him out.

What the …? Jimmy thought. He stood in the hallway for a few seconds, deciding if he should go back inside and demand an explanation or wait for her to reveal things in her own time. He chose to give her some space and bring him in on her secret when she was ready.

***

At home again, his bank accounts fat and happy, Jimmy realized he had not done his due diligence adequately on the Lysts when they hired him. He had done a cursory search on the business and a brief fact-finding exploration of Hillary Lyst. It wasn't Jimmy's custom to do a run-down of all the employees in a company, and Wendi had told him from the outset that she was Mr. Lyst's personal secretary.

Jimmy tried to recall what Hillary Lyst had said about his wife and son.

> *"I had a child, a son. Charles Jefferson. He was born five years before I started this publishing company. He would be forty-three now. I lost him three years ago. He was killed in a collision with a semi on I95 on a rainy night. He was returning home and hydroplaned on the road, crossing three lanes and the center median before the semi-truck broadsided his vehicle. He was killed instantly. As was his mother."*

Jimmy's fingers flashed across the keyboard's keys, entering the pertinent details. In less than a half-second, he had the information about the crash. It happened in 2019. *"… three years ago,"* Mr. Lyst had said.

The local stories about the crash all said essentially the same thing. Charles Lyst had lost control of his car and hydroplaned, ending up in the oncoming lanes where a semi had been unable to avoid colliding with Lyst's car. Both persons in Lyst's car were killed in the wreck. The semi-driver was absolved of any responsibility.

Jimmy leaned back in his chair and stared at the screen, his eyes unfocused while his brain processed the possibilities. Sitting forward, he clicked the keys again and waited while the screen refreshed to the home page of the Oxley-Heard Funeral Home in Fernandina. Jimmy found the archives and sorted the list of deaths, obituaries, and memorials by date and last name and quickly found the two he was searching for: the obituaries—the site called them Life Stories, not obituaries—for Charles Jefferson Lyst and his mother, Amanda Elizabeth Lyst, née Strickland.

Amanda Lyst's obituary included her vital statistics – when and where born and to whom; when married and children – only one, Charles Jefferson. Jimmy noticed that Hillary and Amanda Elizabeth – "*Elly as her friends called her*" – had been married for forty-five years. There was a lengthy write-up, but Jimmy skipped it for the time being. He was more interested in a list of facts.

Moving to Charles Jefferson Lyst's obituary, Jimmy took in the data as he read. Born in 1979 to Hillary and Amanda Elizabeth (Elly) Lyst. Graduated from Fernandina High School. Went to college in Gainesville – go Gators – and was employed with an accounting firm in Jacksonville. He married Wendi Carter in 2002. *What?* Jimmy scrolled through the other information until he came to the part that said, "Left to mourn his memory, his wife, Wendi (Carter) Lyst; his father, Hillary Lyst …" He stopped reading.

Jimmy sat back and pushed away from the desk, his chair rolling backward smoothly. Wendi had told him she was Hillary's wife. Hadn't she? When Jimmy first talked to her on the phone, he asked if she was his daughter, and she giggled and said no. He questioned if she was his sister, and she laughed again and answered negatively. She said she was "Mrs. Lyst."

When Jimmy first met with Hillary Lyst, Mr. Lyst asked him if Wendi had told him about their *relationship*. Jimmy replied that she had told him she was Mrs. Lyst. He remembered the older man had grinned when Jimmy said that. Not a lecherous grin but a private joke grin!

He had said, *"Allow me to put your mind at rest, Mr. Favreaux. She is. And she has been invaluable these past several years in helping me to recover from my grief."*

Wendi was indeed *Mrs. Lyst* but not Hillary's. She wasn't his daughter; she was his daughter-in-law!

Chapter 25

JIMMY HAD ALREADY PARKED IN front of Staples when Wendi arrived the following day. However, he hadn't parked in his usual spot, trying to remain unnoticed. For now. He had parked farther back in the lot, under some trees and close enough for him to walk to Starbucks to get some coffee while he waited for "Mrs. Lyst" to arrive.

He slowly and quietly exited his car when she walked toward their office's front door. Jimmy carefully closed the distance between them, and as she unlocked the door, he put his hand on hers.

She screamed, turned toward Jimmy, lifted the arm he was holding – knocking his hand away – and lashed out with adrenaline-stiffened fingers, punching Jimmy straight in his Adam's apple.

Jimmy immediately bent over, grasping at his throat with both hands. He couldn't make any sounds, nor could he get any air into his lungs.

"Jimmy!" Wendi was yelling at him. "What were you doing? You scared the holy crap out of me!"

Jimmy was still trying to breathe through his damaged throat. He felt sick to his stomach, and without a constant source of oxygen, he was starting to see black spots in front of his eyes. He backed up against the building and slid down into a sitting position with his knees bent.

"Oh … oh! Jimmy! I'm so sorry! I didn't mean to hurt you. Can you talk?"

Jimmy shook his head weakly.

"Can you breathe?"

He again shook his head.

"Oh, Jimmy! I'm so very sorry! Put your head down between your knees."

Jimmy followed her directions, but it wasn't helping. In fact, it was making it worse. The black spots were getting bigger, and then … everything went black.

***

Jimmy became aware of himself again and opened his eyes. He couldn't focus, but ... yes, *someone* had their face on his, their *mouth* on his, and they were breathing air into his lungs. He realized he tasted … *cinnamon?* Suddenly, he focused on an eyeball looking directly into his. The eye immediately moved back and away; the mouth, the breath, and the cinnamon moved away, too.

"Jimmy! Oh, my stars! Are you okay? You had me so scared! When you crumpled into a heap, I thought I had killed you. Can you breathe now?" Wendi was talking very loudly, very closely.

Is this what it's like to be reborn? Jimmy thought.

Jimmy tried to take a breath and found that he could get air into his lungs again. He took a couple of tiny breaths and then nodded his head. The ability to speak was still eluding him, however.

Jimmy draped his arms over his knees and sat, just breathing, against the wall while Wendi crouched in front of him, her hands on his arms. She was peering into his face, concern etched into her eyes and expression.

After another couple of tiny breaths, he whispered, "I think I'm okay."

Relief flooded across her features, only to be replaced immediately by anger.

"What were you thinking? Don't you know better than to surprise a woman in a parking lot? Especially a woman who has taken self-defense classes?"

Great! he thought. *I had to pick on a black belt!*

Jimmy held up a finger to indicate he wanted to say something. She stopped chastising him momentarily, and he crooked his finger in a come-closer gesture. He whispered, "I had no idea you could do that."

"Well, what idea *did* you have, smart guy?"

She turned to sit next to him against the wall. She pushed her hair back from her forehead and looked to the sky.

Jimmy continued breathing since that seemed like the most prudent thing to do. After a couple of minutes of silence, Wendi turned her head and looked at him.

"Your color is better," she said. "Can you breathe alright now?"

He nodded. They sat silently for another minute before he huskily said, "I know who you are."

She turned her face toward him again, her eyes looking deeply into his. He nodded.

She turned and looked straight ahead again, gazing out over the parking lot. People were beginning to walk by on their way to Staples and Publix, some carrying Starbucks coffee cups. None gave them a second glance. People were used to seeing homeless people seated by stores, panhandling.

"It's what I do," he said, trying unsuccessfully to clear his throat. "I find … people …" He took a breath.

"And places and things," she finished for him. "But you didn't search for information about me when you started the case, did you? Why not?"

"You weren't the boss, the client. You were just making the appointment for the boss. I looked up Hillary, but even then, it didn't occur to me to look back to check for traumas and big events in his past. I guess I was distracted. By you. Even before I met you in person," Jimmy said, his voice still gravelly.

"When did you find out?"

"I was clueless until you said the Thanksgiving dinner would be at *your* house. I went home and looked up the accident from three years ago and found the obituaries for Charles and Elly. Charles's obit said he married Wendi Carter in 2002."

It was Wendi's turn to respond with a simple nod.

"Seventeen years is a pretty good stretch in today's market," Jimmy rasped.

"It's a pretty good stretch in any market," Wendi replied. "Except it wasn't seventeen years. It was fifteen. We had simply grown apart and were separated for the last two years. We didn't have anything in common anymore, and – this sounds horrible, but – the divorce decree came a month after Charles died."

"But you kept the same last name?"

"I had everything connected to the business under that name, and it would have muddied the waters if I had changed. How would it have looked if I had changed my last name a month after Charles died? It could have hurt the company. And Hillary. He and I helped each other get through the shock and sorrow after the accident. This business is all he has left of his family. And me."

"So why did you tell me you were Mrs. Lyst? I mean, you are, kind of, but why did you tell me that? And why do you still wear your wedding ring?" Jimmy thought he knew the answer but wanted to hear it from Wendi.

"It keeps the riff-raff out," she said and laughed softly. "I had no idea if you were a jerk or a womanizer, so I used the Mrs. Lyst gambit. Hillary knows, and he's okay with the ruse. It's like a force field, a zone of protection. It would either stop you or it wouldn't, and if it didn't, I would take more drastic measures." She raised her hands in a classic karate pose.

"Like a punch to the throat?" Jimmy asked, lightly massaging his throat where her fingers had tried to perform a makeshift tracheotomy.

"Exactly," she said, laughing. She rose to her feet and reached a hand down to Jimmy. "Ready to try walking again?"

He took her hand and pulled himself to his feet. He stood for a moment to make sure everything still worked, then nodded, and she opened the door. They walked down the hallway to the office.

Wendi unlocked the inside door, stepped inside, and turned on the lights. Jimmy followed at her heels. He walked over to her desk and sat on the corner, still feeling his throat with his fingers, gently probing for potentially-chronic damage. Jimmy was pretty confident he'd live, but he knew he would never sneak up on a woman again unless it was in the line of duty and he was wearing a metal throat collar.

Wendi came over and stood in front of Jimmy. She extended a hand and asked, "Do you forgive me for protecting myself?"

He shook hands with her and laughed. "I do. It's also good to know that you *can* protect yourself."

Her hand lingered in his.

Suddenly, Jimmy dropped her hand, and both his hands went to his throat. He began making loud, gasping noises.

"What is it, Jimmy?" she asked quickly, her voice filled with concern.

He rasped out, "Can't breathe. Need more mouth-to-mouth."

Wendi's eyes opened wide, and she started to step back, but Jimmy caught her arm and twirled her around in a dance step, ending by folding her into his embrace. She didn't resist.

This time, Jimmy provided the mouth-to-mouth.

Epilogue

J IMMY DROVE BACK TO BRUNSWICK a week later, but alone this time. He parked in the parking lot at the Sunnyside Rest Home for the Elderly just off Fourth Street. Jimmy walked up and saw a few people sitting outside on the porch. He saw only two chairs for visitors, but they were occupied by residents, and the others sitting on the porch were all in wheelchairs, so it was a moot point. Jimmy mounted the steps, taking note of the long wheelchair ramp to the right that would have gotten him to the same place, just a little more slowly.

He said hello to the residents sitting on the porch, but most barely acknowledged his presence. One lady did, though, excitedly taking his hand and pulling him close. She looked intently into Jimmy's eyes and made some noises but no words. Jimmy patiently stood next to her for a moment, then patted her hand, freed himself gently, and went inside.

"I'm, uh, Jimmy Favreaux. I called ahead?" Jimmy told the nurse at the front desk. He wrinkled his nose involuntarily at the odor in the air.

"Yes, that's right," the nurse said. "You wanted to see Viola. She's just down the hall in room 242. Go right on. I'll poke my head in after a bit to see if you need anything."

"Thanks, uh, Carla," Jimmy replied, taking note of her nametag on the lanyard around her neck.

Jimmy walked down the hall, wondering if the building had always been a nursing home and how long it had been there. He pondered if they had ever changed the yellowish-tan wall color or the 1940s flooring made with little tile circles. The silence in the hallway made him reflexively think, *It's too quiet,* something a movie hero usually says right before all hell breaks loose.

But nothing broke loose. Jimmy could see into the rooms as he passed them; most held someone looking very old lying in a hospital bed, a few moaning softly. Some rooms' residents were sitting in their wheelchairs, some napping, and some sitting with their heads bowed, their foreheads resting on one hand as though deep in thought. Or sorrow. To Jimmy, it looked as though the weight of their thoughts—or sorrow—was too heavy for them to bear without some assistance.

The little black rectangular plate with white letters read "Room 242."

Jimmy had found Viola's room. His hand was automatically raised to knock, but the door was open, and the only thing to knock on was the plastered wall or the metal and concrete door frame, and he knew a knock would be ineffectual. So he walked in, hoping Viola was decent.

She was. She was sitting in a wheelchair near the bed, and as Jimmy entered the room, she turned to look at him.

"Yes?"

"Miss Viola?" Jimmy asked.

"Yes, I'm Viola," she answered. She was wearing a pastel-striped top, her hair curly and white—naturally curly, he would later find out from her—and she was wearing navy blue slacks and no shoes. It should have been no shock that she was shoeless because she was also footless. Both legs stopped at the knee. Jimmy couldn't help but think of Lieutenant Dan from *Forrest Gump*.

"Miss Viola, my name is Jimmy Favreaux. I was hoping to be able to speak with you for a little bit this afternoon and ask you some questions. Would that be all right?"

Miss Viola's eyes crinkled a little, the corners of her mouth rose slightly, and she asked, "Where are you from, child? I can tell you are not from around here."

Jimmy grinned, blushed a little, and answered, "I'm from up north, ma'am. I'm from Minnesota, but originally from Winnipeg, up in Canada."

"You are a long way from your people, Mr. Favreaux. What brings you all the way to Georgia and the Golden Isles?"

"Well, ma'am, these days, I live by the St. Marys River, just across the line in Florida on Highway 17." Jimmy paused to make sure she was hearing him well enough. Then he added, "But I got here as quick as I could ..."

Miss Viola smirked, then broke out into a big grin.

"So, you brought jokes, did you? That's good. I like jokes. Too many people in here never laugh. Nothing much for them to laugh about, I guess. Look at me. Did you ever see such a mess? I lost both my feet and the lower parts of my legs from the sugar diabetes." She pronounced it dy-uh-bee-tees. Now it was Jimmy's turn to smile.

"I don't think you're a mess, ma'am. And I love your hair. It makes me think of my mama's – so curly, white, and soft-looking."

"It's naturally curly," she said. "Always has been. Ever since I's a little girl, my hair has been curly. I tell you a secret." She motioned Jimmy to come closer. In a conspiratorial whisper, she said, "I've never had bangs. As soon as my hair touches my forehead, it jumps back and curls up on top." Jimmy snorted with laughter at the mental image of her hair recoiling from her forehead. He couldn't help it.

"Is there someplace I could sit?" he asked, looking around the spartan room.

"I reckon you could sit on my lap, but the nurse would probably shoo you out if you did. I reckon I could sit on *your* lap, but I know the nurse would shoo you out then!" Miss Viola laughed at her own joke, then she patted the bed.

"You go ahead and sit on the bed, Mr. Favreaux. I never use the bottom half of it anyway." And Jimmy laughed again as she poked fun at her disability.

"Please call me Jimmy," he said as he sat on the bed. "When someone calls me Mr. Favreaux, I think my daddy's here, and he's been dead for some time!" Although Jimmy had always called his father Dad, he used the more southern "daddy" for this conversation.

Miss Viola laughed at Jimmy's joke. He wasn't sure if it was genuine or just polite, but he enjoyed hearing her laugh. And she was right: the nursing home was too quiet. It needed some sounds of life.

"Well, if I's going to call you Jimmy, you need to call me Miss Viola and quit ma'aming me."

"Yes, ma'am, I mean Miss Viola," Jimmy responded, grinning as he did.

"Now, what did you want to talk to this old lady about, Jimmy?" Miss Viola asked.

"Just some questions," Jimmy replied. "Like, how long have you lived here?"

"In the nursing home or in Brunswick? Or are you just trying to find out how old I am? I can assure you that I am not a minor." She winked slyly at Jimmy.

Jimmy chuckled. "How long have you lived in or around Brunswick, Miss Viola?"

"All my life, Jimmy, which means eighty-seven years. I'll be eighty-eight in three months, so I am eighty-seven and three-quarters. Once you get over eighty-five, those partial years become important to reckonize. When you are a little child, they's important because you haven't had that many birthdays yet. And when you are as old as me, they's important because you don't know how many birthdays you'll be having!" And Miss Viola laughed at her homespun wisdom. Jimmy did, too.

"Were you married, Miss Viola?" Jimmy asked.

"I was," she answered. "Not for as long as I wanted, but for as long as the good Lord allowed. Twenty-two years, and then my Darrell died in an explosion."

Jimmy was surprised, and he was sure his face showed it.

"He was working at a munitions plant in Camden County, and one day, it just blowed up. Twenny-nine people was killed, including my Darrell." She paused and got quiet, looking down at her missing legs. Jimmy knew she referred to the Thiokol chemical plant explosion in 1971.

"I was left with my four-year-old boy to raise by myself. So I did. I did the best that I could. He never went hungry, never missed school—not on my account anyway—and always went to church. Do you know my son, Jimmy? His name is Trevor Mcintosh. He lives out on Jekyll Island. He had a book out once."

"Yes, ma'am … I mean, Miss Viola. I have met your son and talked with him several times. I know about the book, *Growing Up Southern*."

Miss Viola was nodding and smiling.

Jimmy took their discussion in a different direction. "When I first arrived, you said I was a long ways from my people. Where are your people from, Miss Viola?"

"Well, some of them are right here. My daddy's side has always lived in this area. Generations have lived here." Jimmy had seen the Mcintosh Sugar Mill tabby ruins near the Kings Bay Sub Base and the Mcintosh housing subdivision not far from it.

"And your mama's side?" Jimmy prompted.

"Like you, they come from up north, but that was long ago. My paw-paw came from up north, and if you can believe it, he actually fought in the War of Northern Aggression."

Jimmy mentally translated the term to "the Civil War." It was one of those things that hadn't entirely disappeared from the local dialect yet.

"He did?" Jimmy responded, sounding quite surprised.

"Yes, he did. He was born in 1848 and enlisted when he was sixteen in 1864. He had two uncles in the army, and one was killed. So, he felt it was his duty to replace the one who had fallen. He served with the Third Iowa Infantry."

"Iowa? That's a long way from Georgia," Jimmy said.

"I tol' you they were from up north. In July of 1864, the Third Iowa was rolled together with the Second Iowa, and they were part of Sherman's March to the Sea—from Atlanta to Savannah. By the time they got to Savannah, my paw-paw was tired of marching and fighting, and he decided to stay in Savannah rather than march up to Washington, DC. Once the rest of the Second Iowa was gone, he drifted further south, ending up here."

"And then …?" Jimmy asked, trying to keep her talking.

"He worked on some farms and later some boats. And then he met a girl and they got married in 1900. He was fifty-two years old—she was all of fifteen years old. He was old enough to be her paw-paw. I guess he had been too busy making up for the time when he was in the war and then trying to build a new life afterwards. Time just got away from him, I s'pose. But my mama was born in 1915, and she had me in 1935. My paw-paw died in 1927, eight years before I was born, so I never got to know him."

"Did your paw-paw ever write about his life here in Georgia? I mean, it was a big difference from Iowa," Jimmy prodded.

It was like a curtain had been drawn across the window on a sunny day. The smile went away, the spark of life, the laughter – all of it dried up in a flash.

"Who are you, Mr. Favreaux? Why are you pokin' around in ol' stories and ol' business that's none of yours?" Miss Viola snapped at Jimmy.

"Ma'am? Miss Viola? I'm still Jimmy. And I'm afraid that 'old business' you mentioned is my business. I'm a private investigator, and I work for a publishing house down in Fernandina. They held a contest, and Trevor almost won. I mean, he *did* win—a big prize, too—but they found out he had not really written the manuscript he turned in as his own. So, they had to take the prize away before ever even giving it to him."

Miss Viola's mouth was turned down in a harsh frown, and she turned her head away from Jimmy. He kept going.

"Like I said, I've met Trevor a couple of times and talked with him. That manuscript he tried to take credit for? It was written by a fellow who had been a doctor here in Brunswick for a while. Then this doctor fella decided he wanted to see the world, and he left the hospital and signed up on one of those big container ships that dock here in Brunswick. Well, he kept a journal of his travels on the boat, like a diary. Trevor ended up with the journal after the doctor died in 2021. That's the manuscript that Trevor turned in."

Miss Viola said nothing.

"I was just wondering, ma'am, if you might have an idea where Trevor would get the notion that turning in a manuscript like that as his own was a good idea? It wouldn't be because he had done it before and gotten away with it, was it?"

Miss Viola's bottom lip started to tremble. She lifted a hand to brush away a tear.

"That boy couldn't do anything, you know? He had no gumption, no ambition. He couldn't work at any of the plants here in Brunswick, and regular retail work didn't work for him neither. He was always mouthing off at the customers, so the stores always let him go."

It was Jimmy's turn to stay silent and let the absence of sound fill the room.

"I – I had found this old diary of my paw-paw's when I was young, and my me-maw didn't care if I read it. I had it in my room when my me-maw died, and no one ever asked about it, so I kept it in my closet. It just seemed like something that shouldn't get throwed out. When Trevor couldn't get any work, I finally gave the journal to him. I told him to type it up, give it a title, and we'd try to get it published. It worked."

She let her head hang down for a bit before she spoke again.

"I guess that's why he thought he could get away with it. Because he had before. And now people would be expecting him to write something again since it had been so long since the first book."

Jimmy put a hand on her shoulder. After a bit, she put her hand on his and patted it.

"How did that doctor die? The one who wrote the book?" Miss Viola looked and sounded all of her eighty-seven and three-quarters years.

"COVID." One word was all that was needed. Since the pandemic, everybody knew it could take anyone it chose.

"What was his name?" she asked.

"Epps. John Epps." Jimmy felt the old woman's shoulder stiffen under his hand, and she sat a little straighter.

"Did you say Epps?" she asked.

"Yes, ma'am. Dr. John Epps."

"My mama was an Epps. My paw-paw was an Epps. He was Alexander Epps. Alexander Hamilton Epps. I always thought that it was funny that they named him after one of our Founding Fathers. Like he had two last names." Miss Viola had relaxed a little. Jimmy wondered if she was feeling the lightening in her soul from finally admitting to a wrongdoing.

"Your paw-paw had a brother named Christopher Columbus Epps; did you know that?" Jimmy asked.

Miss Viola smiled a little and said, "That's even better than Alexander Hamilton Epps."

"It also means that Trevor and the doctor who died were distantly related, very distant cousins. It's too bad they didn't know that while the doctor was alive."

Jimmy decided that Miss Viola didn't need to know that John Epps's chance meeting with Trevor in a bar was likely how the doctor had contracted COVID. There was no way to prove it, so no need to say it.

As Jimmy stood up to leave, Miss Viola took his hand in hers and asked, "Will anything happen to Trevor because he didn't write his first book?"

"I don't think so, Miss Viola. It happened so long ago, and as it turns out, it's in the family, so I think it'll just stay between you and me. If that's all right with you."

She patted the hand she was holding. "That's all right with me," she said.

When Jimmy started to release her hand, she tightened her grip and said, "At least this way, my paw-paw's book got read by lots of people, right?"

"Yes, ma'am. It got read a lot," Jimmy answered.

Miss Viola continued to hold Jimmy's hand.

After a moment, he asked, "How would you like to go for a little ride around the nursing home, and maybe even get a little fresh air out on the porch, Miss Viola? The sun is shining, and the birds are singing."

She squeezed his hand and said, "I'd like that, Jimmy."

Loose Threads

THIS IS WHERE WE IDENTIFY fact from fiction and truth from the author's fertile imagination. It's okay. This is a fiction book. Stuff gets made up. But not everything, so read on.

The 1881 story of the death of Dr. John Epps is true. I knew about his murder long before I started writing this story. But when I decided to use his name here, it caused me to research the event again. And just like Jimmy, I discovered new information had been added to the story since last I looked. In particular, I uncovered the fate of his killer, F.W. George, who died while waiting for the Iowa State Supreme Court to hear his appeal.

Charlotte Temple Carter Evans was widowed in 1848 when her first-husband George Wesley Carter, died. John Epps and Charlotte married in 1850 and had a son named Christopher Columbus Epps in 1851. That's where I got the name Christopher Evans.

By 1877, she was married to a Swedish shoemaker, John Anderson, in Greene County, Iowa, sixty-six miles northwest of Des Moines. Perhaps her remarriage caused John Epps to list himself as a widower in the 1880 census. Perhaps he was saying, "she's dead to me."

George Carter and Charlotte had a son named William Elijah Carter. He was my great-great-grandfather – my grandmother's great-grandfather.

Records indicate Christopher Columbus Epps was somewhat of a womanizer, with five wives I have discovered and verified through census data and marriage records. Sometimes he was already married to a new wife before becoming disentangled from the previous one. It's too bad I used him up in this story. I could have woven him into another story somewhere! I'll sit him on a shelf for now.

Like Christopher Columbus Epps, his half-brother, William Elijah Carter, was married at least five times, possibly six, and wasn't always able to make it to the clerk of court to file papers of divorce before taking a new bride *(Genealogy is fun and enlightening!)*. The Carter and Epps children seemed to marry with unrestraint. But apples don't fall far from the tree …

Charlotte Temple Carter Evans Epps was married at least three times, possibly five. Although John Epps listed himself as a widower in the 1880 census, in reality, Charlotte lived until at least 1899, possibly later. Census records weren't as carefully recorded back then, and for some reason, my relatives had a bad habit of giving different birthdates and birthplaces in nearly every census. It makes creating a family tree much more challenging!

Another interesting point is that newspaper accounts of Dr. John Epps from 1881 refer to him as an Indian doctor. A little poking through the files explains that that does not mean he was a physician to the Native Americans. Many of the children and grandchildren of mixed race in that era were referred to as halfbreeds, Spaniards, or Indians, so a more likely explanation is that John Epps may have been of mixed-race parentage.

Family stories about John Epps's mother, Patsy Potts, said she was at least partially Black and may have been born a slave. The 1840 census from Tennessee lists the family as Free Colored People (if it is the same family). Patsy died in Tennessee before her husband, George Washington Epps, moved the family to Iowa. The 1880 census in Iowa lists them as white. Whether they were of mixed racial background is difficult to verify so many years later, but census and marriage records list the family members as white.

I have taken quite a few liberties with the genealogy of the Epps family. *But why not? They did!* There were a few brothers of John Epps who served during the Civil War, but not any of John's children.

The Georgia connection with the Epps family is completely made up, at least the one in this book. Also, unfortunately, the manuscript written by the fictitious Dr. Epps of Jekyll Island about going to sea is not real.

✳✳✳

Sadly, there is no small hallway and office space next to Staples in Fernandina. Lyst Publishing is a creation from the author's mind, but it will return in book number three. But happily, Peterbrook Chocolatiers is just a few doors down.

***

I stole the name of the character, Pepé, from my friend Robert (Pepé) Perez. I want to clarify that the book character, Pepé, is very loosely based on Real-Life (RL) Robert, but they are not the same. For one thing, RL Robert laughs easily, but it's not an embarrassing laugh. RL Robert is a former Charleston police officer and Navy Watch Commander, but he is not a private investigator. He is my go-to guy for real-life law enforcement and firearms questions. I only recently learned RL Robert was a certified sharpshooter, so don't be surprised if that shows up somehow in the future. RL Robert's wife, Karen, makes a cameo in this story, too, appearing as Gwynn. They are wonderful friends of this author and his wife.

***

The International Seafarers' Center (ISC) is real and was established in 1982 as a 501(C)(3) non-profit Christian organization. They have two locations in the Brunswick, GA, area – at 307 Newcastle Street and at Colonel's Island.

According to their website, "Commercial shipping is the most globalized industry in the world, and over 1.5 million seafarers deliver 90% of the world's goods so that we can live in ease and comfort. The seafarers come from all over the world.

The Port of Brunswick, GA, receives more than 16,000 seafarer visits annually, and the number is increasing. Seafarers have very little access to conveniences and comfort while at sea. Seafarers are apart from their families and friends at least 6-10 months a year. (During the pandemic, this has increased to as much as 18 months since seafarers are often not allowed to return home.). Common issues that seafarers face include fear of pirate attacks, unpaid wages, loneliness, maltreatment, lack of internet and phone access while at sea that inhibits their communication with loved ones and many more.

ISC centers are staffed by volunteers who are friendly faces in a strange place to make the seafarers feel more at home. The volunteers visit the ships, drive the vans, and staff the two centers, interacting with seafarers and port workers to be the hands of God when and where needed.

The ISC's Christmas-at-Sea program is a favorite of seafarers and volunteers alike. It began many years ago and grew out of a desire to bring a little Christmas cheer to the many seafarers who visit the Port of Brunswick during the holidays.

Seafarers are so far away from home and family that the ditty bags and shoeboxes have become the highlight of the season. The seafarers have often expressed how appreciative they are and how much the gifts mean to them."

To contact the ISC, email info@seafarerscenter.org

About the Author

MIKE ZIMMERLI IS AN AUTHOR, ghostwriter, and editor whose fingerprints can be found in over two dozen books, usually intentionally. Although most of his previous work has been as an editor, he is now writing and publishing his own series, *The Blue Bridge Mysteries*, featuring Jimmy Favreaux. He continues to work as a freelance editor.

A Minnesota native, he has lived in several places between the northern and southern borders of the Gopher State. In 2004, Mike and his beautiful bride, Mary, abandoned their empty nest, sold everything, and moved to St. Marys, Georgia – as far south as you can go without stepping into Florida and as far east as you can go without getting your feet wet in the Atlantic.

After a lifetime of writing words for others – through radio, newspaper, blogs, and full-time ministry, Mike –

prompted in part by the pandemic – became a freelance writer and editor in 2021. That year, he published his dad's memoirs, *One Soldier's Story* by Jacob Wesley Zimmerli, which recounts his experiences in the Pacific Theater of War in 1944-45, and began fulltime freelance editing.

Two years later, after editing or ghostwriting over two dozen books, it was time for Mike to write under his own name, and Jimmy Favreaux was "born." *Zamboni Is Not A Pasta* became the first installment of The Blue Bridge Mysteries, and *Wanted: Dead or Alive (Again)* continues where *Zamboni* left off. There's more fun to come, too!

Books with Mike Zimmerli Fingerprints

The Blue Bridge Mysteries:

#1 Zamboni Is Not A Pasta — (2022)

#2 Wanted: Dead or Alive (Again) — (2023)

#3 To The Last Breath — (Coming 2023)

#4 The 7 O'clock Man (working title) — (2024)

***

Select books edited by Michael Zimmerli

- *One Soldier's Story: WWII Service Record: Leyte & Okinawa* – Jacob Wesley Zimmerli
- *Nine Days: A Time to Heal* – Delphine W. Berry
- *In Between (From Calling to Fulfillment)* – Jeanine Kabasakalian
- *Ending the Power Struggle: 5 Strategies for Parents of Children with Disabilities* – Heather McMillan
- *Faith In Deep Waters* – Maya R. Calhoun
- *My Life is Series of Songs* – Amy Clay Jones
- *How to Write Better Songs* – Ashley Scott
- *A Safe Pair of Hands: Achieving Business Success* – Robin Royals
- *Life, Death, and a Stroke in Between* – Aaron Kinne

www.ingramcontent.com/pod-product-compliance
Lightning Source LLC
Chambersburg PA
CBHW051213130726
47988CB00001B/79